inSyte

Greg Kiser

For Serena, Grace, and Miller -- my reason.

ACKNOWLEDGEMENTS

I'd like to recognize Steve, Bill, Matt, Larry and Mimi – five pioneers brave enough to read early versions of my novel. A feat of extreme patience and virtue.

And my wife, Serena, who helped me 'keep it real'.

And my mother, Carlene, who always challenged me to learn.

For real.

In some respects, we're past the era of the PC and into the era of extrasensory computing. These mobile phones have eyes. They've got a camera. They've got ears. Every one of them has a microphone. They've got skin. You can touch them. And they're increasingly augmenting our own senses.

Vic Gundotra, VP of Engineering, Google, 2009

Over the past two decades a series of profoundly important advances have occurred in both the philosophy of mind and the empirical mind/brain sciences that, taken together, are finally opening the way to a new understanding of breakthrough creativity. Three developments are of particular significance: recognition that the mind extends beyond the brain, a renewed interest in the mind's imaginative faculties and the analogical reasoning that underlies them, and the emergence of a new science of networks.

Richard Ogle, Introduction to Smart World, 2007

And I stood upon the sand of the sea, and saw a beast rise up out of the sea, having seven heads and ten horns, and upon his horns ten crowns, and upon his heads the name of blasphemy.

Revelation 13:1

1   Tuesday July 15, 2014
Bushehr, Iran

"What do you think those guys are doing back at the bar?" Woody asked.

"Picking up teeth. Calling their associates," Mitch said. "Come on, we need to hurry."

Mitch broad-jumped a black puddle and followed Woody toward the open street. Jesus, like following a runaway bus. Mitch knew they were made by now. The assholes in the Samshiri were figuring out they'd been hit by a covert. Slit right up the middle.

He passed a dirty steel dumpster and there it was, the dusty pick-up. The Saipa had come out of its Korean factory canary yellow. Now it was dented and scratched to hell and Mitch thought it looked like a million bucks. He jumped in and revved the engine. Woody retrieved their sniper rifles from behind the driver's seat and both men began stuffing extra magazines into the wide, deep pockets of their cloaks.

Mitch looked up and spotted the angry black eyes of a Mullah warrior sixty meters out. Eleven O'clock.

The man wore a dirty houndstooth turban and pointed an RPG at the Saipa.

"MOVE!" Mitch shouted and dove through the passenger door with Woody as the truck ignited into a fireball that blew him sideways across the sidewalk into a brick wall.

Mitch struck the wall upside down and twirling, right shoulder first. Felt something crack, pain flowing immediate and intense. He bounced to the sidewalk in a thick shower of glass and debris. Couldn't breathe, surrounded by a darkness he could feel but not hear. His eyesight cleared, thick black smoke everywhere and his ears only registered a dull ring. His arms and legs still worked so it could be worse. He felt Woody's arm.

"FALL BACK before he fires into the SMOKE!" Mitch yelled.

Both men were up and running low to the ground back toward the alley. They cleared the smoke field and met gunfire seemingly coming from every direction. Two bullets hit Mitch's vest and it felt like battering rams. He bounced off the wall again and kept running and another rocket struck and he was falling forward. The second grenade saved his life, dropping him twenty meters horizontally through the air to escape the deadly swarm of bullets. Felt like free fall, except accelerating sideways instead of down and all he could do was hold onto his M25 like a lifeline a line to life a guardrail to keep from going over the cliff and he kept pumping his legs like he was running through the air then he skid across dirty concrete and was running on the ground. His jeans were shredded and his thighs were bloody but he was shrapnel free and hadn't been shot, at least not so his vest couldn't handle and he uttered a little laugh.

Woody slammed into the small steel dumpster at a dead run and it slid in front of the alley's mouth as Mitch slipped past and hit the deck.

Mitch assumed a prone position covering the east flank, Woody took west. Mitch stole a glance at his friend who looked back, nodded once.

The fury of bullets found them again. Mortar danced off walls, dirt rose from the ground. Angry red dirt swarmed into the air and dusted their mouths and Mitch was grateful for the cover but even more grateful for the steel dumpster that screeched like an innocent victim tortured by sharp metal hail.

But now the SEALs were dug into position. Though greatly outnumbered, Mitch knew they had the advantage over these amateurs. He and Woody had vastly superior training and weaponry and were ready to take the fight to the Mullahs. Mitch swept the street through his sniper scope, past the burning truck. Bingo, the houndstooth turban sixty meters east. Bastard was kneeling in the street to line up a shot at the dumpster. He noted the RPG 7, maximum practical range of fifty meters. Glad it wasn't the V, accurate to five hundred. The man's thick beard was covered in dust. Mitch squeezed the trigger and blew his head off.

One down. Mitch conducted a rapid search and counted at least thirty armed warriors firing at his position. They shouted and pointed and shot toward the dumpster with little discipline. Good. Most were in shadows. Not good. Some ventured into the street. Good.

Mitch lined up a warrior in his crosshairs, pulled the trigger, watched him drop. Slow, deliberate search and kill. Boom. Take your time. Boom. Take your time. Who's next? Boom.

He emptied his clip, slammed a new magazine into the breech, glanced skyward and continued firing. Weather conditions were favorable. Only a slight breeze. Superb light from the Mid afternoon sun. He and Woody had visibility looking out below the haze of dirt. Much harder for the Mullahs to see under and in. Dusk wouldn't be a problem if the Iranian's lacked night vision technology. Terrain was mostly positive. AK-47's were inaccurate as hell beyond a hundred meters while his M25 could pick a cigarette out of a man's teeth at one thousand meters. At least, the way he and Woody knew how to shoot. So the Mullah's couldn't close inside a hundred meter perimeter without getting smoked. Sincerely. Mitch emptied another clip and started firing left handed to minimize eye fatigue.

The key variables were total combatant count, rocket launch technology, leadership. He and the Woodman had dropped at least forty warriors so far. Good. No break in return fire. Not good. For every Mullah warrior that dropped, another stepped into place. Could be two hundred of the sonsabitches out there. Not a show stopper. He and Woody had more than four hundred rounds combined. And they weren't missing. He was still breathing, so the Iranians must be limited to RPG 7's. The leadership was obviously slim to none. Tactically, they should be trying to flank the SEALs by coming over the rooftops and up the alley from the Samshiri. Of course, Mitch immediately took out anyone who tried to cross the street. But he couldn't cover past the turn maybe a hundred meters east. Mitch glanced at the rooftops and hoped to Christ these guys really were as green as they seemed.

"How you doing, buddy?" Mitch yelled. The noise was deafening.

"Petrified, chicken fried, run and hide. Bout a hundred rounds left. You?"

"Bout the same."

The SEALs continued firing and warriors continued falling. More moved in to take their place and the SEALs continued firing. Uncompromising, steady, professional. Surrender was not an option. Mitch wasn't much in the mood for an acid bath.

An hour went by and, incredibly, the hail of bullets from the AK-47's did not let up. Neither did the methodical firing from the SEAL sniper rifles. Warriors dropped in the street and fell from rooftops. RPG rounds exploded against the walls around the SEAL position.

"Playing whack a mole here, man!" Woody yelled. "Every time I ventilate one motherfucker another motherfucker pops up. Jesus, Mitch. How many are there?"

That was the question, alright.

Mitch kept hoping for a lull in the gunfire that would indicate the warriors were falling back, preferably running out of men or ordnance or both. But so far the return fire remained constant. Mitch had killed at least fifty fighters and thought Woody must be close to that.

"They must have two hundred men to keep this up," Mitch finally said.

If anything the volume of gunfire grew more intense.

"We gotta get some back up, Mitch. Just a matter of time before they flank our asses up this alley. We gotta open a comm channel to QRF."

"Roger that." They had to reach the Quick Reaction Force on the carrier. Mitch reached into his jeans and pulled out his PRC 152. The multiband radio was compact, flexible and nearly indestructible. Unfortunately, the wireless speaker mic wasn't as rugged. The initial RPG blasts had torn it the hell up. He continued firing with his right hand and brought the PRC to his face with his left.

He shouted into it. "Alpha One, Alpha One! Blue Dog Charlie calling Alpha One! Do you read? Alpha One we are pinned down and require assistance. Do you read, over?"

No response.

"Alpha One, do you copy?"

No response.

Mitch checked to make sure the radio was in bird mode. It was. He looked up. The satellite was in the eastern sky but the walls obscured his line of sight. He had to get the antenna into an open position.

Mitch stood to position the antenna a little higher. "Alpha One this is Blue Dog Charlie! Do you copy? We are in a major engagement. Repeat, major engagement and require immediate assistance."

He continued firing the M25 from his shoulder but lost accuracy as he fumbled with the radio's push-to-talk button.

"We require immediate air support and pick-up at these coordinates. Now, Alpha One! Repeat, NOW! We are pinned and taking heavy fire. Repeat, heavy fire! Surrounded by---"

Mitch felt an impact like a stick of dynamite going off in his shirt pocket followed by somebody swinging a sledge hammer into his back. He reeled sideways and dropped. Adrenaline flooded his body like a heavy drug as his central nervous system fired out of control and the outside world was transformed into a macabre slow motion picture show. A strobe light flicked off and on like someone beating a drum in his brain.

Then the pain stopped and he lost his eyesight and his world went perfectly quiet.

The world didn't go black, more like a white out on a winter mountain. He felt like he was sliding down a soft hill, falling to whatever awaited him at the bottom.

He saw a shape and as he began to pick up speed he knew someone somehow shared this odd journey. He was conscious of his heart the way you might be conscious of your hand if someone held it. He knew who was with him.

"I'm coming to be with you," he said.

"Son, I'm not ready for you to come home just yet," his mother said with a translucent smile.

"Not sure I have much choice, here," he said.

"You always have a choice. About everything. It's up to you if you'd rather live or die."

"How is it up---"

"And it's not just you, now, is it? Goodness, no. You've got your friend out there who can't make it through this without you."

It was important for him to get a point across. He knew this was fleeting and he fought an overwhelming sense of urgency. "Mom, I still have so much to learn. But I've learned a lot, haven't I?"

His mother's spirit smiled and her aged eyes looked weary. "Not enough, I'm afraid. You don't belong here. Go back and help your friend and you'll see. God has special plans for you, son. Special plans. You will learn so much."

He thought about trying to slow his descent. But the temptation to close his eyes and accept the fall was overwhelming.

Part 1

Turning On

2 Friday, March 6, 2020
Tampa, Florida

Midway through her second vodka martini something cast a shadow over Jessica's face. She opened her eyes and was startled to see the dark form of an enormous man. The sun was at his back so he was only an outline.

"The water is magnificent this time of morning, is it not?"

His voice sounded dark. Incredibly low and deep.

She smiled uncertainly. "Yes, it is."

From nowhere she remembered a comic strip she'd seen as a little girl. A vampire held a noose and the caption read, 'Tall, Dark, and Hang-some'. *Where did that come from? Must be the martinis. Christ, get a grip.*

She shielded her eyes. He returned her smile and she could see he was a good looking man. Hmmm, there was something wrong but before she could put her finger on it he narrowed his eyes and looked out at the bay.

"The sea reminds me of my childhood," he said.

His English was good. "And just where were you raised?"

"A long way from here. Russia. Off the Black Sea."

"Oh my. A long way indeed."

"Yes. In my country we do not allow beautiful women to drink alone. Not good for the balance."

"The balance?"

"The balance of the universe." He took her small hand lightly in his. "Cheslov. Cheslov Kirill," he said with a slight bow.

She gave him a small nod. "Jessica. Jessica Hart."

She looked at the large hand that held hers and was a little creeped out by the long fingernails. They looked clean and oddly strong and the sun actually *glinted* from their tips. Maybe he was a musician?

The paramedic told her the global position lock failed and the kids weren't paying attention so nobody was steering. The lane departure alarm didn't work either – beyond belief --and the hydrogen coupe slammed into the bridge doing a hundred thirty. Looked like her hair was long and blond before…

Jessica suppressed a shudder and maintained her smile.

"May I join you, Miss Hart?"

"Please do. I could use some company this morning. And call me Jessica."

"Thank you, Jessica."

Cheslov sat across the small table, the sun hit his face and Jessica looked into black eyes.

Not black as though someone had punched him. Black as in zero eye color. Each eye appeared as one large pupil and she realized he had Aniridia. She vaguely remembered this condition from nursing school. Congenital, only a few documented cases. Something about under-development of the iris color. Gene responsible for retinal growth didn't do its job. Bad gene. Bad, bad gene.

He wore a faded chocolate tee shirt over faded khakis. He pulled a surprisingly long cigar from his shirt pocket and severed the tip using a cutting device that looked old and worn and dangerously sharp. He lit the dark cigar with a gunmetal Zippo, leaned back, crossed a long leg over a tall knee. She noticed he wore hobnailed work boots. He set the Zippo on the table and Jessica squinted to read tiny letters scratched into the lighter's innocent face.

QUIT YOURSELVES LIKE MEN.

She frowned and her eyebrows climbed ever so slightly.

The man was completely and attractively bald. Thick dark brows shielded black eyes and the effect was dramatic and a little creepy until he smiled. Then his huge half crescent grin emasculated the black eyes and rendered his entire countenance harmless and playful as if to ask... *how can you take me too seriously?*

"What brings a stunning young lady out on such a beautiful morning?" he asked.

Blood in the teenager's eyes and he didn't seem to realize his girlfriend was dead. What went through his mind? Hope? Or something closer to fear? She couldn't stop asking the question and, well, here she was.

"Might be Friday morning to you," Jessica said with a chuckle. "But it's Friday night to me."

"Ah. You work the night-shift where?"

19

The young boy holding the dead hand. The girlfriend's hand being held because, of course, it could never hold again and...

"Tampa General. Can we talk about something else?"

"Of course, Jessica." Cheslov smiled his charming smile and looked toward the bay. "The gulf waters are God's own hospital, yes? What cannot be healed by fishing in bright sun with cold vodka?"

She finished her drink and thought he might be in his mid forties. A little rough around the edges but overall he showed potential.

Four martinis later, she had to admit the man had a helluva sensa humor.

He described a pet Sheppard he'd owned as a young man. To honor his love of the animal, Cheslov approached a taxidermist to investigate mounting the dog's head on a base of dark Russian cedar.

Jessica knew he was pulling her leg. Black humor, certainly. Exactly the kind she enjoyed. Not unlike many in her profession.

Closer to fear or closer to hope?

"There was a certain expression I wanted to capture," he was saying. "The look of eagerness Helsing had during the hunt."

"What did Helsing hunt?"

"Helsing loved to hunt any animal that walked or crawled or flew over God's Earth."

"Come on." Jessica smiled and recognized a pleasant feeling of unfeeling and knew she was getting smashed. "Must've had a favorite."

"Indeed. His favorite was the wolf. Helsing was fast and strong. On occasion he would outrun and take down a black wolf in an open field. He would kill the animal by breaking its neck in his great jaws.

Few dogs can take down a wolf, let me assure you. I cannot say how often I pulled Helsing from his prey to prevent my excited pet from overindulging in fresh organs." Cheslov shook his head, clearly relishing the memory. "A smile on a dog is a delight, is it not?"

"You didn't actually do it, did you? Mount your poor dog's head in your living room?"

"Alas, I did not. The talent did not exist then to capture the right expression. Then one day Helsing met a certain wolf and … well, that was not a good day for my fine –"

"Hey, you could've topped it off with glasses? Sunglasses I mean. And stuffed one of your cigars into his mouth?" She pushed her foot forward, brushed the inside of Cheslov's boot.

Cheslov frowned. "Nyet. That would be---"

"In poor taste?" she laughed out loud and she thought a little too loud or maybe not because a moment later Cheslov started to laugh, his dark face full of merriment.

Hope, definitely hope. How else could one be expected to cope? Please, God.

The warning signs were there, she had simply chosen to ignore them. On the surface his dark eyes held a look of constant amusement. But when he laughed she watched his black eyes go somewhere else. Laugh at something else. Something of which she had no awareness.

When Cheslov suggested lunch on his boat, she pronounced carefully that dinner sounded mighty good to her.

She just wanted to spend more time near the water. Just a little more time. Was that so bad? She hated the idea of going back to her barren apartment to empty dreams of lifeless hands, she just couldn't handle that right now. God not right now. She knew what she'd do. She'd open a bottle of Absolute and she'd call Janet and Janet wouldn't answer and she'd hang up but not before leaving a message she'd regret tomorrow. Then she'd call Margot and good ole Margot would come running like a puppy. Been that, done there. Wait a minute, that's not right.

Like a gentlemen, he picked up the tab. Hopefully he wouldn't count her drinks. But if he did, fuck it. A girl had to have her fun, right? He actually used cash. Too funny. What an old school gent. She had no business driving so she thought she'd try out his big black Jaguar. He pulled out of the parking lot of the Sandpiper Beach Shack, seashells popping in protest beneath the tires of his silent vehicle.

An old MP5 by Led Zeppelin screamed through his stereo.

Hey, hey mama said the way you move.

What was the name of that one? Something about a Black Dog? Name didn't make any sense but it sure sounded good.

His boat was a freaking yacht. A mile long and OH MY GOD gorgeous. She stumbled from one end to the other while he opened a bottle of something and by the time she came up from the ladies room he handed her a cold glass and she had to sit for just a minute so she leaned into some warm leather high chair on the back of the boat and looked out over the water. The air was so hot she took off her shirt and sipped her drink, just what the doctor ordered iced vodka with a few black oranges thrown in. *My goodness.* Not oranges. Get a gip. Grip. Olives. Delicious. Strong and dry.

She swooshed the vodka around her tongue and the ship rocked gently like a hammock and her eyes were so heavy she had to close them for just a moment.

The last thought Jessica had was the boy holding the dead girl's hand. And then she knew. Hope is abandoned with intense sadness. And there's simply no time for fear. You're past that before you feel it. In the end with blood in your eyes and broken bones, sadly it's all about ... *resignation.*

Soon after Cheslov captained the boat southwest into the Gulf of Mexico. He knew of a large shiver of sharks twelve leagues from shore, quite active this time of year.

3

Daylight was fading. Downtown Tampa rolled away to the north of the Planetcom building. The bay glistened to the south. Margot looked at row upon row of cubicles. Most everyone had left for the day, so the floor was quiet. Most of the cubicles looked the same.

Occasionally an individual tendency emerged. Oh look, there's a balloon in the shape of a palm tree. And there's a poster of a beach. Margot liked to see a little individuality. She considered corporate America way too conservative and buttoned down and boring. At twenty three, she may have some things to learn in life. But she knew boring when she saw it.

She played along during work hours. Her long skirts looked conformist. But in the evenings her short hair became a loose brown bob and she liked to walk on the wild freakin side. She lived in an Always-On Surveillance Society. And that was just fine with Margot. Her latest fave gridsite recorded public flashers. Of course she loved to watch. But she also enjoyed acting as the trigger for such recordings.

Oh yes they call it the streak... lookiedat, lookiedat.

She had several girlfriends and a couple of boy toys and her very favorite pastime was to get dolled up and roll into the beach bars. She enjoyed playing pool in a short skirt and thong panties. Or no panties. If the girls sitting near the table were really cute she'd lean way over to make the shot, letting her dress ride up and putting it all out there for people to appreciate.

She smiled and thought about the effect she had on most of the employees at Planetcom. Even though they'd been with the company longer and held higher positions they treated her with the utmost respect. She held the keys, they knew, to performance evaluations. Performance evaluations held the keys to pay raises. She welded a certain influence -- unforeseen, a bit intangible, but real. Being in Human Resources did have its perks.

But it was all so incredibly boring. Here she was asking her micro for a summary of the key attributes to look for in hiring executives. She had to complete this stupid form so the micro could correlate the data and create a presentation by Tuesday.

Her thoughts were interrupted by the approach of a dark shape.

Margot recognized the new lobbyist and absently reached up to twirl her hair. She had filled in the paperwork to retain Cheslov's service for the Wireless World contract.

OMG how boring!

"Good evening, Mr. Kirill."

Cheslov looked toward her and his dark face erupted into a huge and utterly charming smile.

"How are you this evening, Margot?"

"Friday night in Tampa, right? I'm ready to head home after a long week and curl up with my dog. Maybe some wine. Just relax, you know?"

"Indeed." His voice was so low. It positively rumbled.

"You got some sun today," she observed.

Cheslov offered an exaggerated shrug and a wink. "I confess, I enjoyed a glass of vodka on my modest boat far out in the Gulf."

"And?" she prodded.

Cheslov stared.

"Come clean, Mr. Kirill. I happened to drive by Sandpipers on my way in and guess whose car I saw? That's right. The Jag with the black package? I'm pretty sure that's the one we're leasing for yours truly."

Cheslov smiled with shy contrition. "A man has his needs, yes?"

"Well, what did you think? Was that place as awesome as I said it would be?"

"I think the view is to die for," Cheslov said.

Margot nodded. "I'm so glad you liked my little suggestion. Heading to the docks, now?"

"Yes, Margot, to my home at the docks. I shall have a glass of Stoli and I shall perform a small toast to you and your dog...?" He raised his dark brows, imploring.

"Pretzel. My dog's name is Pretzel."

Cheslov's eyes absolutely sparkled with mirth. "Of course. I shall perform a small toast to you and Pretzel. Perhaps you'll be kind enough to have a drink towards my health as well. Good evening, my Margot."

Cheslov moved toward the elevators and a not unpleasant chill glided through Margot starting in her mind and heading south. Deep South. He was so smooth, like an animal built for speed. Just a hint of what's there.

Thick, dark brows over black eyes. Eyes so dark they were black. Maybe not the kind of eyes you wanted gazing into yours. For long. And that head that was brazenly bald. Yeah, he was seriously sexy. If you're into darkness. Margot admitted that on a certain level she was. She thought many women were.

His fingernails were long, creepy long. But he kept them clean, hey the man obviously took great pride in his appearance. Maybe the fingernails were a European thing. Or Russian. Whatever. She would have to ask him if he played guitar.

On rare occasions, the left side of his face pulled together. She knew the tic was involuntary. But it seemed to be in response to other people. Sort of an involuntary grimace of disagreement.

She watched him enter the elevator and shook her head. Cheslov Kirill. She had no idea what he could do to help the company with Wireless World. But she had to admit, she enjoyed having him around. He definitely spiced things up.

4

Cheslov rode the elevator down to the parking garage and considered the silly tart, Margot. The inane woman sat at her desk as though it were a throne. She would not last two minutes in Rostov. All prim and proper and waiting to put a knife into the back of anyone who does not show her the respect she so vehemently does not deserve. Only in America could such a shrew end up with any façade of authority in a large firm where men worked hard to provide for their families and make their lives.

Cheslov smiled and considered what he would do in one evening with a child such as Margot. He thought about the woman from the Tiki Hut and his smile turned to a frown. What had happened, exactly? He honestly wasn't sure. He thought he was simply going to have fun with her. He was not surprised when she drained two stiff vodkas on his boat. She'd slipped off her clothes and pranced about naked and asked if he thought she was pretty. Quite the show. Then she started to cry and talked of breaking up a marriage because she lusted after another woman, a mother of young children.

That's when the images went dark for Cheslov.

Next thing he knew he was disposing of her corpse among the sharks.

It was during such introspective moments that Cheslov wondered if he were losing his mind.

The Margot bitch had witnessed his location this morning. Events were getting too hot, too fast. He considered his exit strategy, sailing north up the coast. But first the contract award must occur. The delusional Mayor must be satisfied.

His micro chimed and the sound created reflecting echoes in the chamber of the large concrete garage. He slid his finger across his watch to direct a narrow ray of audio toward his ear. The sound was as compact as a beam of light. A person standing one meter away would hear nothing.

"Speak," he commanded.

"Cheslov? This is Paxton. How are you this evening?"

Paxton Phelps. A man no better than the little tart upstairs. Bothersome, incompetent.

"Speak," he repeated.

"Cheslov, we have a little problem on our hands. Wanda Deter on the Citizen's Coalition committee's not rolling over on this one. She could knock our team to the ground at the Council meeting."

Cheslov smiled because Phelps seemed to wait for a response.

Receiving none, Phelps continued.

"Cheslov I think we need to do something about this."

"You say this on a wireless connection?"

"Don't worry, our channels are fully encrypted. You know what the Mayor's going to say if this doesn't go our way."

Cheslov said nothing.

"Miss Deter would rather see the City apply these funds to our, how should I say …"

Cheslov heard the man exhale.

"Social unrest. Cheslov, are you there?"

"Da. Make your point."

"Don't take this lightly, Kirill. Deter has friends in Tallahassee. She can push us pretty hard. If she diverts our funding to some sort of welfare program … well, I don't think I have to tell you what that would do to our program."

"Meet me at the landing at dawn."

"Cheslov, I'm not sure that I can do that. I'm in St. Pete tomorrow morning at my daughter's soccer game---," Phelps began.

Cheslov disconnected.

5

"Where we going?" Mitch asked, taking the bags from Kate.

"Up the beach," Kate said.

"Whatcha got in the bags?" Woody asked.

"Extra food from the kitchen. Cheeseburgers and grouper."

Molly and Woody drifted ahead of Mitch and Kate. Woody rushed knee high into the waves and Mitch could tell his friend was tempted to strip and dive into the gulf. He hoped Woody wouldn't try that shit on their first night with these girls.

They headed north along the shore in the cool night. Mitch listened to the surf, a sound he'd heard many days and nights on coastlines around the world laying in water so cold you couldn't breathe. This girl was pretty special and he tuned into a soft jazz station in his mind and started to look at the classes she was taking. Hmmm, business technology. Interesting stuff there, for sure. Her Facebook page was intense too. So she liked music from the seventies? Alright.

Suddenly his head felt light. Like someone lifted a heavy helmet he forgot he was wearing. No signal on this part of the beach. Damn it. The coverage around this town sucked. He hated going in and out of signals. Well, mostly he hated going out of signal. It was painful and a major buzz-kill.

He glanced at Kate. She smiled at him and dark hair blew across her eyes. He smiled back and didn't say anything. He didn't have to. Mitch's eyes followed the coastline. A figure appeared above inland dunes. He came closer and Mitch saw it was an older man.

"Please. My family just over hill," the man pointed. "Is cold tonight. Anything, please, would be appreciate."

"Sorry, buddy. All I got is a micro," Woody said. "I don't have any cash on me."

Mitch and Kate caught up.

"Your family?" Kate prompted.

"Yes, just over hill. Anything would be appreciate."

"Let's take a look." Kate and Molly headed inland. Mitch glanced at Woody and they followed the girls.

Crossing over the dunes, Mitch saw a dozen women dressed in rags gathered around a fire. He shook his head. The Union's move to a cashless society was hard on the lowest rung of the population. People no longer carried wallets or purses. No cash, no change, no way for the poor to accept money transfers from micros. How many people lived like this around here? Couldn't look it up without a signal. But it was unbelievable the level of poverty. Everywhere he went, it seemed. Abandoned property, vast tent cities. People living in areas filled with filth, debris.

Without a word, Kate handed the bags of food to the old man. She removed her hoodie, knelt in the sand and smiled into a little girl's eyes.

"Hello there, honey. What's your name?"

"Maribel," the little girl said and Mitch was amazed at how pretty she was.

"Maribel. So beautiful I should have guessed. I'm Kate."

Mitch could just make out men talking. He looked toward a line of palms.

Maribel glanced down. She looked up and tears formed in her eyes.

"I want you to have this," Kate handed her hoodie to Maribel. "This is a magic sweatshirt. Do you know why?"

Maribel shook her head slowly.

The voices grew louder.

"It's magic. Keeps little girls safe."

"Safe from what?" Maribel asked.

"Safe from the world. Safe from everything."

Maribel took the sweatshirt and put it on. She wrapped her little arms around herself and closed her eyes.

"Thank you, Kate," Maribel said.

Mitch and Molly handed over their sweatshirts. Woody unbuttoned the last few buttons of his shirt and handed it to the old man who lead them in.

An argument erupted among the men nearby. Mitch made eye contact with Woody and they eased into the shadows beyond the perimeter of the firelight.

"Thank you for your kindness," Maribel's father said to Kate. "Much appreciate."

"She's so lovely," Kate said. "I only wish I could do---"

A group of men approached the fire.

"What is this?" the tallest pointed toward Kate and Molly.

"Marcus," Maribel's father said. "These are friends."

Marcus shoved Maribel's father and the old man stumbled into the fire. Woody's shirt caught and the man leapt out of the fire and rolled across the sand without making a sound.

"Daddy!" Maribel shrieked.

"What are you doing?" Molly cried. "You could've burned him badly!"

Kate rushed to the old man who lay smoldering. "Are you alright?"

"Leave him," Marcus commanded.

"This is my camp," a fat man standing with Marcus said. His face was dark. He looked at Kate and Molly. "Where's our food? What is for me?"

The men stared.

Kate and Molly self consciously crossed their arms.

Mitch and Woody stepped into the firelight.

"Y'all need to back on outta here," Woody said.

The group of men turned.

"There's no more food," Mitch said. He looked at the old man in the sand the said in a low voice, "You need to leave now."

The men stared.

"I think maybe no one will leave," Marcus said with an ugly sneer.

The fat man pulled a machete and held it over the fire. "I think maybe they have food after all, eh Marcus?"

34

Marcus smiled. "Yes, I think so." He pointed at Molly and Kate. "You and you. Take off your clothes and throw them into fire."

Mitch considered the odds. Twelve against two. Impossible odds.

But at the moment they were not a group of twelve. They were twelve separate men, each trying to size up an unfamiliar situation. Two new men in their camp, one the size of Frankenstein's monster.

Twelve individuals.

But in about five seconds the moment would pass. They'd tighten ranks and be a group again. Then he and Woody would be back to impossible odds.

Mitch had to change the dynamic.

Establish who was in charge.

He rotated his shoulders, lead with his hips and whipped his open palm into the fat man's face. The lateral cartilage in the man's nose compressed and exploded in a bloody red shower. The machete dropped and the fat man collapsed into the sand with a high pitched wail. Spewing blood made it difficult to breathe so Mitch figured the man wouldn't scream for long. Otherwise he might've hit him again just to shut him the fuck up. Either way, this asshole was out of the fight.

He looked up as Woody grabbed Marcus by the hair and slammed his head into his knee. Marcus's skull flung back like a punted melon and he fell next to the fat man in the sand. Mitch watched his concave face unfurl like a bloody sponge.

Two seconds, two methods, two faces crushed.

The remaining men stepped back.

Woody and Mitch stared.

No longer any question who was in charge.

"Git," Woody growled.

Two men in back broke and ran. Mitch and Woody stepped forward and the remaining men stumbled and fled.

Mitch helped Maribel's father to his feet. He looked into the old man's face and expected to see anger. Embarrassment. Mitch was surprised to read an eagerness he did not at first comprehend. Then he did.

Maribel and another woman emerged from the shadows with carving knives.

"Let's go. Now!" Mitch grabbed Kate's hand and they sprinted toward the beach. The old man's voice faded in the wind. "Analyn, Maribel. Prepare this meat while is fresh. Remove the clothes and prepare …"

Kate started to speak but Mitch put his finger to her lips and shook his head. Eventually they slowed. Away from the fire the night grew cool again. Kate leaned into him. He put his arm around her waist and held her tight.

6

"What are you wearing?"

"Oh Bob, you're such a flirt. Why don't you just take a look?" Wanda flicked on her wall display and watched his eyes widen. She strolled across the room, conscious of her long, dark legs beneath a short, white robe. "OK, keep your hands where I can see 'em," she said with a smile.

"Wanda, when can I see you for real?" Bob said.

"Next week. Let's do Destin." She splashed vodka over ice and returned to her recliner. She sat slowly, holding the robe in place. She didn't need Bob getting too excited. "I have something to discuss." He lifted his head, trying to see her legs. "Something serious."

He looked disappointed.

She pushed on. "Did you hear about the Anderson riot?"

"Yeah, I did. They figure out how many folks were killed?"

"Something like forty Troopers and two hundred Nomads."

Bob winced. One of the things she loved about Bob, he'd be a terrible poker player. "Jesus. What in the hell happened?" he asked.

"Nomads tried to organize a march. Expressly forbidden by our esteemed Mayor Delaney."

"That goddamn guy."

She nodded. "So he orders a dozen troopers in there to break it up. With Goodbye Guns. Can you believe that noise? It escalates, the Nomads grow from a hundred to a thousand. They go at the troopers, it turns violent."

"IEDs?"

"Just rocks and clubs. More Troopers move in and it's something out of Detroit in fifteen. Or Los Angeles in sixty five. Take your pick. It was bad."

"Any arrests?"

"No. Where would he put them?" She sipped her drink. "More like clearing the back forty of bothersome varmints. Did you hear what the Mayor said?"

"Yeah. Said it was like dealing with monkeys that belonged in the zoo."

"Black hole of idiocy."

"I got my eye on that Mayor of yours. He's trying to do something slippery with his budget. Real slippery. Wants to build himself some kind of wireless shrine. He's got a bid out but one of the bidders is wasting their time. Mr. Delaney knows who he wants. Foregone conclusion."

"Do you have proof?"

"Not yet. But we'll find something. Just a matter of time."

"I'll be at the council meeting to keep an eye on him."

"Good. And one more thing. He's hired some kind of muscle. Russian bastard. Fella's bad news, Wanda. Seriously bad news."

"What's his story?" she asked.

Bob said nothing. His eyes went distant and he looked away. Finally he looked back.

"Not a hundred percent sure on that one. I know he spent some time in New York but I can't trace him before that. Really sort of odd. Anyway, just do me a favor and stay away from him."

Wanda nodded. "OK, Bob. Thanks for the heads up."

"And I need you to do me one more little favor."

"What's that?"

Bob smiled. "Open up that robe for me, darlin."

7   Saturday, March 7, 2020

Just before dawn, Cheslov stood at the pier admiring his yacht, a Carver 12 meter Super Sport. Here was an example of American ingenuity at its finest. She was a beautiful vessel. Twin Volvo IPS hydrogen engines provided a range of six hundred nautical miles. The Swedes were good for only two things – banking and hydrogen motors. Quiet, responsive engines. The way he liked all his vessels. He smiled at the weak double entendre.

Cheslov named his vessel *Chorny Volk* in honor of the hunts he'd had as a child through the dense forests north of Rostov. He and his father hunted boar and brown bear and Chorny Volk which meant Black Wolf. Beast of prey. Dangerous in every situation.

He thought of the fishing vessels in his home village of Rostov, just off the Black Sea. Weeks at sea with dozens of men in vessels half the size of the Carver. Vessels made of wood and held together by twine navigated waves the size of houses. He spent more time at sea than on land as a youth. To this day he could not fall asleep on a bed with no movement. Unnatural in a dynamic world to sleep in such stillness. Such quiet.

It would have been good to have had this Carver as a younger man. Not that the Carver would be a good vessel from which to fish with a dozen men. You could not get lines into the water, not enough open space around the perimeter. But it would have been wonderful to strap into the captain's chair and cast a line with a vodka in the cup holder. He smiled at the thought. This vessel could handle whatever the Black Sea could throw at a man in a winter storm.

His father's shack stood a good distance from the village off a dusty dirt road. He remembered the stone walls, cold enough in winter to numb his fingertips.

His father had fished the entire eighty one years of his life. He had yellow eyes and a greenish face that was always angry. Cheslov, a little boy who smoked and drank and used the worst profanity at the age of ten. He acted tough because he wasn't, really. His father and their friends made fun of the runt with the facial tic.

"Come over here, pussy boy. Come let me see the way your pussy face twitches." the men laughed. His father joined them. Young Cheslov had shuffled away and cried.

He worked hard to control his facial spasms. After a time, he did. As a small boy, he could not go more than a few seconds without a violent muscular contraction. By the time he was a young man, Cheslov displayed a mild contraction on rare occasions. Mainly when he lost control due to anger. Or contempt.

He had overcome his obstacle by learning to maintain control. He then applied the lesson to the rest of his life. Absolute control. He rarely showed anger. To anyone. For any reason.

Not that Cheslov didn't feel anger. He simply did not, could not show it.

Pleasant emotion, on the other hand, had the opposite effect. To smile and laugh soothed his soul and the impulse to twitch went away. He therefore tried hard to fill his life with activities and material belongings he enjoyed.

Cheslov grew into a large young man. He was fifteen and one of his father's friends asked him to show his pussy face. Cheslov beat him until the man screamed. Cheslov found the sound delightful.

After that, the jokes stopped.

One night his father's friends spoke in urgent disbelief around a large fire. News of the massacre, all murdered in the same room by the Bolsheviks. Bloody Nicholas, his wife, son, daughters.

Here's where events grew hazy. Bloody Sunday occurred in 1918. Was this a memory or a dream? He just could not connect the dots between being a young man and becoming a grown man. Something was missing.

Something had happened in the woods of Rostov.

It was clear from his first day that people in America had no nerve. From a glorious history that peaked in World War Two, the American children and grandchildren of that great generation were weak and spoiled. This land of great riches was primed and ready for anyone who had the fortitude and resolve to simply take what they wanted.

With respect to Cheslov's line of work, New York was crowded and territories claimed. So he migrated to Tampa where a man could establish roots and grow his business. And the climate was to die for.

Tampa was a long way from Rostov, and the Carver was a far cry from the fishing vessels of his unnaturally distant youth. Interior space made full use of the beam. Cheslov at a height of two meters could move about the cabin freely. And the best thing about the Carver was each yacht was custom manufactured. Cheslov specified a lower bridge configuration for better maneuverability during storms. He designed his galley and sleeping quarters with full handcrafted cherry cabinetry and paneling. The paneling hid another specification – one centimeter hollow core steel plating throughout the smaller stateroom. The additional weight cost a mere five centimeters of draft at rest, less than two centimeters at forty knots. Well worth it. The ostensible reason was so the stateroom could substitute as a freezer on extended journeys.

And should the need arise, as had happened from time to time, the stateroom could secure a guest who may not otherwise wish to ride along.

He lived on his yacht. He cooked in her gourmet galley, large tuna he deep sea fished from her aft captain's chair that came only with the sports package. He wrote poetry from his master stateroom on a built-in roll top desk with serpentine drawers to secure loose items at sea. He slept in the king sized bed that easily accommodated his large frame. He fired at buoys from six hundred meters with his Groza OC-16 assault rifle. The Groza was manufactured by the Tula weapons plant in Russia. It was a solid weapon built for a man and he rarely missed. The holographic scope presented easy targets, day or night. He sang Russian folksongs from the bridge while he drank vodka and enjoyed gazing at the lights off Florida's west coast. And he murdered men on the stern then fed their bodies to sharks in the deep blue waters ten to twenty leagues into the Gulf of Mexico.

Cheslov once had a man on his vessel, Charles Johnson, a successful American businessman. Charles was a prominent citizen in the community, active in the megachurch and local politics. Charles promoted family values and thought the best way to reduce teen pregnancy and venereal disease was pure abstinence. If not factually accurate, well, it didn't matter. God did not want American teenagers to fuck before marriage and He surely didn't want man to lay with man or woman with woman. Hell, it was right there in the bible for anyone to read.

The megachurch where Charles was assistant minister believed he made his living as a wholesale shoe distributor. Business took him to Russia two to three times a year. For years Charles lured beautiful young Russian teenagers to America with empty promises of stardom as models and entertainers.

Though a man of questionable ethics himself, Cheslov harbored a protective streak when it came to children. Like a pack leader, he possessed a strong paternal instinct. One that he did not entirely understand.

For fun, Cheslov pretended to be a smuggling agent who could help Charles snare girls by acting as his point man in Russia. He took Charles fishing hundreds of kilometers into the Gulf so they could enjoy secure business discussions. On the second bottle of Stoli, Charles really opened up.

He indentured the young Russian girls into prostitution, forced them to live in squalor, and routinely beat them into submission. He told the young girls their parents sold them, they were forgotten by their families, they were his property.

The twelve year olds believed this absolutely. Some older tuna were skeptical. (Cheslov was long accustomed to weasel wording by fools such as Charles in an attempt to conceal distasteful business). Occasionally he had to carve an older girl and leave her body in the common quarters for a few days. Charles made sure her dead eyelids were open. He told the living tuna he could see them through the dead tuna's eyes. Charles always rubbed his belly with a hearty laugh when he told this part of his tale. He confided with Cheslov that the empty eyes really closed the deal on the other tuna. Calmed them the hell down.

Charles enjoyed his vodka with fresh grapefruit juice so Cheslov purchased a pewter spoon just for their trips. Essential for anyone who enjoys eating grapefruit, his well-balanced citrus spoon had a finely serrated edge so fruit separated easily from the membrane.

On one particular voyage after softening his target with the usual bottle of Stoli, Cheslov used the grapefruit spoon to carve out Charles' right eye. He found it to be the perfect utensil for severing ocular muscles. He performed the act so quickly and his intoxicated guest was so surprised that Charles did not scream.

Cheslov held the bloody bubble up to his own eye, winked solemnly, then pushed the sphere onto a three centimeter cedar plug. Big game fishing lure. Cheslov hoped for tuna. He had found that adding a small slice of bait to a lure attracted big fish through their sense of smell. An uneven orb also contributed to an erratic swim action that helped incite the fish to go after the lure. Baiting was an art, and Cheslov knew it was important to draw Tuna, not feed them.

By the time Charles started to scream, Cheslov was already removing the man's left eye with the dirty spoon.

His bull pup Groza housed a Russian AKM bayonet on its muzzle. Cheslov normally used the bayonet to filet fish at sea. On this occasion he slid the blade into Charles's stomach and cut a 'Z' pattern to ensure a clean breach of the large intestines. Charles turned his head left and right, attempting to look around and comprehend what had happened in the past forty seconds. To no avail, of course. Charles had two bloody holes where his eyes had been and his bowels hung over the big silver buckle of his PGA golf belt. Absurdly, he still held his drink. Took a large gulp. Cheslov could appreciate the need and gave Charles a refill. The result of an intestinal breach was a lot of blood and also a lot of pain for the victim. Quiet pain as the victim lost energy and air.

Cheslov threaded the second eyeball onto a black and red Conehead Tuna lure. He lowered both poles into separate rigs and they trolled for tuna using Charles' eyes. Cheslov hoped the scent from the eyes would really bring the point home to the tuna.

And he hadn't been disappointed.

In less than an hour a fifty-five pound Yellowfin hammered a lure. Cheslov grabbed the line and the tuna ran one hundred meters straight off the bow and seventy meters deep. The bent pole and spooling line sprayed saltwater into the air and onto Cheslov's face and he laughed like a schoolboy. He eventually pulled the fish into the vessel and prepared the tuna exquisitely in the Carver's contemporary galley. By then Charles had no appetite so Cheslov dined alone.

After dinner, Cheslov poured a healthy shot of Stoli, lit a Cohiba Maduro and pushed Charles onto the deck at the stern of the vessel. In no time the blood trail attracted seven large bull sharks. Cheslov shot one through the head with the Groza, partly for fun and partly to stimulate the other sharks. He pushed Charles, still sobbing and holding his drink, into the dark, foamy water and watched the frenzy.

One anonymous phone call later the young girls were in custody of the Tampa police. Cheslov used his connections on the City Council to ensure the girl's parents were properly notified. He funded airfare and most of the girls made it back home. Sadly, some decided to stay and work at a local strip club. Perhaps a few degrees removed from prostitution, perhaps not removed at all. At least it was their choice.

His thoughts returned to the present. He thought about Wireless World. Why did the government not just do what they wanted? Was that not their right? At any rate, it was fine with Cheslov. Convincing Planetcom he was the man for the job was simple. Convincing the Deter bitch that the future lay with Planetcom would be just as easy. These weak rats did not stand up to anyone who had the courage to play outside the lines.

He heard footsteps, turned and watched Paxton Phelps approach. Another weak rat. Phelps actually thought Cheslov was here to play by the rules. To persuade the various factions through logical argument to support the Planetcom contract.

Did Phelps not realize people made decisions that served their own interests, and their interests alone?

Cheslov smiled. He would get the job done, would certainly persuade. But it would not be by the rules.

"Mr. Kirill, I don't understand why we must have all this cloak and dagger business." Phelps spoke slowly and with a pronounced southern accent. "Your insistence that I miss my daughter's soccer game simply because you're afraid to have a conversation on a micro, even when I assure you we have full encryption … well, I just don't understand and frankly don't appreciate your tactics here."

Cheslov did not always understand this little man, nor did he think it was necessary. "The docks are where we can truly have a private conversation. The Mayor has killed the video and audio on all cameras in this sector. This is our quiet space where we can talk like men."

"I realize that, Mr. Kirill. I just don't understand the need when we have the same protection using encrypted channels."

"I prefer to conduct certain business face to face." Cheslov's dark eyes danced with amusement.

"I see." Phelps said and Cheslov could tell the little man was thinking just the opposite. "At any rate, we have a real problem here. This citizen's coalition is not going to roll over. I'd like to understand your strategy to deal with and resolve the situation."

Before Cheslov could respond, Phelps continued. "I think you need to schedule a sit down with this Miss Deter. See if you can reach some kind of understanding. After all, you are the City's new *lobbyist*, " Phelps pronounced Cheslov's title with obvious disdain. "And I have been lead to believe you have powerful forms of persuasion. She'll have to see that it's in everybody's long term interest to move forward with Planetcom's bid on Wireless World."

"Mr. Phelps, please stop your description at the problem and allow me to prescribe the solution. That is why I am here." Cheslov's smile broadened.

"Mr. Kirill, I assure you, the last thing I want to do tonight is drive down here and have any discussion with you, let alone tell you how to do your job. Frankly, I'm upset at having to do so. But since you insisted I come here you will show me the courtesy of listening to my description of the problem as well as my prescription of the solution."

Cheslov felt a slight contraction on the left side of his face.

"I'll be frank with you, Mr. Kirill. I don't like you. I did not hire you nor do I approve of the City's decision to retain your services. We are quite capable of securing this contract award without your influence on the decision makers. But retain your services we did, so as far as I'm concerned you work for me. And you'd better understand I'm the man who controls decisions in this City. So in the future when I call you on a secure channel…"

Cheslov stopped listening to the little man. The thick accent distorted many of his words, but Cheslov could discern the meaning. Like so many Americans, he attempted to hide behind process and take charge through status. Time to bring the weak rat down to reality. To the real world. To the street level where men ruled. Men like Cheslov who got things done.

"Mr. Phelps, let me tell you a story." Phelps started to speak again, but Cheslov's deep voice easily silenced the other man. "I was a young man. On a dock not unlike this one. Surrounded by waters black like these." Cheslov gestured toward the water that appeared shadowy dark in the bloodless light before dawn. "A man who worked for my father was rude and unpleasant. Not unlike yourself."

Cheslov stepped forward. Phelps stepped backwards, then apparently decided to hold his position.

Cheslov's tone was soft, conversational. "We were discussing a difficulty that night. Again not unlike you and I. Do you know how I solved our problem that evening?"

"Mr. Kirill, if you're attempting to intimidate me I can assure you---"

Cheslov held the AKM bayonet in his right hand and Phelps' throat in his left.

"I slid this very knife into his belly and twisted."

All fight drained from Phelps.

"I twisted through flesh until I felt bone. Then I cut along bone while I looked into his eyes and blood soaked my hands. I carved while he wondered how he had misread the situation so severely. I can assure you, Mr. Phelps, the problem ended then and there. So I implore you, do not prescribe solutions to me. Simply stay out of my way like a rat avoids a snake and we shall get all that we desire. We shall live long lives and watch our daughter's plays while we hold the hands of our whores and our wives in our safe and prosperous worlds."

His black eyes absolutely danced with secret glee.

"Do you agree, Mr. Phelps? Can I count on your cooperation?"

He could.

8

Kate's eyes were closed and she was sweating profusely. She kicked into a jog and forced her body to accept that she was on this treadmill for forty-five minutes so no use complaining. She increased the incline five degrees. Her legs protested then settled into a rhythm. She moved to a full run. Loud protest, then the adrenaline kicked in, her body responded and she glided.

Woody and Molly had flirted all night, couldn't keep their hands off each other. And my-oh-my the conversations she'd had with Mitch. Mitch Downing. Get-down, Mitch. He could really turn it on. Talk about left brain, right brain.

He took that fat man down like a wolf on a rabbit. Get-down.

The sunset, the crowded dance floor, finding an open booth. Mitch and Woody drinking shots of Jack Daniels. She and Molly sharing raspberry Jell-O shooters. Woody made a sissification joke. Molly defended their drink choice, claimed the bartender used a unique recipe that allowed the highest concentration of alcohol attainable in a Jell-O shot while maintaining structural integrity. Molly and Kate high fived and celebrated that retort with another shooter. Woody asked her to define structural integrity and Molly fumbled the ball. Then Mitch picked it up and scored by defining structural integrity as the ability of gelatin to hold its shape when removed from its container.

The fat man dropped like dead weight. Except he wasn't dead. That's the first time Kate ever heard a grown man scream.

Molly lead Woody in a game of 'choice'. Molly selected two celebrities and Woody told her who was hot. If the 'choice' was far from obvious Molly insisted on justification. This lead to a discussion on the true nature of beauty. A discussion lead, of course, by Mitch.

A fine art indeed to have so much to say while never dominating a conversation. A refreshing change from most of the men Kate dated who had so very little to say while controlling every discussion.

She'd read about snow at the Donner Pass. Thirty-one immigrants. Hey, thirty-one flavors, right? Wrong. They only had one flavor.

A mild burst of static. She frowned at the end of her finger, the micro painted onto her nail. Amazing how they could integrate the electronics into a resin that was essentially disposable. Painted onto her fingernail today, removed tonight. Reapplied tomorrow in a different color.

Mitch Downing. Darkest eyes she'd ever seen, with a twinkle like polished mahogany. Get down, Mr. Brown eyes. Sounded like a teacher. One minute quoting Dickenson, the next minute Albert freaking

Einstein. But didn't push too hard. In fact, he seemed the quiet sort.

Would it taste like chicken? A bit bland? Not with the Colonel's secret recipe of eleven herbs and spices.

She'd ask a question and he'd glance at his feet as though he didn't have anything to say. Except he did. And not just a little. He'd start slowly, then look into her eyes and say the most incredible things. Only in response to a direct question. A first she wanted to challenge him, to find the limits of his knowledge. The night progressed, the drinks flowed, and her attitude changed to appreciation at having him around to provide objective data on any subject. Like an oracle. Or a computer.

Beautiful Maribel who deserved so much better than to be homeless and hungry. She'd wake up with a full belly this morning. Cheeseburgers and Grouper and plenty of Marcus to go around. But a steak without A1 sauce isn't a steak, it's a mistake, a mistake, a mistake...

She couldn't think about that. She just couldn't. So she focused on the words. The gridcast, stepping through a history of the micro. The cast stated that cell phones were popular at the turn of the century. Then MP3 players merged with cell phones. Wireless networks sprang up everywhere and suddenly everyone had affordable high speed connections. The name change from Net to Grid indicated an increased density as internet traffic exploded and the planetary backbone multiplied with astonishing speed.

Silicon nano-photonics in the early teens reduced microprocessor size by magnitudes, removed all the heat, and presto – enter the personal *micro* for everything a twenty-first century neo-human could ever need. ID, electronic payment, photos, keys, music, video player, cell phone, Grid connection -- the micro did it *all*. The most basic models worked only in vicinity of the person to whom they were validated. The owner's biometrics were measured and recorded upon activation. The micro learned the unique way its owner talked, one hundred percent impossible to replicate or clone.

The micro evolved into a fun fashion statement. Different forms reflected an individual's personal expression. Everybody had one and wasn't it fun to see how the next person hid it on their body? Old folks used ceramic clips on their belt. *Boring*. Others hid micros in earrings, watches, rings. Teenagers didn't screw around. Skin patches. Tattoo ink. Breast implants.

Kate was old fashioned. She painted her fingernails with an electronic resin that had been on the market for six months. She could capture any color whim or choose French Buff if she felt naughtily au naturale. A society that produces disposable e-resins with the ultimate wear, strength and shine for your nails while providing ubiquitous communications … well, that's just fabulous.

She flicked again. The e-resin on her fingernail detected the motion and toggled the gridcast. A young woman droned in her ear about local politics. Boring, except that her Dad was in politics. If you call being the Mayor of Tampa involved with politics, that is. Wait a minute, this gridcast was actually talking about her Dad's Wireless World thing.

She glided her finger sideways in the air and video appeared on her bedroom wall. Her Daddy was chatting with a young blogger in the lobby of the government center. The blogger wore jeans and a pink halter top. Long black hair was tied into a puffy plait with a soft red floral headband.

Kate liked the way her Dad's electric tie picked up the blue from his navy blazer. He looked fine for a man pushing fifty. Tall and trim and his dark hair showed just a hint of distinguished gray. Her Dad was good at these interviews. He wore a constant little smile on his face no matter how abusive the question.

"---home grown network goes down and my people can't talk and there's not a damn thing I can do about it. Ramona, that's why it's critical that a new network be installed and run by professionals. And that's it. That's my concept."

"And you're referring to this new wireless contract as, um, Wireless World?"

"That's right. That's my vision for our city."

"Sir, if I may ask---"

"You deserve this, our agencies deserve this, and it's the responsible thing to do."

"Mayor Delaney, I understand two firms are bidding on the project – Planetcom and New Light Corporation."

"Yes, that's right."

"Which way is the City leaning?"

"Ramona, let me ask you something. You a radio expert?"

Ramona shook her head.

"No, but---"

"Have a degree in network communications?"

"No sir, but I have a CCNA in routing and switching and---"

"Then please, let our people do their jobs. And don't pay so much attention to self serving rhetoric you're going to hear from one vendor or another."

"*What about the Citizen's Coalition? Is it true that Wanda Deter is organizing her troops for the City Council meeting next week?*"

"*If so this is the first I'm hearing about it.*"

"*I see. Mr. Mayor, the recent census shows over a hundred thousand of our citizens are homeless. So called Nomads. Up over a thousand percent from the turn of the century. Half are children.*"

"*A result of the banking meltdowns a decade ago. You know that.*"

"*A lot of experts feel it's related to the technology gap in our work force. The City could have a big impact through aggressive training and education.*"

"*Yes, and my experts are studying the situation quite carefully.*"

"*Meanwhile the City has earmarked a billion for a new wireless system. That's…*"

Ramona appeared to look directly at the camera which meant she was reading notes from her micro.

"*That's forty-two percent of the City's total budget. Can you comment on that, Mr. Mayor?*"

"*Well within our target for technology and innovation as well as police, fire and rescue expenditure.*"

"*But at the cost of depleting budgets for everything else. How will that impact Tampa's economy long term?*"

A broad smile appear on her Dad's face. He reached out and touched Ramona's arm as though they shared a small joke.

"*Now that's a loaded question if I ever heard one. Look, Ramona, there's lots more to consider than you have in these sound bites. Let me tell you something, I need you to listen carefully to what I'm saying. I've prayed for the Lord's enlightenment, here. Big time. And I can assure you we are on the right path."*

The Mayor glanced at his watch.

"If you'll excuse me, darlin', I've got to run."

Ramona looked straight at the camera on her micro again.

"There you have it, as always, the news Reasonable and Stabilized, from Ramonaonthestreet.com."

Kate adjusted the incline angle to zero and moved into cool down mode. She would have to talk to her Dad about the religious comments. Again. People would think he wasn't open to other points of view. And they'd be right.

She heard a soft drum beat. Molly calling. She flicked her finger and Molly's grinning face appeared on her bedroom screen.

"How can you look so glib after last night?" Kate asked.

"Last night was wonderful. I had a great time. What are you talking about?" Molly said.

"I'm referring to what happened in the camp."

"You know what?" Molly said calmly. "That's none of our business. If you try to worry about how they live, Katie, it'll drive you nuts. Just forget about it."

Kate chewed her lower lip. "I guess you're right."

"So what do you think about Woody?" Molly asked with a grin.

"Pretty hot," Kate said. *But not as hot as Mitch.*

"He's a cage fighter."

"A what?"

"You heard me."

"I thought he was a student."

"He's both," Molly said. "Woody said they learned how to fight in the Navy. Now he cage fights to earn money for tuition. What do you think about that?"

"I think they were paying attention."

"Well, I'm not sure I want to have a boyfriend who fights. In cages. Then again, I'm not looking for a boyfriend, just a good time. And Woody is *definitely* a good time."

"Physically he's got the package, no doubt."

"What do you think about Mitch?" Molly asked.

Kate stepped off her treadmill, wrapped a towel around her neck, smiled at her friend.

"Don't tell me, let me guess," Molly said. "Too short. What is he, five-eight? Nine?"

"Sounds about right."

"Well, he is handsome."

"Devilishly. And there's something else."

"He's too cool for school. Smart as hell."

"True. But not arrogant. In fact, he has a certain shyness. Did you pick up on that?"

"Yeah, I did. He's humble. I like that in a smart guy."

Kate nodded. "You don't see that very often. Like a rare gem. Still trying to get my arms around him. So to speak. But, hey, I'm not looking for a boyfriend either."

"Woody said they'd be at the Undertow tonight. You want to head over there?"

9

Woody was late and the only open seat was in the front row. Professor Martin was already speaking. Mildly annoying but not a mood killer since Woody's mind was on the night before. He spotted Mitch a few rows back. Mitch smiled and gave him a thumbs up.

"...no longer a middle class in our society," said Professor Martin. "That class's contribution to the social order has been replaced by the personal computer."

Those girls were so hot. He asked Molly to zap her profile to his micro, but she just laughed and danced and smiled and her eyes man-oh-man her eyes were time warpers.

"The computer was designed to free our minds and unleash the full potential of our society," Professor Martin said. "Perhaps that could have occurred with severe population control."

He looked into her eyes and he lost track of time. Seriously. Nine, ten, eleven. Then three am. Her eyes did that, created a hole in time.

"There is no debating the notion that the computer, in its ever evolving form, has profoundly increased efficiency and productivity. This has occurred, however, over a half century during which the educated workforce has declined with a corresponding explosion of the unskilled."

OK, maybe it was the booze. But her eyes were part of it. And it was sort of nice to hang out with a chick who at least came up to his chin.

"Today we have reached the point where the uneducated masses no longer bother trying to compete. May as well ask a legless man to try out for professional soccer."

God, she must work out every day to keep a bod like that. Four in the morning and she finally gave him the password to her Facebook profile - Norma Jeane.

"The end result of the great invention that Bill Gates proclaimed would change our lives and free mankind from the burden of manual labor? Simply this. A massive separation of societal classes. The evidence is right outside those doors. Homeless people, Nomads by the tens of thousands in our city. Tens of millions across the Union. Billions around the globe."

Wasn't that Marilyn Monroe's real name?

"We are witnessing class separation, levels of poverty not seen since the Middle Ages. In addition to the obvious suffering, the burden on our government is tremendous. Rather like a large sucking sound. Survival crimes are driving immense cost in parallel with a greatly reduced tax base to fund law enforcement. The center cannot hold."

Woody's fingertip buzzed. He slipped his hand beneath the table and toggled his micro's hologram mode. A tiny naked girl emerged from his palm. She leaned back and rocked little shoulders to silent music. Lilliputian boobs shook and colorful lifeless hair whirled across his fingers. He couldn't help enjoying the show, but his mind was on Molly and he sort of resented the intrusion. He glanced around and spotted her two rows back, throwing a smile and a wink his way. He gave a polite little wave then flicked the tiny dancer from his palm and killed his micro's troll mode. Sometimes these damn things were just annoying.

"And what of the impact to the educated class? Certainly the computer has expanded our ability to process large amounts of data. Mankind's overall knowledge has grown exponentially. But what of an individual's average intelligence?"

And wasn't Marilyn Monroe the first girl to pose naked for Playboy? Molly could sure as hell pose naked for him, any damn day of the---

"Mr. Logan. Do bless the room with your opinion on this grand and noble point."

Woody looked up, wondering for a moment where he was. "My opinion on ….?"

Professor Martin stared down from the stage through thick glasses. "Micro technology for people. Good or bad?"

"Um." Woody tilted his head sideways. "Good? Probably?"

"Mr. Logan, please indulge the class for one moment by pretending you have the mental capacity to be in a position of authority. A position that could make a decision on the very option of the North American Government to shut down the world-wide Grid. Would that you were in such a position, what decision might you make?"

"I'd leave the Grid up. For sure. That's a no-brainer."

"Mr. Logan, MR. LOGAN! You have just DESTROYED the future of mankind."

The auditorium was suddenly silent.

"How's that?" Woody asked quietly.

"Well, Mr. Logan, it is none other than the very Grid you love that has given us the ability to network with many people. E-mail, texting, Twitter, social networking sites… they all provide the ability to keep in touch."

Woody tried to see where this was going but couldn't make it out. "And that's a bad thing." he finally said.

"Indeed, Mr. Logan, it is terrible because we keep in touch without direct contact. Relying on technology to communicate our ideas has lead to diminished interpersonal skills. In simple terms, we have become stupid. Don't you agree?"

"I'm not sure. I mean, at least I keep in touch. Hell, if I didn't have my micro I don't know when I'd have time. What am I supposed to do, make *voice* calls to my Mom?" Woody looked around with a grin and several students nodded agreement. "I mean, come on. That's preposterous. It would take forever."

"My, my," Professor Martin said. "Taking the time to have an actual conversation. Horror of horrors."

Woody thought for a moment. "Besides, I think I'm more expressive with technology. It sort of forces me to get to the point, you know? I mean, I can only send a few sentences at a time. Do you see my point?"

"Indeed, Mr. Logan. Microscopic but I do believe I can just discern its outline. But the fact remains, current forms of communication do not expand our thoughts. Quite the contrary. And Grid search engines make us dumber. It's too easy to obtain information. We do not think. We simply go online and search a particular topic then receive a bounty of information."

"Are you saying it's impossible to critically analyze information to decide the truth for ourselves?" Mitch interjected.

Professor Martin shifted his pinched gaze to Mitch and Woody appreciated his friend's attempt to draw fire.

"Mr. Downing anything is possible. I am not debating what may or may not be possible. I am attempting, struggling in this case, to have you understand reality. Not a Pollyanna view of the world we desire, but the reality of the world in which we live."

Woody drew the fire back his way. "I'd like to go back to an earlier point you were making."

Professor Martin nodded. "Quickly, please."

"You're talking about the poverty level driving crime," Woody said.

"Yes. Cause and effect."

"OK, so we got this problem. But what do we do about it?"

"About what, exactly?"

"Well, do we spend money on helping the Nomads get jobs? Or do we spend money on helping the police fight the crime?"

The Professor shook his head. "Mr. Logan, I would suggest you consider whether you want to apply a Band-Aid or address what causes the wound. The fact that you would ask that question, I mean really. Clearly this is beyond your ability to comprehend, let alone discuss intelligently. Why do I waste my time?"

Professor Martin looked at his audience and smiled, apparently pleased with himself. Woody waited for the man to take a bow.

"Going forward I suggest you read the assignment or do not bother showing up to class. Unlike you, Mr. Logan, my time is EXTREMELY valuable." Professor Martin glared at Woody.

Woody stared back calmly.

"Anything to add, Mr. Downing?" Professor Martin turned away before Mitch could answer. "Didn't think so. Now class, what does this all mean to world markets?"

10

Mayor Delaney watched his daughter fill a tall plastic cup from the sink. How could she drink that pissy tap water? He opened the fridge and grabbed a bottled water. He leaned back and tipped the bottle until it was empty. He wiped his mouth with the back of his hand and looked at her hands.

"Right here," Kate smiled and wriggled her index finger.

He examined the blue micro resin painted onto her fingernail. "That still amazes me," he said.

"Oh, Daddy. This is the twenties. Not the nineties. We have technology now."

"I'll say."

"Speaking of which, I was listening to a gridcast upstairs. The interview you had with that blogger. Talking about the wireless contract."

The Mayor shut his eyes. "Please. Wireless World."

"It does sound odd. Why should the city spend a billion with Planetcom? There's a lot of other stuff you could do with that money."

He opened his eyes and looked at his daughter. "My God, Kate. Do you really want to talk about this?"

"I don't understand the gives and takes the way you do. But I'd like to know more about what goes into this kind of decision. I am working on a graduate degree in Business Technology, after all." Kate fluttered her eyelids in exaggeration.

He smiled. "Angel, mostly it's politics going into that decision. There's always other things you can do with the money. Everybody has a say in it. But that's why I was elected. To make decisions to benefit the most people for the longest period."

Kate took a deep drink followed by a soft exhale. "So tell me what will this Wireless World do for the most people for the longest time?"

"Well, in managing a city, public safety's the foundation for everything."

"But we already have wireless access everywhere you---"

"Ad hoc, sure. But what happens when a firefighter goes into a building and needs schematics and he's in a tight spot and can't get any coverage?"

"Hmmm. Can't that happen with a new system?"

"Well, I suppose, but we'll map those areas with better accuracy."

"I don't think the voters are going to understand that nuance. It's too much money. And I don't understand how two companies can bid on the same thing but one costs twice as much."

The Mayor looked at the large wooden cross above the picture window, then through the glass to the blue Bay beyond the fence line. Lots of boats sailing today. He'd be joining them soon enough. "Like I said, Angel, it's complicated."

"Come on, Dad. New Light's a multi-national. I can't believe they'd risk a global reputation by getting sloppy with Tampa's network. Sounds to me like they're trying to buy our business. Loss leader. Why don't we let them?"

He saw his opening and took it. "God Bless you, Kate. I wish your mom were here and could listen to you. But hey, we have a consultant who's handling this whole thing. He's the expert."

Kate nodded. "Dad, did you hear? A friend in my ethics class? Her brother was murdered in Seminole Heights last week."

"I did hear about that," the Mayor said with a frown.

She threw up her hands. "What's wrong with the world today? Can't you just send more troopers in there?"

"Wish it were that easy. People in that area are animals. Sometimes you need to stay away and let evolution cull the herd."

"Excuse me?"

"We just don't have funding to address every issue." The Mayor sipped his water. Much better than tap. Better still if he poured in a little Scotch. "Those neighborhoods don't pay taxes as it is. Frankly it's tough to spend more money patrolling on top of what we already spend on housing subsidies."

"Well, I guess I'll have to take your word for it. But, Daddy?"

"Yes, Angel?"

"You need to cool it with the religious references."

Kids these days. "How do you mean?"

"When you tell people God wants the new contract... well, it doesn't help your case. That's all. Sounds like an excuse. God told me to do it this way."

"Honey you're part of the new generation. Young, hip, you got it going on. But everyone's not like you. There are lots of folks out there who have deep faith."

"That's fine, Dad."

"They'll never get all the bits and bytes. What's important to them is that I have a relationship with our Lord." He gave his daughter his firm look. "People need to know that."

"People like me vote too. Just cool it a little. OK?" She placed her cup in the dishwasher.

"Where you heading tonight?" he asked. "Any plans?"

"Molly and I might hit the Undertow."

"Special occasion?"

"Just blowing off steam."

"Oh? Why do you need to relieve steam pressure? What's going on?"

"Oh Daddy, just stuff. Life."

"I see," he said with a chuckle. "Checking out the boys."

She smiled. "Molly's thing, not mine."

"Tick tock. You're twenty-four years old, you know."

"I know, I know."

"What about Robbie? He's a good looking kid."

"And doesn't he know it," she said. "That's just it, I'm not looking for a pretty boy."

"What are you looking for?"

"I'm looking for someone I can talk to. Someone who can talk to me. Somebody smart, who knows how things work. Like my Daddy." She winked.

11

"What a prick." Woody slogged across campus with Mitch after class. Five minutes in a cage with Martin. That's all he asked. Hell, make it one minute.

"You got that right," Mitch said. "I thought you asked a pretty good question."

"Me too. Cause you know the city's getting ready to spend a pile a money on that new wireless network."

"Wireless World. Yeah, I heard about that," Mitch said with a smile. "Suits me, I need the coverage for my project."

"Sure. To hell with everyone else. How's your little covert coming along, anyway? Ready to come clean?"

"Getting there. Just give me another day or two."

"At least tell me this," Woody pressed. "Can you really beam that stuff into a person's eyes?"

"That's the easy part, actually. Your optic nerve naturally demodulates signals in a fractional area of the exahertz band."

"Can I get that one more time in English?" Woody asked. *God, here we go.* "You saying your eyes will see what's in the signal?"

"Your eyes don't *see* anything. This has nothing to do with light. Your optic nerve decodes the signal and passes it to your brain."

"Umm... if that's true, then how come we don't see weird stuff coming in that way all the time?"

Mitch shrugged. "On occasion something natural might hit that range. Sun spot, maybe. The odd cosmic radiation. Who knows? Maybe that's where Moses got his idea for the tablets."

"Just how in the hell did you stumble upon this weirdness, anyway?"

"University optics lab figured it out a couple years ago. They modulated a high def photo of a carrot, aimed it at rats. Eventually hit pay dirt in the exahertz band. Hey, it's not rocket science."

"You mean rabbits?"

"Rats, man. Rats."

"Why in the hell did they send a picture of a carrot to a rat? Why not cheese?"

"Rats and mice don't like dairy. They generally prefer grains and vegetables."

"Are you shittin me? Jesus, is anything simple anymore?" Woody shook his head. "And why did they think of that, anyway? Who guessed that your eyes---"

"Your optic nerves."

"Whatever. I may be a country boy but you and I have gone through the same radio training. Who guessed your freaking body decodes RF signals like that?"

"Well, about five years ago grad students in Columbia identified physical characteristics of modulation. Your ears have physical attributes that align with demodulation of sound."

"That's different," Woody said. "The whole set up is mechanical. I mean, little bones and drums."

"True enough. And those same little bone and drum patterns exist on a molecular level. We just never knew it until nanotechnology. Once we could examine parts of the body at the molecular level and look for specific patterns, lo and behold we discovered the optic nerve had the right blueprint."

"And how does this relate back to your project, again?"

"I'm close, let's just leave it at that. In fact, I'm heading to the lab now to get back on it."

"One more question. How much you gonna make on this?"

Mitch smiled. "I've promoted the hell out of the upside. Now the Buyer wants me to outline potential downside. Then we'll talk price."

"Is there potential downside?"

Mitch hesitated then shook his head. "Not that I'm aware of."

"Well, then. Looks like you're in the catbird seat," Woody said. Then he remembered something simple and easy that even he could understand. "One other thing, Einstein. We're going out tonight."

"We are? Where?"

"Undertow. Molly and Kate are going to meet us."

"No shit? You talked to Molly?"

"Sent her a text letting her know we'd be there. She said she'd talk to Kate." Woody reached down and rubbed his thigh.

"Leg sore from last night?" Mitch asked.

"Nah. Little sore from the tournament Wednesday." Woody lifted his palms and wriggled them while he said in a sing song voice, "Rage in the Cage."

Mitch smiled. "Somebody finally landed a blow on the Woodman?"

"No, I just didn't stretch out like I should have."

"Hey old man. What do you think? You're a teenager?" Mitch slapped Woody's shoulder. "How'd you do? As if I have to ask. Nobody ever touches you."

"You know what? I did OK. Got in the zone pretty good."

"You get into that Muay Thai, don't you? I've seen you fight. You don't use the soft techniques. You go for the straight line attacks. Over powering force."

"That's the quickest way to win."

"So did you win on points or what?"

"No, I put him down. Asshole tried to get inside and I landed a clean hook kick. Got his attention pretty quick. He hit the mat and, ya know, I don't recall seeing the gentleman get back up."

Mitch winced. "You kick him as hard as you could?"

"Sixty percent."

"Can't they just step out of the way when you kick that slow?"

"Not this guy, he was coming too fast. But sometimes people duck out of the way, sure. I still earn earn points because obviously if I don't pull back I'll kill the son of a bitch. That's OK. These cage fights are just a show."

Mitch nodded. "Long way from Bushehr."

Woody looked at his friend. His eyes were wide as he nodded his head. "That's right, my friend. A very long way from Bushehr."

12

Margot was surfing and eating wheat divine ice cream in bed when she saw it. A little blue hyperlink texted to her micro as a Grid alert. The story contained the name of a Grid pal.

<u>Local nurse missing since Friday morning</u>

Margot selected the link and when she saw the smiling face of a woman wearing dark nursing scrubs, she dropped her ice cream spoon.

When she didn't show for her shift at Tampa General, Jessica Hart's supervisor called 911. Soon after, her Mini-Cooper was found abandoned at Sandpipers, a local bayside bar. A garment bag with her nurse's uniform was found in the vehicle.

No husband or local family, no immediate suspects in her disappearance. Bar staff remember the woman sat alone on the back deck and ordered several drinks. No one noticed her leave but they were certain there were no other customers on the deck that morning. An apparent malfunction of the area surveillance systems prevented any clues as to when she left or which direction she may have taken.

Margot scanned the opinion journalist's response to the story.

DOESN'T THIS PROVE THE GUN CONTROL LEGISLATION IS A FAILURE? CLEARLY, IT'S ONLY THE CRIMINAL ELEMENT THAT HAS THE GUN IN THE CITY AND JUST WHY IS A BAR WHERE THEY SERVE THE LIKKER A SO CALLED GUN-FREE ZONE? JUST WHY IS THAT? SO CRIMINALS CAN SHOOT GOD-FEARIN FOLK? AND JUST AS I PREDICTED IT WOULD THE FAT TAX IS DESTROYING MERICAN ICE CREAM AND LEADING TO THE DEMISE OF THE POOR PISTACHIO PEANUT, WHICH AFFECTS MILLIONS OF OUR FARMERS ACROSS THE---

Margot stopped reading. Her mind was numb and her body felt as though it were sinking into the bed like dead weight.

The Sandpiper was Jessica's favorite spot to get laid. Margot met her there all the time for appletinis. In fact, Margot had invited Cheslov to join them and the smug bastard didn't show any interest. Now Cheslov goes to the Piper and her friend comes up missing? She needed to see that big Russian.

Who knows, maybe he knew something. Besides, here was the perfect excuse to get his sexy ass out. On her terms. Someplace that would lure him away from his arrogant zone. Knock him down a peg. Hopefully turn him on. And boy-oh-boy she knew just the place.

13

Mitch's mother was old-school strong, raised on a farm with eleven sisters and two brothers. She found a job in the city and that was no hayride, either. Secretary by day, odd jobs at night, saving every dime and living off egg sandwiches. The best time of her life was the decade married to Bill Downing. Then Mitch's Dad passed away it was back to nickel wages with two boys to support.

All because she didn't know anything. She'd set Mitch on her lap as a young boy and say, "Son, you got to learn everything you can in this old life. Knowledge is power, you better believe it. Promise me you'll work hard and know everything one day. Promise your mama."

"I will," he'd say and hug her neck hard as he could and he didn't know how but he planned to keep his promise. Wouldn't be enough to know a lot. He needed to know everything.

Everything.

Most of the Optical Lab was built underground like a stingray concealed in the sand. Mitch pulled open the main door then rode the elevator to the lowest level.

Last night hadn't been a complete disaster. Couple of hiccups, but he'd adjust by inserting a feedback loop into the tuner.

He peered through the microscope at what appeared to be tiny grains of rice. They were actually nanotubes transmitters the size of hairs on a fly's ass. His eyes shifted to a small amber vial that contained a pure form of free-base micro resin that held a five gig connection courtesy of the manufacturer. A large pipe that's always 'open and smoken' to the Grid. He'd enriched the e-resin with millions of his nanomitters and cooked the mixture down to a milky white crystal with only minor modification in the overall chemical structure.

Kate Delaney. Katie D. What a beautiful woman. What an athlete. She was into him. Whenever he looked at her she gave him a smile. Her smiles got bigger as the night wore on.

Until that scene around the campfire. Hopefully she wasn't too freaked out. He'd call her later, just to make sure she's OK. And her Dad was the Mayor. Wow. Man had a big ego, no doubt. He seemed sort of strange from what Mitch could see. And he was pushing some kind of Wireless World vision the City obviously couldn't afford.

The software algorithm for the new feedback loop was fully compiled. If it worked properly, the images would remain locked in high def. No more blurring. His palms were sweating. The back of his neck tingled.

He was ready to turn on.

"Elephant," he said.

The monitor displayed a large African Elephant. Loxodonta Africana. Big ears. The program was responding to audio. Good.

Mitch hit the button and started the sequential modulation. He looked across the room at a dry erase board filled with equations. The 'two's' had looping curves at the base of each digit.

The Buyer insisted on a comprehensive list of downside potential before signing a contract. That was a bit melodramatic. Everything has *potential* downside. Everything in the world. Come on, that's elemental physics. Newton's Third Law. For every action there's an equal and opposite reaction. Did the bank ask Henry Ford to list downside potential to the automobile? It'll change the world, move mankind to the next level. Downside? A little pollution, some global warming. Did I mention hundreds of thousands of deaths every year? No problem, that's collateral damage well within acceptable limits.

How about the upside? If he did this right the possibilities were mind boggling. A blind man could wear a camera smaller than a button and literally see again. In resolution exceeding that of natural sight. And that's just for starters. The real upside was accelerating people's ability to think. People's ability to analyze, to solve problems. Raising the power of the human race as a whole. The sort of advance that could, over time, eliminate poverty.

Screw the downside. The upside potential was off-scale, out of this world. Those were the stakes and Mitch intended to fly this rocket ship all the way to the moon, baby, all the way to---

Something large and gray flew past his mind and he ducked. The dark shape was in his head for a moment, then gone. Not a picture, just a blur. The way you'd see a grease spot flash by on the runway the moment your flight lifts off. He stopped the sequencing and slowly reversed the scale.

15.577, 15.576, 15.574...

And there it was, an African elephant. Clear as a blue sky in his mind's eye. In perfect focus and staying that way.

A warm sensation draped over his mind. A perception of sound within his ear, odd due to the absence of noise in the lab.

He looked at the dry erase board. He could see the looping two's as though the elephant were in his near field vision and the equations in his far field. Not like the elephant obscured the twos. More like the elephant was in the corner of the picture. He was tempted to move his eyes to look from the elephant to the erase board. But he only needed to refocus. Not his eyes, exactly. More like his thoughts.

"Theory of Relativity," he said.

The elephant was replaced by paragraphs of text describing Einstein's theories of relativity.

Mitch luxuriated in a sense of relaxation as he read aloud. "The development of general relativity begins with the equivalence principle, under which the states of accelerated motion and being at rest in a gravitational field are physically identical."

Clear as a computer screen in his head, and that's how he visualized it. Projected onto a screen in his mind. The first screen was the television set in the 1950's. The second was the personal computer monitor in the 1980's. The third screen was the cell phone display in the 90's. Mitch had created a fourth screen – his mind's eye. He could project any information from the Grid directly into his head for easy viewing. Of course a casual observer would be unaware that he was reading anything. A casual observer would assume he knew the material cold.

He once had a class where the professor showed an old television concept called commercials. The idea was that during a program the broadcaster actually interrupted the show to advertise product sales. Ghastly concept, but prevalent in its day.

Some were mildly entertaining. A man walks into a bar and asks the barkeep if she has a juke box. She points to the corner. The man asks about the music selection. The barkeep looks him in the eye and tells him the device contains every song ever recorded by any artist. The man looks incredulous and asks how is that possible.

The point of the commercial was that in time all recorded music would become digitized and stored somewhere on the Grid. The jukebox was just an interface. The commercial was simple, powerful, prophetic.

In the quarter century since that commercial aired, every recorded song had indeed been digitized. More than just music -- every book, magazine, research document, opinion paper, news article and blueprint. Twitter and blogs captured practically every new thought. Nothing short of the aggregate sum of all human knowledge developed and recorded over the past five thousand years down to the last bit and byte. And available to anyone who carried a micro smaller than a peanut. And that meant everyone.

If knowledge was power, Mitch had become the strongest man in the world.

What a rush. Wonderful. Awakened. Powerful. His mother would be so proud.

He smiled and shook his head. Wait until the Buyer tasted *this* shit. It was almost too pure. Almost.

14

"Jesus Christ, Paxton. Calm down."

"I'm telling you, that man is stone cold crazy."

"That may well be true," Mayor Delaney acknowledged as he sliced a piece of sausage and stabbed it with his fork. "Let's just say Cheslov came highly recommended by certain friends who shall remain nameless. Let's leave it at that and let the man do his job."

Mayor Delaney swallowed the sausage and chased it down his throat with a large swig of coffee. He could not remember seeing Paxton this upset. Sure, the man was a pain in the ass but his nerves were normally rock steady.

"Mr. Mayor, I will not be threatened. In any fashion. I did not graduate from U of M Law College, ace the bar, claw my way up to Hillsborough County ADA to ---"

"Lower your voice, Paxton."

Phelps leaned forward and poked the air with a thin finger to enforce his point. "To Chair of the City

Council to be threatened and manhandled by some sick Russian gangster."

"You will get hold of yourself. Right now. We are dining in a public fucking restaurant," Mayor Delaney hissed.

Phelps leaned back and sighed. "I'm telling you as plain as I can. Cheslov Kirill is not a man who can be controlled. In this business, that means he's not a man who can be trusted."

"So now I have to repeat myself? Unbelievable."

"I understand what's at stake here. I understand we are talking hundreds of millions. I understand there are forces at play."

A waitress appeared, offered to freshen their coffees. Both men declined. Mayor Delaney sipped his cup, frowned at the lukewarm coffee, tried to reign in his growing impatience. He swung his index finger in a circle as a motion for Phelps to continue.

"But letting that man into this process is like letting the fox into the hen house. No, it's like letting a wolf into your bedroom. He may help you reach your goal but he will eat you alive in the process. No good can come of this."

"I can handle him," the Mayor said. "And face it, Paxton, he does possess... certain powers of persuasion. Wouldn't you agree?

Phelps snorted. "That notion is rather like sending a Sumo wrestler to ballet school because he's a fine athlete."

Mayor Delaney leaned back and drummed his fingers on the table. "Meaning it sounds silly but you might be surprised at the results. Paxton, let me tell you something. The Lord is with us on this one."

"Oh, please," Phelps said.

"Now, now. Hear me out," the Mayor continued. "You're right, there are also Earthly forces at play here. Powerful forces you cannot imagine. We're talking about money. Real money. There are people…" He paused, carefully choosing his words. "… people who have strongly urged us to let Mr. Kirill into this process. Let's just leave it at that. Keep in mind, Mr. Kirill works for Planetcom. Not the City of Tampa."

"Oh come on. We have him on retainer too. And you could change that in a heartbeat."

"No I cannot change that in a heartbeat," the Mayor snapped. "Are you listening to me? I just said the man came highly recommended."

Phelps shook his head and scowled as he stared across the table.

"People you do not want to mess with, Paxton. I can't say it any simpler than that. End of discussion." Mayor Delaney softened. "Come on Paxton, just play ball, here. Let Mr. Kirill focus on the citizen's coalition. That's what he's been hired to do. He's just a lobbyist at the end of the day---"

"More like hired muscle," Phelps scoffed.

"---and his job is to persuade Deter and her people that Wireless World is a good move for everybody."

"And how do you think he intends to persuade her, Mr. Mayor? Just how do you think he intends to do that?"

"That's not my concern. Nor yours."

"Just look the other way?"

"This is not a college debate, Paxton. This is the major leagues. Suck it up and do your job. Leverage the consultant's data to support our result. Lead the City Council to the conclusion we desire. Total Cost of Ownership, apples versus oranges, my way or the highway, I don't give a shit just get it done. Explain it in terms the people accept."

Phelps held up his hands. "Alright, alright. You're the boss. But I think you're making a big mistake if you think that Russian is going to play our game." Phelps leaned back and his eyes were hard. "Cause he's not playing our game. He's playing his game."

Mayor Delaney stood. "Look here, I'll call Cheslov and have a talk with him. And we're still running our ads against Deter in Google Tampa and Craigslist?"

"The ads calling her a terrorist? Yeah, we're still doing that."

"Hell yes, that's what the bitch is." The Mayor winked. "Look, I'm sorry you got yourself so riled up. But I shouldn't have to tell you how to do your job. You're a smart guy. Just do it, goddamn it."

15

"Why'd you break up with her?" Mitch asked, glancing around the bar.

"Same reason I break up with every chick. Starts out hot. Then just sorta fizzles out til it's nothing but a pain in my ass," Woody said.

"How do you mean?"

"She worried about every little thing all the time."

"Give me an example." Mitch absently considered crowd control modeling. Risk assessment. Threat identification.

"She had a puppy. Cool little guy named Rusty," Woody said. "Mutt developed a rash so I bought some flea shampoo. But was that good enough?"

"I'm guessing not." Petite redhead at the bar ordered her third vodka and Red Bull. At her size that could get real interesting.

"No sir. She had to take Rusty to the vet for a full check-up. All these tests. Of course, she's broke so guess who gets stuck with the bill?" Woody shook his head.

One-man band setting up shop near the entrance. Guy wearing a blue Hawaiian shirt with pink palm trees and Mitch thought anyone wearing a shirt like that had nothing to hide, absolutely nothing. "Well?" he asked.

Woody turned to look at his friend. "Well, what?"

"Well, what did the vet say?"

Woody thought for a minute. "I think he said it was ringworm."

"Ringworm."

"Yeah, you know. Those little worms. Curl up in rings."

"So the flea shampoo idea. Swing and a miss, huh?" The music man wore an acoustic guitar, a harp rack and a loop router to auto-tune his vocals. Doctored karaoke at its finest.

Woody shrugged and pretended to swing a bat in slow motion.

"Do you remember that purser in San Diego?" Mitch asked.

Woody chuckled. "What an asshole. Didn't matter what you needed or how little it cost, his first answer was always no. I mean, you could ask him for a dime to buy a pencil and he'd tell you to pound sand."

"He was a pain in the ass, wasn't he? Kind of like your girlfriends."

"Dude was a little bitch."

"But think about it, Woody. If you're running a business, he's the perfect person to watch the money. Right?"

"Well, hmmm. Maybe."

"Women are the same way. They worry about everything. Eighty percent of the time it's pointless. Maybe ninety percent."

"Ninety-nine."

"Guys like you and me, we'll ignore a situation. Throw flea shampoo at it and be done, right?"

"Where you going with this?"

"What if it'd been a child instead of a dog? You and I maybe give him some aspirin, tell the kid to man-up. But women are different."

"You know that's right."

"She'll take your kid to see a pediatrician. And when the first one says the kid's fine, that's when you and I would definitely let it go."

"Well of course."

"But she'll take the kid to see another doctor and then you find out he's got a rare infection and you realize their nature, a woman's character, is perfect for raising children. If it were up to us the kids wouldn't live. Hell, could be early man would not have survived." Mitch took a long, slow drink from his beer. Two guys in the back of the bar playing darts. One wearing a tee shirt with sleeves cut off. Biceps like Armour hams.

"So you're saying it's the way God wired women. To promote survival of the species. He could've done it to us, but He didn't. He chose to take it easy on men. A little gift, if you will."

"You could look at it that way. Sort of like a spiritual sedative," Mitch said. "But the point I'm trying to make is it's important to understand where the other person's coming from. That's all. Once you understand why things are the way they are then you can get along with people." The other guy was tall and wore a lemon colored shirt. Something about those two bothered Mitch.

"Maybe you should be a marriage counselor." Woody tilted his head and displayed an artificial smile of maniacal proportion.

"What are you boys talking about?" Kate said.

"Why do you look like a freak?" Molly asked Woody.

Molly and Kate stood in front of the booth looking tall and lean and tanned. Mitch looked at Woody who flashed a quick wink and they stood like gentlemen. Mitch gave Kate a shy kiss on the cheek while Woody and Molly melted into a bonafide lip lock.

"Get a room, will ya?" Kate smiled and slipped into the booth beside Mitch.

"What are the ladies drinking tonight?" Woody asked. "Jell-O shooters?"

"Raspberry!" Molly responded with enthusiasm, and the night was off.

They talked of life and they talked of love but they stayed away from politics. They were just four young people drinking and enjoying the laughter and delight that come through the exploration of serious sexual chemistry.

Woody looked at Molly. "You know, you might be asked to leave soon."

"Why's that?"

"You're making the other women look really bad."

Molly frowned. "Why don't you button up your shirt?"

"Might interfere with my ability to dance."

"I see. You're a moron."

"No mamm. It's just that you never know when someone might ask you to perform."

"You don't have to worry there, my friend. No one's going to ask you to perform wearing a shirt like that."

"Guess I won't ask you to dance," Woody muttered.

"What did you say, mumbling man?"

"You have such a beautiful tan." Woody reached out and brushed Molly's arm. "You must spend a lot of time in the sun."

"Natural skin color. Basically the same color as my butt."

"Prove it."

"You would say that."

"Chicken?"

"Hardly. I have dignity and tact."

"Me too."

"How wise of you to know."

"No, I'm serious. Honest to shit." Woody raised his palm like a man swearing an oath.

Molly rolled her eyes and looked away. "I don't know where you come from, country boy, but in my neck of the woods we wouldn't consider that a binding vow."

"Can I still smell your hair?"

"Still? That was never in the---"

"I repeat. Get a room, will ya?" Kate said with a big smile. "Hey Woody. Has Molly told you she's a closet Marilyn Monroe fangirl?"

Just then the one-man band at the front started to play *Red, Red Wine*. Molly crossed her eyes, brought her index finger to her temple and pulled an imaginary trigger.

Woody laughed. "It is interesting, you have to admit."

"What's that?" Kate asked.

"Every time you go into a bar for like the past fifty years you hear the same music."

"Fucken A, the same goddamn song," Molly added. "What's up with that?"

Mitch opened his mouth but it was Kate who jumped in first. "That's because this is universally accepted music. Everybody loves this. It doesn't matter what else you're plugged into, this is good stuff."

"You're kidding." Molly gaped at her friend. "You think *this* is good music?"

"Not this song, necessarily," Kate said. "I'm saying music from this period, in general. You can't beat it."

"What makes it so good?" Woody asked.

"I don't have the..." Kate smiled and shrugged soft, round shoulders. "I can't articulate why that is, it just is. If you look it's evident, it's obvious. There's something specific and tangible about that timeframe. Yeah. Before and since, until today, that timeframe of that generation."

Dark hair fell across her face and Mitch thought she looked... well, his Navy buddies would've said *wicked delicious*.

"What timeframe are we talking about?" Molly asked.

"Late sixties, early seventies," Mitch said.

"But *Red, Red Wine* is from the eighties," Molly said.

Mitch watched the man in the lemon shirt tap pig arms on the shoulder and point their way.

"You've got certain standards in Florida beach bars," Mitch said. "But it's the same point. Kate, when you say 'that generation'. You mean the Beatles, but who else? The Stones? The Animals?"

"All those bands. All of them," Kate said with a nod. "The British bands, obviously. And the American bands. I mean, look at what was going on culturally. I don't want to get into a dissertation. Just pick up, read any edition of Rolling Stone during that timeframe and what they had to say. It's, you know, great music. It'll never go away, God---"

"Or be repeated?" Mitch asked.

"---willing. Huh?"

"Or be repeated?" Mitch asked again.

"Or be repeated. Which is weird. Which is sad. I mean, you wonder why. Why not." Kate looked around the table and shrugged once more. "I don't know. There's probably another Elton John out there who can't make it commercially today. Especially with auto-tune software propping voices and killing any passion that might have been there."

Mitch watched her blue eyes sparkle. Her hands moved in front of her face like they were catching and forging her words into final shapes.

"My grandmother would've told you the same thing," Woody said. "They don't write 'em like they did in the fifties."

Kate cocked her head and dropped a half smile. "You cannot compare the crooners and the Sinatra's and all that, which were lovely in their own way, but you can't compare that to the folk melodies and all the music that was made in the sixties and early seventies. It's completely different. Don't you agree?"

"I totally agree," Woody said.

"Well there you go," Kate said. "Then why are you arguing with me?"

The passion, Mitch thought. The pure passion that allowed her words to flow like clear water from her mind through her hands to the people around her. His little experiment seemed puny and slight in contrast. Access to all the knowledge in the universe couldn't replicate the way she formed her thoughts and expressed herself. He shook his head and smiled to realize he was a little bit in awe of this girl. OK, maybe a lot.

He sipped his beer. Watched lemon man glance at their table for the fourth time.

"I know," Molly said. "Let's play 'I never'."

"How do you play?" Woody asked.

"Simple. I tell the table something I've never done. If you have done it, then you drink."

"Can I drink if I haven't done it?" Woody asked.

Molly smiled. "Sure. Drinking is mandatory if you have done it, optional if you haven't."

"Got it."

Molly frowned and flicked her micro. "Jesus, I'm getting pinged from half the guys in this bar. Time to turn the damn thing off."

"Hell yeah, baby," Woody said. "No trolling tonight. You're closed."

"Too right." Molly smiled. "To everyone but you."

"But here's the most important rule of all," Kate said. "Absolutely no questions. We have to be one hundred percent honest. No joke. This game can reveal weird and wonderful confessions. If you want to offer an explanation, that's up to you. But no one can ask you to explain. Agreed?"

They were all in agreement.

"Alrighty then. I'll start," Kate said. "I've never... been out of the Union."

Mitch and Woody raised their glasses.

"Where have you guys gone?" Molly asked.

"Hell, all over the Med and the Persian Gulf," Woody said. "In the Navy we---"

"No questions, Molly," Kate said. "Those are the rules."

"Of course. How silly," Molly said. "I never... went streaking."

Mitch and Woody drank.

"The English Navy was involved." Woody offered.

"Say no more. Please," Molly said. "Alright, Woody. Your turn."

"I never... slept with my boss," Woody said.

The girls hesitated. Kate tilted her head sternly and Molly drank.

Woody sighed and wiped his chin with the back of his hand. "Ladies, please excuse me. I gotta hit the head."

"I'll go with you," Mitch said.

"I thought only girls went to the bathroom in pairs," Kate said.

Mitch smiled. "We had a head start on you."

Kate couldn't believe it. The moment the boys left, none other than Robbie Phillips showed up at her booth. She'd met Robbie at a dinner party hosted by her Dad last year. Robbie's father was a large corporate donor to her Dad's campaign.

The first date consisted of a stiff evening in a formal restaurant and a never ending monologue describing Robbie's future in politics, sports, education, music, hunting and world travel. Kate asked what sports he played. He mentioned volleyball and Kate started to tell him about the beach games she and Molly picked up. Robbie flashed an annoyed look and said football was his game, deftly changing the subject back to Robbie.

She only went out again on her Dad's absolute insistence that she give him another chance. Her Dad said it was important to cultivate a relationship with the boy's father. Kate remembered thinking what the hell, she'd take one for the team.

The second date was a different restaurant, same bland meal, same weary monologue. Then Robbie drove to the causeway and parked his hybrid Jeepster in the sand off the shoulder of the road. He leaned over to kiss her and she pushed him away. He must've taken that as an invitation since his next move was to grab her breast and she had slapped him hard across his face. His shocked look was full of such brooding that Kate actually laughed out loud. She remembered watching the anger spread across his face like a marching colony of ants. He grabbed her wrist and squeezed too hard and that's when she got scared. He glowered and she tried to pull away. After a moment he let go, called her a whore and drove home in sullen silence.

That's the last she'd seen of Robbie. Until now. Of all the lousy beach joints. He stood by their booth and stared down at Kate and Molly. He wore a loud saffron shirt and his friend looked like a big redneck.

"Well, well. Look who's here," Robbie said with a tight grin. "Little Miss Hot Shit. And you must be her volleyball lover."

Molly rolled her eyes. "Get lost, creep."

Kate stood and glared into Robbie's face. "Keep moving, Robbie. I have neither the time nor the inclination."

Robbie stepped back then glanced at his friend and regained his composure.

"Couple of real whores, here, Vince."

"Watch your mouth."

Robbie whirled and stared down at Mitch. "Who are you?" he said with a sneer.

Kate watched Mitch stare calmly into the taller man's face.

"You need to get the hell out of here," Mitch said.

"What the fuck? Why are you even talking to me?" Robbie's tone was clipped. He stepped from one foot to the next and slid his sleeves halfway up each forearm. He glanced sideways at Vince, then glared down at Mitch. "You best keep moving, little man, before I get angry."

Mitch stepped closer to Robbie.

"You don't want to do that," he said quietly and his eyes never left the taller man's.

Robbie looked less certain. "Kate, you better tell this guy to---"

"Not here." Mitch's voice sounded low and dangerous.

Robbie glanced at his big friend. Back to Mitch.

"Not with me." Mitch gave Robbie a small grin.

Robbie hesitated and Kate knew he was going to slink right out of here with Vince. Something in Mitch's voice. A quiet command. Robbie looked like a child in the presence of an adult.

"Come on, Vince," Robbie shook his head. "Let's get the hell out of here before I hurt someone. Couple a real whores, here, Vince. Couple a real---"

Robbie slammed to the floor on his back and Mitch's foot was on his neck. Robbie's lips pulled apart in pain and he thrashed at Mitch's leg but couldn't get any leverage. Mitch bore down, Robbie's lips turned lavender and he stopped struggling.

Mitch glared up at Vince. "Make your move, fat man."

Molly brought her hands to her mouth.

Kate held her breath.

Vince stood frozen.

Mitch leaned down and whispered into Robbie's ear. Anger drained from the bigger man's face and was replaced by a dead calm.

Then Mitch rose and smiled his boyish grin. "These assholes were just leaving."

Robbie climbed slowly to his feet, brushed off his shirt and made a half hearted effort to tuck it into the front of his pants. "I'm sorry to have bothered you, Kate," he said with his head slightly bowed. Then he turned and walked away.

Mitch looked at Vince.

"It's OK. You can go now," Molly said. She raised her hand and flicked fingers at Vince, the way someone would shoo a fly. Vince turned and hurried after his friend.

Kate sat down and Mitch slid beside her.

Molly tried unsuccessfully to suppress a smile.

Kate took a long drink of Mitch's beer then turned to face him. Apparently height didn't matter in a guy like Mitch.

Woody returned and slid into the booth beside Molly.

"What did I miss?"

"Oh, nothing much," Molly said. "Your friend here just helped two ladies in distress. Asked a rude man to leave."

Woody looked at Mitch and raised his eyebrows. Kate saw Mitch shake his head slowly.

"Who?" Woody asked.

"Some guy I went out with a couple of times." Kate looked from Woody to Mitch. "Am I missing something, here?"

"No explanations. Come on now, those are the rules." Mitch said.

Kate shook her head and a smile spread across her face. "Thank you, Mitch. The situation could have turned ugly. For us, I mean. You defused it like a true gentleman."

"I've never seen anything like it," Molly said.

Mitch and Woody raised their glasses high.

16

The music was loud but Margot didn't hear. She only saw and felt. Appletinis harmonized with XTC and the melody was dazzling. Shirley dealt the occasional shit, but today she'd really come through. The pills were stamped with little playboy bunnies and Margot thought that was perfect considering the evening's destination.

Roosters was one of the few clubs in town where the talent were real humans *and* tolerated a little hanky-panky with clientele. Hell, you might even say encouraged. God it was wonderful to touch an actual person sometimes.

The bass subsided and Margot transferred fifty Ameros to the digital screen wrapped around the dancer's shapely thigh. She watched a computer generated pile of cash expand, accompanied by notes climbing the musical scale like a slot machine payoff.

The dancer leaned low, a slight toss of bleached bangs away from dark eyes. "I can do you and your friend for five hundred," she whispered.

"Not tonight," Margot said. "He's all mine, honey. Get the fuck outta here, will ya?"

"Anything for you, baby," the dancer said. She sauntered away on high heeled stilettos. Margot watched her hips recede into the smoky darkness.

Depending on how the evening progressed, Margot thought she might revisit the idea of a threesome. A chunk of change, but she *was* discussing business with Planetcom's lobbyist so the charges *could* be expensed.

"I'm really glad you agreed to meet me," she said, then flashed what she considered her best *fuck-me* smile. She strove for a look that said open and irresistible but not too obvious. "Why did you?"

"Must a man state a reason to spend an evening with a beautiful young lady?" Cheslov looked around and waved his drink expansively. "In the presence of so many beautiful women?"

"You've got a point there," Margot acknowledged. "Can I ask you something?"

"Anything, my Margot."

"Do you play guitar?"

Cheslov raised a thick index finger and Margot was startled to see her reflection in the long nail. "I play many instruments, my dear," he said.

She needed him to play her instrument. "I've never seen such long fingernails on a man. Sincerely. Is that a European thing?"

Cheslov's black eyes danced. "I would say it is more of an inherited trait."

Margot listened to the peculiar sound of her laughter. The X was really kicking into fifth gear. "So how's our friend the Mayor doing?"

"He is doing exactly as we wish him to do."

Margot smiled, relishing in the mysterious nature of HR. She had hacked a certain file. But how was Cheslov to know she wasn't part of the inner loop? "So our arrangement is in order?"

Cheslov frowned while his eyes continued to smile. "Da."

Now she had his attention. "He hands Planetcom the contract and we cut two percent to his personal account. Am I right? Son of a bitch pays our asking price and it's off to the races. Two percent of a billion's a lot of incentive. Am I right or am I right?"

"Da, he has already selected his boat," Cheslov said and there it was, that weird twitch in his face. "You talk as though you are truly part of the equation, my Margot," he said with a huge, black grin. "But in reality you're just a child."

"Don't be an asshole," Margot said with a frown. "You know I'm right about this." He was making fun of her, the son of a bitch. She needed to regain the upper hand. "So tell me something. Delaney's record is clear. Never a hint of scandal. Why does this cracker suddenly put everything on the line to trade us a contract for a goddamn boat? Huh? And he's a Jesus freak. I thought Jesus freaks were supposed to be better than the rest of us? What gives?"

"I cannot say with absolute precision." To her great dismay Cheslov looked bored. "But I have a theory."

Margot raised her eyebrows and waited. This fucker was something else. She could actually hear the music again and it sounded like shit. What a buzz-kill, this one.

"He uses religion to mask his true motives. His heart cannot admit that he is merely a man who naturally wishes for finer things in his life. He therefore hides behind the conviction that a God wants the people of Tampa to have the Planetcom system. Not the Mayor's plan but the plan of a God." Cheslov shook his head. "As if a God would concern Itself with such tedious affairs."

"Hey, I don't give a rat's ass if he thinks it's the Antichrist's plan as long as he awards that fucking Wireless World to Planetcom." Margot tipped back her drink and raised an empty glass. A topless waitress appeared with a refill and Margot trained her eyes on the woman's breasts.

"Did you put more vodka in this one like I asked?" The key to having your way with these bitches was to keep 'em on the defensive.

"I asked Walter to do that."

"Good. The first one was a little weak. But the second one was better. This one better be the bomb. OK, you can vamoose now." Margot turned back to Cheslov. She had the same problem here, she thought. She needed to put this jackass on the defensive. "I wouldn't be so cocky if I were you. I could get you fired, Mr. Kirill. Don't think I can't make it happen. I sure as shit can." She tilted her head down and glared across the table with what she considered her best *don't-fuck-with-me* look.

Cheslov pulled a long cigar from his shirt pocket. He flipped open an old lighter and as he brought the fire toward his face she caught her reflection in his black eyes and for a moment, just a microsecond really, she saw something hideous and revolting.

She shut her eyes and shuddered. Her throat was dry and she forced a swallow. *What the fuck?* If her X turned out to be rotten she'd have Shirley's ass under a strap across her fucking lap. She opened her eyes and drank deeply from her martini. And again. The soothing numbness returned. Damn drink still needed more vodka.

Time to bring the conversation back around to herself.

"OK, come clean. What were you doing at the Sandpiper? Looking for me?" This morning she drove right by the Piper on her way to work. She was trying to get around some slow-ass motherfucker when she glanced over and spotted the black Jag in the parking lot. She wanted to stop but she was late for a Telepresence session with Singapore. Her boss expected her to set up the connection, the retard.

"I was merely seeking cold vodka," Cheslov said. "And warm sunlight."

"Did you see Jessica? About five ten, dark hair? Bangs?"

Cheslov frowned and this time it reached his eyes. "A friend of yours?"

"Yes, you heard me talk about her. Remember? I've invited you out with us. You don't know what you're missing, Mister." Margot leaned her head back and gave him a small smile.

"Is she a beautiful woman like you?"

"Jessica's very pretty." Margot cocked her head sideways and laughed. "Especially her tits. I can't believe you haven't taken me up on my invitations, Cheslov. I swear. Sometimes you're such a loser."

Cheslov chuckled. This inane woman's company was worse than the Mayor's. Sitting there with her whore legs spread, rambling about the deal with the Mayor as though she were anything other than a low life cyka who did not deserve to sit at a table with men. Her rudeness knew no bounds, treating the young prostitutes at this dance hall like chattel.

Interesting that she had invited him to Sandpipers to meet her and a friend. He did not understand why he could not recall that. He thought he'd been there by chance. Was he going mad? Perhaps. Such a shame.

Cheslov listened to the cackle of her laughter and made mental calculations. The award occurred in four days. *Check.* He hit the high seas in five days. *Check.* Margot would read more newscasts about her missing friend and even a bitch as dense and clueless as she would eventually put two and two together. *Check.* And just what were the odds that he would be associated with Margot's disappearance before he made his great escape? Less than zero. *Checkmate.*

"Have you seen the inside of my Jaguar, my dear? Still synonymous with old-world English luxury. I would consider it an honor for you to warm the black leather." Cheslov smiled his charming smile and his eyes reflected all the desire the crazy bitch imagined.

Margot grinned eagerly. "Great idea. Maybe you're not such a loser after all."

Margot wanted to stare into his black eyes forever. They brimmed with bottomless warmth and humor. Fuck the Jag, she'd take it standing in the alley where she'd ravished many a dancer and the best part was when other people strode by and looked in. *M'm!, M'm! Good!* She just didn't give a shit and wanted the whole world to know it.

She took his hand (ouch those nails were long), led him into the alley, and kicked off her tiny skirt while Cheslov lead her deeper into another darkness and his eyes were like headlights shining brightly until a short time later when she was horrified by what lived beneath.

17 Sunday March 8, 2020

Mitch saw that Kate was online so he pinged her. He hoped she would respond. If her name turned blue he'd open an audio channel. Audio only, not video. Video might be a bit presumptuous. Her name remained black.

She stood at the bar. Hair waving in a sea breeze blowing in from the gulf.

Her name remained black.

Her eyes soft and gentle, he caressed her hair and touched her face then tasted her soft kiss.

Her name remained black.

Her smile glowed in the soft light on the beach, dark Irish looks. Irresistible.

Her name turned blue. Just like her eyes.

"Hi Kate."

"Hello Mitch."

They were quiet.

"Can I see you tonight?" he asked.

"Hello there, young man. You must be Mitch."

"Good evening, sir."

"Call me Chase. Come in, come in." Mayor Delaney opened the door and ushered Mitch into his home. "Please, join me in the family room. Can I get you anything? Drink?"

"No thanks," Mitch said, and followed the Mayor into a cavernous room decorated in white with blue accents. Beachy. Two large picture windows looked over a lanai, then an expanse of green grass and the blue water of Tampa Bay. The windows framed what looked like a two hundred inch organic LED television. The screen displayed a news channel and the sound was muted. Above the TV was a simple wooden cross.

"Kate'll be down in a few minutes. I'm just watching a little tube. Please, sit. Sure I can't offer you a drink?"

"Quite certain, thanks." Mitch was mildly shocked to see the Mayor drinking a bottled water. Those little bottles were banned in the US what, ten years ago? Ridiculously high carbon footprint. What would he do next, mix it with booze?

"Kate tells me you're in grad school too."

"That's right, sir," Mitch replied.

Mayor Delaney nodded. "Studying nanotech over at the college, son?"

"That's right."

"When do you get your sheepskin?"

"Three months. Graduate in June."

"God bless you, son, that's wonderful. Interviewing with any particular firm?" The Mayor tipped his water bottle while his eyes remained on Mitch.

Mitch lifted his palms and smiled. "I'm afraid of all that structure. Too much time in the Navy, I suppose. Think I'll strike out on my own, go after venture capital, try to bring something to market. I have some ideas."

"Navy, you say? What did you study there?"

"Electronics, at first --"

"Hell, if you have product ideas you may get something to market faster with resources available at a larger firm. I've got contacts at Planetcom. Be happy to help you out."

"I appreciate that. But I'd give up too much creative license at a larger firm."

"God bless you, son. You have a lot to think about and some interesting options. Please excuse me, I do believe it's time to upgrade to Scotch."

"Sure thing," Mitch said. "Pleasure meeting you."

"Likewise. Kate should be down in a shake." The Mayor disappeared into the kitchen.

Mitch sat on the sofa and used his micro to flip through channels. Then stopped, unmuted the audio.

He loved this old show. Trebek was a little long in the tooth but his voice was strong and clear. Mitch appreciated the way Alex spoke every phrase with perfect pronunciation, no matter the language.

"Ancient history for three thousand," a contestant said.

Mitch glanced over his shoulder. The coast was clear. He couldn't resist. He tapped his resin finger on the sofa.

Mayor Delaney helped himself to a thick, green glass from the cabinet, poured two fingers of twelve year old Scotch followed by the last of his water. He took a slow sip, savored the smoky blend of heather on his tongue. He'd better go upstairs and let Kate know her guest had arrived. Decent kid. He appreciated Mitch's formality. Asking the boy to call him Chase was a little test. Anyone who tried to become informal too early was not the sort of person who properly respected class. Kid looked a little rough around the edges with that hair. Hadn't shaved today. Oh well, enjoy your college freedom while you can. A little indecisive about his future, but seemed sharp. The Mayor stepped into the archway framing the family room.

The boy was watching Jeopardy with his back to the Mayor. Great old show.

"Geometry for two thousand."

"Here is your answer … A triangle with all sides of different length, all angles different degrees."

The contestant hesitated. The Mayor heard Mitch ask in a soft voice, "What is a scalene triangle?"

"What is a scalene triangle?" the contestant finally asked.

"'What is a scalene or oblique triangle' is the correct question," confirmed Alex. "Next category?"

"Dante's Inferno for two thousand."

"Here is your answer. These allegorical depictions of temptation assailed Dante before his visit by Virgil."

"What is a lion, a leopard, and a wolf?" Mitch asked.

"What is a lion, a leopard, and a wolf?" the contestant asked.

"Yes, that is the correct question," Alex agreed.

The Mayor sipped his drink. *Jesus Christ, what have we here?*

"Let's try Dante's Inferno for three thousand."

"They are concentric and represent a gradual increase in wickedness," Alex said.

"What are the Nine Circles of Hell?" Mitch and the contestant asked simultaneously.

"Nine Circles of Hell is the correct question," Alex said.

"Dante's Inferno for four thousand."

"These three traitors are chewed in the vicious mouths of Satan in the very center of Hell."

"Who are Brutus, Judas and Cassius?" Mitch asked.

"Who is Brutus, Judas and Cain?" a contestant asked.

"Yes, that is the correct question," Alex said.

The Mayor shrugged. Oh well, can't be right all the time, son. Nice run, though. Damn nice run.

"Wait, I have a correction. I'm very sorry," Alex said. "Brutus, Cain and Judas is not the correct question. Does anyone else have the proper question?"

The buzzer sounded.

"'Who are Brutus, Judas and Cassius?'" Alex asked. "Brutus and Cassius betrayed Julius Caesar. According to Dante, this act represented the destruction of unified Italy. Judas, of course, is the biblical betrayer of Christ."

Well I'll be dipped in shit.

"We'll continue the category with Dante's Inferno for five thousand. Here is your answer. These are the people in Dante's Hell. These are the people in Dante's Hell."

"Who are the unrepentant?" Mitch asked.

"Who tried to justify their sins?" a contestant asked.

"Yes, that is the correct question," Alex said. "Those in Hell are people who tried to justify their sins. The unrepentant. People who sinned but prayed for forgiveness before their deaths are found in Purgatory, where they labor to be free of their sins."

Well God Bless and God damn. The Mayor sipped his drink. He couldn't believe it. Damn kid ran the table in every category.

"Dad, you're not spying, are you?" Kate asked, softly hugging her Dad from behind.

Startled, the Mayor almost spilled his drink. "As a matter of fact, I am. Come on, Angel."

He lead his daughter into the room. Mitch looked up, muted the television, and stood. His wore a big smile. So did Kate.

"Hello, Kate."

"Hi there."

"Mitch, I'd like to have a word with you," Mayor Delaney said.

"Oh?"

"I wonder if you could help me with a little problem, son."

"I will if I can. What's the problem?"

Mayor Delaney told Mitch about Wireless World.

18

Mitch wished the Mayor hadn't laid that on him. Wireless World was a huge waste of money. Come on, who couldn't see that? Just driving to the fair they passed acres and acres of tent cities. Government couldn't afford housing projects. And why bother? Tents were way less expensive. Thousands, tens of thousands *out of work* (according to the opinion journalists). *Adopting to a new life style otherwise known as survival* (according to bloggers). Hundreds of thousands of people migrating south for the winter. Refugees. Nomads. No different from birds. Living off recycled waste from landfills. Rumors of cannibalism. More than rumors based on what Maribel was sharpening last time he saw her.

And the Mayor wanted to hand Planetcom a billion? Sonofabitch should be shot for even thinking it.

Except for … well, except for one little obsession scurrying and gnawing at the back of his mind. *InSyte* needed coverage. *Of course it did.* And wasn't that important, too? Important for what? *People, that's what.* Do you merely treat the symptoms or do you attack the root of the problem? *InSyte* could change the---

"Mitch, why did my father ask you to do that?" Kate asked.

Mitch looked at her then back at the road. "I'm not sure."

"What did the two of you discuss when you arrived?"

"Just your basic meet and greet. He asked me about school, my plans after graduation. Nothing too exciting."

"Well, you must've said something that caught his attention. I mean, I can't get him to say boo about that contract." She shook her head. "I can't believe he asked you to meet his staff to discuss an issue his experts have studied forever."

Mitch glanced at her as he changed lanes. "Your Dad wants to leverage an average citizen to support his position. He needs someone like me to offset someone like Wanda Deter."

"Wanda who?"

"Deter. She leads the Citizen's Coalition. Local org. Damn effective at influencing politics."

"Do *you* support Wireless World?" she asked.

"It's probably a good idea for the City to take control of its network." He reached over and gently touched the top of her thigh. She turned slightly, moving her knees closer to the center console, closer to him.

"That contract is about more than taking control," she said. "The City could easily take over the existing home-grown networks. Wouldn't cost much. Or they could go with the New Light bid.

That's the part I don't understand. Why do you think my Dad wants to spend a billion with Planetcom when he can do the same thing for half the price?"

"I don't get that, either. That's why he wants me to talk to Mr. Phelps tomorrow, I suppose, so I can learn more about it. Then if I support his position, I might speak at the Council meeting Tuesday night."

"Did you hear about the riots last night?" Kate asked.

Mitch shook his head and followed the Grid search her question induced.

"Another food riot near that big landfill off Anderson. Two hundred refugees were killed, Mitch. *Killed*."

Mitch opened his mouth to ask her why did it always have to be about the goddamn Nomads. Then he stopped. *Where did that thought even come from?* He didn't really wonder that. Surely the Mayor had an obligation to help people living in poverty. And yet… Mitch needed more wireless coverage, man, he *needed* it. He felt like battle lines were being drawn. In his head. Which side was he on? He had to decide before---

---movement in his peripheral vision. This time it wasn't Kate and wasn't exactly his vision, more like his peripheral *perception* because the actual *vision* was unfolding inside his mind like a stranger crawling out from under the bed after lights out, standing to shake dust from ragged clothes and showing sharp teeth---

---*through a red haze the Mayor vows to quell the Godless rebellion, troopers spray thousands of Nomads with heat rays mounted on truck beds, an olive drab Humvee explodes careening into the sky to flip slowly, an improbable gainer, Nomads detonating*

IEDs remotely with micros, twirling into a brick wall shoulder first, FALL BACK, FALL BACK, FALL BACK before they fire into the---

"Mitch, what's wrong?"

Kate. Far away.

Whiskey Tango Foxtrot?

Mitch shook his head and willed his eyes to focus on the negative of the road slowly dissolving before him.

Now what? Hallucinations?

"Nothing, Kate. Little headache." He smiled and coughed softly. "I knew I should've turned down that final shot of Jack last night."

"Nonsense," Kate said matching his grin. "There it is. Take this right. Yep."

Mitch pulled into a large gravel lot, found a slot, parked. He exited the car, stepped to Kate's side, opened her door.

"I got this," he said as they approached the main entrance. Their hands touched and she slipped hers into his.

"If you insist." Kate smiled and flicked her micro to protected mode.

They stepped through the RF field of the fair's entrance and a pleasant female voice welcomed them to the one hundred forty third annual County Fair and Mitch's micro was debited ninety Ameros. The voice suggested they try the pulled barbeque pork at the northeast corner of the park. Mitch thought they might head that way. Barbeque was one of his favorite foods. The fair program knew this, of course, from scanning Mitch's profile and purchase history while debiting his micro.

"Where to?" Mitch asked.

Kate looked around and Mitch watched her chew ever so slightly on her lower lip. Bright red and white striped tents loomed on both sides of the entrance. A John Philip Sousa grand march permeated the night from small speakers mounted on tall poles. The music mixed with the sound of young teenagers laughing and talking excitedly. Rides of all sizes were filled with children of all ages. Human and holographic vendors hawked ice cream, cotton candy, popcorn, sodas and challenged all-comers to step right up and try your hand at various virtual tests of skill. In the center of the fairgrounds a huge Ferris Wheel towered above all else.

"Let's just grab a snack and see where we end up, shall we?" Kate asked.

"Wonderful plan," Mitch said.

They stood and watched a gray machine spin warm liquid sugar into blue and pink cotton candy. Mitch purchased two cones and off they went. They lost a few Ameros on the virtual ring toss. They both knew it was designed to miss ninety nine percent of the time but the sound effects were splendid and it was fascinating how the programmers allowed you to hold and toss a virtual ring. They rode the whirly bird and the motion pushed their bodies close together. They tried their luck at the shooting gallery. Mitch leaned close to Kate to help her align her sights. She smelled terrific. The lasers were set to random so it was impossible to hit anything. But it was fun and when the occasional digital duck fell from the digital sky Kate laughed herself silly.

She laughed again at the gamer tent. So many people engaged in activities that just looked ridiculous to an observer. People wore headsets and body harnesses and some eager young boys wore uniforms of light armor complete with shields and homemade coats of arms. They engaged in everything from virtual sword fights to virtual bowling.

Kate challenged Mitch to a tennis match. He looked across the net and a girl who looked nothing like Kate hit a big serve. He felt the clay court beneath his feet as he dove wide for the return. He felt his virtual racket hit the virtual yellow ball and watched it loop fuzzily cross court with loads of topspin from his virtual forehand. A puff of green dust as his shot landed just inside the line. But the virtual female anticipated a cross court return and she blistered a forehand down the line. Since the serve pulled him wide, Mitch could only watch the virtual ball bounce inside the line across his court. They played a complete set and Kate won six games to four. The gaming space was heavily air conditioned, so they hardly broke a sweat.

Eventually they found themselves at the Ferris Wheel. They were lead to a cage by a teenaged attendant. She wore a large paper nametag with a barely legible scrawl. *Phyllis*. Mitch made a small joke that the attendant ignored. They soon spun upwards in their lazily rocking cage.

"Boredom," Kate said. "Remarkable concept."

"Let's just hope our young friend down there can concentrate sufficiently on her current task."

"What do you think causes boredom?"

"The perception of one's environment as boring."

"Oh no you don't," Kate said. "No fair using the word as a part of the definition."

"Fair enough. In her case, I think boredom is caused by something that's too easily understood. Namely, helping people into little cages and pressing a single button over and over."

"I think you just nailed it."

"How about anti-boredom?" Mitch asked.

"What do you mean?"

"Tell me something you've always dreamt of doing."

"Let's see," Kate said. "That's a hard one. I'm the kind of girl who takes it one step at a time."

"So you're climbing a staircase but you don't know where it leads?"

"More like I don't choose the next path until I finish the one I'm on. I'm not overly concerned with my destination. Just choosing the right path. So I know I'll end up in the best place. Just don't know where that place is, necessarily."

"I see," Mitch said and crossed his eyes. Then he smiled. "So you don't have the usual female dream? The mental picture of laying on a beach surrounded by men in Speedos who cater to your every whim?"

"That's no dream. That's a fantasy. Totally different thing altogether. Except for the Speedos. Honestly, Mitch, is there anything you don't know?"

"There is much I could learn of love, my dear. The greatest mystery in the universe."

"You always seem to know just what to say to a girl."

The big wheel spun around and around. Most of the riders sounded like teenaged girls. Delighted screams floated through the air, not entirely unpleasant. The wheel eventually stopped with Mitch and Kate's enclosure rocking gently at the apex. The sun's last rays landed long and low across the fairground before reflecting off the Bay. Beyond the water they could make out a dozen skyscrapers.

"What a view," Mitch said.

"Yes, it's beautiful," Kate agreed. "Thank you, Mitch."

"For what?"

"For bringing me here. It's been too long since I came to the fair."

"How long has it been?"

"I must've been about four. My Mom and Dad brought me. Everything looked bigger but it was the same stuff."

The Ferris Wheel jerked forward with an audible groan. They were high enough so that it was a little scary.

"How often do they test these things, I wonder?" Kate asked.

"They test every day."

"They do?"

"Sure. They're testing right now."

"Oh, you're bad," she said, smiling.

"Good thing too," Mitch continued. "Since every so often they have this little problem."

"What problem is that?"

"This little problem with the lag bolts that hold these cages in place."

"What are you talking about?"

"These cages rock back and forth, right?"

"Yeah. So?"

"So that stresses the bolts and eventually they weaken."

"What are you saying?" Kate grinned.

"No reason to be alarmed. It's just that every so often the bolts fatigue and the inspectors miss it and…"

"And?"

"And the cages fall off. But it's infrequent. I mean just incredibly rare."

"Oh, you're such a liar!" Kate said and grinned wider. The Ferris Wheel lurched bumpily into its spin and their cage rocked creakily back and forth.

"What?" Mitch asked innocently.

He leaned closer, pretending he couldn't hear. Kate slapped his shoulder playfully and he kissed her while their cage whirled around and around the great wheel like a satellite caught in orbit.

19

The Mayor sipped twelve year old whisky and looked out the big Palladian window into bright sky. Hell of a day for the beach. Too cold to swim, but at least you wouldn't roast over the sand with that sea breeze.

Lauren had loved the feel of the morning air riding over the gulf. Scones and strong tea at the Café Continental. Scrabble on a blanket, making up words and laughing the entire day. Lauren packed Cuban sandwiches and a few pale ales for late afternoon and an inflatable water bowl for Demi, their golden retriever. Young Chase Delaney's face flushed after one beer and Lauren would joke about his Irish Tan.

Lauren always stopped to watch the sailboats. She had sailed as a child and often described the feeling of silently cutting through waves. Floating through ocean spray.

"One day," she would say. "Promise me one day we'll have a sailboat, Chase. Please, that's all I ask."

She was tall and lean, long soft hair fell over her face and he swore to God she looked just like an angel. He wanted to hold her and feel her body next to his because she was perfect, just perfect and he could not fathom how God could create a more wonderful woman. On the Spring day in 1995 Lauren agreed to marriage his heart took off like a big C130 and Chase felt the soft hand of God's love.

They wed the summer Chase completed Law School. He passed the bar and became a public defender in the Thirteenth Judicial Circuit. Katie came along a year later and those were the good years. Little Katie on his shoulders as they watched Lauren play beach doubles, two on two. Nothing held Katie's interest more than watching her mom fly into the sky and spike that white orb. Katie's whole face would transform into a huge toothless smile.

The damn good years.

Working as a young public defender was just the opposite. At first, he assumed his clients were innocent and trusted his ability and God's mercy to prove it to the jury. Over time he figured out they weren't so innocent. In fact they were guilty as hell and didn't care who knew it. They resented the whole arrest thing and usually blamed him.

One night he and Lauren lay in bed. She'd played volleyball all afternoon.

"If you imagine your arms panting out of exhaustion. Not your body, just your arms. If they were separate unto themselves they would be gasping for breath right now."

He smiled. "How about your legs? Are they gasping for breath too?"

"Yes. And they desperately need to be kissed."

He rubbed and kissed a long, smooth leg.

"Mmmmm. Coming back to life feels so nice," she purred. "How was your day?"

He shook his head. "Had a kid in, maybe fifteen. Some dumbass left the keys under the seat and he boosted a car. Detectives caught him at a traffic light, I mean he could barely see over the damn wheel. Dead to rights. Mother posts bail and the kid skips his court appearance. Just blows it off. Judge issues a bench warrant and they pick him up last week. I meet him and the kid acts like he doesn't give two shits about the whole thing."

"Is he going back to court?"

"You bet. In handcuffs. He'll do time and there's nothing I can do about it. I met his mom yesterday. She got in my face for taking her son away. Lord have mercy."

Lauren brushed hair from his forehead with gentle fingers. "I tell Katie every day her Daddy loves her and he works so hard to support our family. You're our hero, you know."

"What is wrong with these people?" he asked.

"Well, you know the system's gamed. Kid takes a joyride after somebody leaves the keys on the seat. Come on, that's apple pie on a windowsill."

"Maybe so. But the kid knows it's wrong. I mean, what kind of city do we have if everybody does whatever the hell they want?"

"But you have to understand the people you're sworn to defend. Their circumstance in life. That's all I'm saying. I just want you to try."

But his job, man it beat him down every day. People lied. People cheated. He couldn't stand to be in the same room with his clients. How could he find compassion? Contempt is what they deserved and Lord he had plenty of that. Extra helpings topped off with scorn. These people got into his head and God he couldn't take it.

Charles convinced him that running for Mayor was his *chosen path*. There was no finer man than Charles, no closer friend. The man traveled the world and built a sprawling shoe empire from scratch. Wherever Charles had landed, the Lord had his back and would carry him safely home. That much richer, knowing Charles. Lucky sumbitch probably hit a jackpot overseas.

Chase finally discussed his Mayoral run with Lauren. Just finishing his third scotch and water when he said, "I need you in my corner on this one. Can't do it without you."

Lauren sat at the kitchen table, her voice and eyes were soft. "Honey, I am in your corner. Always. I just want you to run for the right reasons."

"What the hell's that supposed to mean? Do you think I'm running for the wrong reasons?"

"As a matter of fact I do."

"Oh please." He stepped to the counter, poured four fingers of Scotch over rocks, stirred the drink with his pinkie. He spoke with his back to Lauren. "You've seen me with our parishioners."

"Making decisions for a church and for a City are two different things."

He turned to face Lauren. "I don't see any difference. Either way, I consult a Higher Power for my decisions."

"That's just it. You're a wonderful man, but just a man so you're not perfect. You can't be all-knowing. You'll face decisions where God won't give you the answers. He can't. You have to listen to other people."

"Lauren, come on."

"Weigh the evidence, make decisions based on your experience, your principles. What you know and what you don't. That's what makes a great leader."

He ran a hand through his hair and drank deeply and that's when

(the secret voices started to chatter)

he first knew he couldn't trust his wife.

"Faith's what makes a great leader," he said. "Too many forks in the road, way too many rivers to cross to think you can lead a flock without faith."

"Faith is an important part of leadership. That's true. But faith can't be blind. Can't marginalize facts."

"There's lots a facts in this world. Too damn many. They're not irr-futable, you know. Not by a long shot."

"All facts are irrefutable. That's why they're facts."

He slammed his hand against the counter, happy to read surprise in her eyes. "For Chrissakes you're missing my point! There are spirits in the world. You know that. Dark spirits. Little bastards do their damndest to influence a man, knock him off the straight and narrow." He took a drink and ice cubes rattled as he set down the glass. Condensation soaked his hand so he wiped it on the front of his shirt. "Now I'll agree a leader needs men, good men, to focus on the facts and give advice. Just like you're saying. But the man at the top, he's got to be a man of faith."

"I agree that you need faith to lead---"

"Man at the top has to govern for a City of God. Not a City of man. That's the only way."

"---I said that already," she continued. "But don't you see? Blind faith is dangerous."

He filled his tumbler. "Dangerous? Oh please. Such melodrama."

"If you run for Mayor and win, it's not because God hands it to you. It's because you earn it. On your own."

"Damn right."

"Sure, God gives you health and talent but the rest is up to you."

"Wait a minute," he said.

"Some people win and others lose and God, he stays out of it. He pulls for you, sure. He pulls for everybody. He wants us to make the most out of our---"

"Just wait one God damn minute."

"---five senses and remarkable intelligence. The ability to look at something closely, trust what our wits tell us we see, then go from there."

"I don't think God sits back at all," he said. "He's in the boat with me, helping me row."

Lauren gazed evenly at him. "What if you decided to climb Mount Everest? Lead an expedition? Quite an undertaking, right?"

"Well sure it is."

"You have the ultimate responsibility. Other people's lives."

"What's your point?"

"You'd perform your due diligence, wouldn't you? Study the weather to time it right? Examine the terrain, select the best trails? You'd want to talk to men who already made the climb, right?"

"And consult my faith."

"Uh-huh. But you'd also do those other things too." Lauren waited. "Right?"

"Not necessarily."

Lauren shut her eyes.

"Maybe you wouldn't mind telling me why not."

"I don't know. I don't have the …"

Lauren's eyes opened. "You might just start up the mountain without a map? Or maybe with your eyes closed? What difference does it make? You know your God will protect you."

"He's your God too."

"Yes, he is. And He's given me the greatest gift of all. Rational thought."

"You need more than that---"

"That gift bears a responsibility. The obligation to apply it."

"---in an irrational world, my dear."

"Don't equivocate. We're talking about people's lives. Do you hate the pain that much? That heaviness in your chest when you make a wrong decision?"

"What are you talking about?" he said, confused.

"Does blaming God for everything let you off the hook?"

He shook his head in an effort to clear it. "I am so tired of your bullshit."

"Don't get defensive. It's not a personality flaw. It's the natural temptation for politicians. Don't you see?"

"You have no idea what you're talking about. You don't have the courage it… the real faith the... I have courage, Lauren." He jabbed his chest with a broad thumb. "Me."

As he spoke his words felt empty, like sand spilling from a broken vessel.

Lauren stood and her eyes flashed. "You don't have the courage to admit what you don't know."

"I won't let you talk to me…," he said. "Out of my beliefs."

"You're a man. Not an apostle. You're my husband and I love you. But if you insist on going down this path then you'll have to go it alone. I can't support you."

"I won't be moved by evil spirits."

It was Lauren's turn to shake her head. "Who are you, Chase? Honestly, sometimes I wonder if you're losing your mind. You sound like a crazy man."

He would never forget what happened next. The moment. The instant. Lord knows he had replayed it over and over and over. He'd long given up hope that the outcome could somehow be different. But he couldn't stop the reruns. The memory was coated in emotional glue.

He stepped forward and slapped Lauren's beautiful face. He moved in slow motion so she saw it coming but made no move to block it, as though she wanted him to hit her and to this day he did not understand what made her so strong.

She stared at him for a full minute. Her stunned blue eyes were wet. He watched detachment form in her gaze, realization dawning that she was looking at a stranger.

Then she turned away. She left the room, left his life. Then in one hell of an exclamation point she left the world that night four years ago.

Her car was struck head on when a big Chevy van swerved into her lane. The driver of the van tried to flee the scene but stumbled and passed out in a nearby palm grove. The breathalyzer registered zero point three five. Way past legally drunk, more like a medical miracle the son of a bitch could walk. The man was unable to walk, come to think of it. And unable to drive.

She flew through the windshield. Up, up and away. At the hospital the doctor leaned close and whispered to an indifferent trooper that Lauren's femurs shattered when they connected with the top of the van's frame but she kept sailing. Like a beautiful angel.

The Doc said Lauren would not have felt a thing, not one little thing. Your body goes into metabolic shock within microseconds of such trauma. Funny how that happens, a deep lower level something seizes control from the conscious mind. Swipes it the way a mother might snatch a sharp object from her baby. Not funny haha, but, you know. Funny strange.

Chase was shocked and he was numb but he couldn't say he was surprised and at least he had an answer to his question of just how long happiness could last. Twenty one years. Seventy six hundred days. How many seconds had he been blessed enough to actually look into her eyes? One of those numbers in life a man can't count. He would never know but realized with suffocating sadness that the number did exist and was finite. The Lord took Lauren. To balance out the Mayor's hubris. The most serious of the seven deadly sins. The first six the Lord hateth, but pride His soul detesteth. The Mayor might as well have driven that van himself.

He remembered counting the days after her death. Then the weeks. The pain was ripe and fresh for the first twenty. Then he was up to forty. His friends told him even the worst pain had a half life of maybe a year. But at seventy five weeks his pain had only intensified. He prayed for any kind of relief and when he got to three years God finally showed His mercy and the pain mellowed and rotted to a slow burn.

He strove for perfect contrition so the Lord would forgive his transgression and bestow His great compassion. He prayed for God to have mercy upon his sinful soul and cleanse his spirit. Chase made a deal with the Lord that he would atone for his sins. His cilice would come in the form of a great sailboat in which he would sail the seas in honor of his beloved Lauren. He would sail forever or until his soul was whiter than snow and the Lord said enough's enough. That's the only way he could be free again.

He ran for Mayor and handily defeated his Godless liberal foe. The more time he spent talking to God the less he spent focused on his pain and through these conversations he realized he was on a Special Quest. Of course the paeans couldn't see the big picture so he met resistance at every turn. No matter.

Jonathan Swift wrote of true genius that when it appears, you may know it by this sign -- all the dunces are aligned against it.

Forty nine years on this Earth had prepared him for a momentous decision that would affect the lives of millions. He alone would make the decision and his choice would be righteous because the Lord was by his side.

And God help any mortal who got in his way.

20   Friday July 1, 2011
Atlanta, Georgia

The stroke hit his mother the summer Mitch graduated high school. He stood at the side of her bed and thought she didn't look like she belonged in the hospital. Impersonal fluorescent light highlighted soft freckles across her nose. She looked healthy everywhere except her eyes. They were bloodshot and sad, resigned. Her stroke was massive and the doctors told Mitch she was down to the last hours of her forty seven year life.

"Bobby. Where's Bobby?"

Her voice was soft and Mitch leaned down to hear. A single tear trickled past the end of his nose and dropped onto a frayed sheet.

"Mom, don't. Don't think about Bobby. Please."

She shut her eyes.

The week before her stroke Mitch told her he'd joined the Navy and would ship out in thirty days. He hoped his mother would be happy at the news. He hoped she'd be proud of her son who had the inner courage to leave home and strike out on his own.

"Mitch, you disappoint me," she had said.

"Why, Mom? Why does that disappoint you?"

"Son, you know your father wanted you to go to college."

"But Dad was in the service. He didn't go to college. I thought you'd be proud."

"Your father was drafted. He didn't go into the army by choice. Things were different in the seventies."

"This is just a first step. I'll go to college one day."

"No you won't. Everyone says they will but they don't, Mitch. Life goes down a different path and you'll meet a girl and get married and have children and there's never time for an education. You'll see."

"I won't be in the Navy forever. I'll learn a craft and save money and I'll go to school when I get out. I promise."

"Son you don't know how hard it was for me to go back to work after your father died. But I've tried to tell you. I didn't know anything. You need to get a formal education. You need to know everything. That's the only way you'll be happy in life. I tried to explain that to your brother but he wouldn't listen."

Mitch looked around the hospital room. The bed was coated in cold, chipped chrome. The walls and ceiling were painted a washed-out beige. A picture behind the bed depicted a stormy day at the beach. The bedside table held a cracked plate with dividers that sectioned the food as though for a child. The rations looked unappetizing and hadn't been touched.

He wanted to tell her to believe in him. Wanted to tell her to wait, she'd see. But he knew she wouldn't see anything. He took his mother's hand, raised it to his lips and gave it a soft kiss. Already her hand felt cold. The Doctors said that was a first sign of death as the body began a systematic shut down, a diversion of blood away from extremities.

She opened her eyes. "Your father ... loved you ... and your brother."

Mitch looked into her eyes and promised he'd learn everything one day. She smiled and he saw that even now she made an effort to be strong for him and then she was gone.

The equipment around her bed started to alarm. He held her cold hand and gazed into her beautiful face and before the nurses rushed in he promised to have all of the answers one day.

Then someone pushed him out of the room and he exited the hospital all alone.

21

Cheslov sat nude in the darkness and listened to the soft lap of water against the hull. *Thu-thud, thu-thud, thu-thud. Chorny Volk* was anchored half a league from Clearwater Beach. Her running lights were off. He frowned at the headline on his micro.

Headless Body found in Topless Bar

The missing head would soon be so much chum for his friends swimming in the dark Gulf water. He would be long gone before anyone could connect him to the fate of that cyka. Good riddance, my Margot.

Light from the coast formed crimson patterns on clouds high overhead. Cheslov closed his eyes and listened to the faint sounds from the crowd taking pleasure in their nightlife. He leaned into his captain's chair and drank chilled Stoli from Dyatkovsky Crystal. Nightlife had a different meaning for him. A meaning not so much associated with bars and city streets. More associated with forests. Dark woods. Buried prey.

When Cheslov was a young man a bear terrorized his village. Many farmers lost cattle but when the bear killed a young girl, sixteen year old Cheslov set after it alone.

Chorny Volk's gentle sway felt much like the horse carefully stepping down icy mountain trails so long ago.

The shaggy Yakutian steppe horse trotted down the narrow mountain path. The horse's body was dense, massive hind legs shaped like sickles. A thick coat insulated it from the frigid winter air.

Young Cheslov did not understand Western breeds produced only for speed on the racetrack and always at the sacrifice of endurance. A horse is good for nothing in Russia if it cannot find safety through a snow blizzard or the densest of fogs. His Yakutian fended for itself in the forest, finding food beneath one meter of snow.

Young Cheslov thought of the millions of horses killed in open warfare ravaging Europe. His father spoke of Austrian cavalry sweeping across a battlefield to become tangled in barbed wire and decimated by machine gun fire. Cheslov knew this Great War represented the end of cavalry. Man created war but the horse was its innocent victim.

The trail leveled out onto a snow covered plain. He took the reins and kicked the horse into a gallop. Helsing dashed ahead. They were getting close.

He smiled at his father's seafaring life. Twenty men aboard a small ketch working the nets through Black Sea storms. Where was the reward in hauling expressionless fish into the boat by the thousands?

No, fishing was not where his passions lie.

He rubbed the wooden stock of his Mosin rifle protruding from the saddle holster. Accurate to five hundred meters but he had never fired at big game beyond twenty paces. He preferred to look his prey in the eye, to become acquainted on some level. He wanted his victim to read in Cheslov's eyes that death was in the picture. He could see no reason to hunt without reaching this vital conclusion.

Big animals were surprisingly expressive. Almost human.

He had seen many final expressions. Fear was the most common. But hardly the most satisfying. The most fulfilling, far more than any other, was defiance. Such an expression was truly a window into one's soul and who could not respect that final act of courage? Defiance radiated by doomed eyes was the most beautiful expression of God's hand.

Men from the village thought Cheslov had a death wish that he put himself so close to feral boar. Their rifles were old and to be near wild animals with a weapon prone to jamming was a fool's game. He smiled and called them cowards that they took impersonal shots from great distance.

But the men in his village were right. He did have a wish to meet death.

He often dreamt of being devoured and knew that one day he would be consumed by his prey. That was his destiny. This was true as surely as the sun set every evening to change his world from day into night.

The Yakutian trotted steadily through the snowy field. The alabaster plain transformed to a dark wall of thick forest ahead. Freezing wind burned his back through the wooly parka. Helsing yelped in excitement. Cheslov whistled softly and Helsing was silent.

The shepherd and his extreme Russian horse were good examples of Darwin's theory in action. Nature bred for survival and endurance, with speed of secondary importance. He respected the English naturalist who realized that life evolved over time. Species transmutated, altered into something better.

The brown bear stepped from the forest and his horse skidded across hard ground, then seized to a stop. He tightened his legs around the animal's midsection but still slid hard into the pommel. Helsing barked furiously, head low to the ground. The bear stood and its dark body rose toward the sky, massive as the tall cedars from which it emerged. Small brown eyes glared into young Cheslov's blue eyes from a broad head. A large snout bellowed in anger. Large enough to consume a man's entire skull. Flash of red tongue and white teeth like a shark, a killer created only to move and eat.

He whistled softly and his dog went silent. Cheslov stared across the tundra into the eyes of the bear and listened to the wind blow past his freezing ears toward the trees. He smiled and the puzzled bear shook its colossal head. He noticed a silver streak across the bear's dark skull and realized one of the villagers nearly killed the animal with that shot.

The bear snorted. The sound carried upwind like a gunshot and the Yakutian tried desperately to flee. Cheslov pulled the reins in the opposite direction so instead of turning the anxious horse sidestepped thirty meters toward the soaring rock face that formed the base of the western steppes. He yanked hard on the reins but the panicked animal did not respond and before he could leap the horse slammed into the rock wall and there was a loud crack that Cheslov heard more than he felt. He looked down to see a bloody femur jut through the dense cloth of his breeches.

Still he held the reins as the Yakutian reared. Cheslov tugged the horse's head down toward his toes trying to make the animal bend. He whispered soothingly but the frightened horse bucked and Cheslov was thrown to the ground. The Yakutian fled at a full gallop.

He lay weaponless and broken and his eyes never left the bear. The huge animal dropped its great forearms to the ground and loped forward...

Cheslov opened his eyes on *Chorny Volk*, drank from his crystal and looked down at his thigh. Thick black hair but no scar. He rubbed his leg.

What happened after he fell from that horse?

Something about a wolf. And dearest Helsing.

Then his memory picked up in Moscow at the fall of the Soviet Union. Somehow he lost nearly seventy years. Not a complete blank. He had fleeting images. Hunting through dark forests and the dreams were always black and white and included an overpowering sense of... smell. The visions were muddled but the scent of prey was always strong. The oddest part was how he hunted low to the ground.

He was puzzled but not overly concerned. Perhaps he had gone mad. Was that significant? He did not think so. He lit a Cohiba, inhaled the fine aroma. He possessed strength and wits and found his pleasures where he could. That's all that really mattered.

22   Monday March 9, 2020

Brilliant sunlight illuminated the interior of the diner through glass walls. The space was crowded and noisy and Mitch felt… *vivid.*

"Pass the pepper," he said to Woody.

Woody pushed it over. "I swear, man, she grabbed my ass on that dance floor."

"So I noticed."

"Mitch, she was pushing into me, honest to shit. Like she was making love to me and wanted everybody to see." Woody's eyes were wide, mouth pulled down in a puzzled frown. "Is it wrong to be aroused right now?"

"Settle down, Midas dick. We're in public."

"On the beach the other night? I'm telling you, I was this close to stripping off my clothes and diving into that water." Woody raised his hand, index finger nearly touching his thumb. "What do you think would've happened?"

"Well, I think Molly would've followed you while Kate and I kept on trucking."

"Who you kidding? You woulda shucked your drawers in a heartbeat."

"I would've been tempted. But a girl like Kate?" Mitch shook his head. "You don't get naked with her the first night."

"Why not?"

"You take your time. Get to know her, let her get to know you. Getting naked when you first meet? That's a novice error. Amateur hour."

Woody smiled. "Wow. I mean, I knew you liked her. But now I see you *really* like her."

"That's what I'm trying to tell you. Girls like Kate come along once in your lifetime. If you're lucky."

"Get the fuck out," Woody bit into his egg sandwich and bright yolk dripped onto his plate. "You get her token?"

"I did. You get Molly's?"

"Hell yeah," Woody smiled and absently stirred his coffee. "Tell me something. Where'd you get all that crap about bridges?"

Mitch took a bite of his waffle and shrugged.

Woody cocked his head. "I mean, it's sort of amazing any girl asks about bridges in the first place, right? Kate wins kudos for even caring. The Sunshine Skyway looks cool and all, but who really gives a damn?"

Mitch shrugged again.

"Who has time to think about the force distribution to the thingamajigies so some bridge can span a frigging bay?" Woody bit into his oozing sandwich. Mitch didn't respond so Woody wiped his chin with a napkin and continued. "So first I'm thinking, OK, we're buzzed. Let's have some fun. We can speculate on how the bridge is built, right?"

Mitch nodded.

"Then you come outta nowhere with this crap about how the bridge has a cable-stayed main something. But that's not enough for Kate. She's got a bullshit detector and wants to know if you're for real or just making it up. So you start talking about pylons and cantilevers and I'm wondering how come you know so much about bridges? Then we're laying on the beach looking at stars. You point out nine constellations. Nine."

"Come on. You guys pointed some out."

"Yeah. We pointed out the big dipper." Woody leaned back and looked calmly across the table at his friend. "So tell me. What's going on?"

Mitch smiled. The loop lock helped. He had some bugs, he needed some tweaks to do a better job correlating near field speech. But it worked! He was so ready for his meeting with the Buyer Thursday morning.

He had tried to cool it with his friends. But goddamn, when you have all the answers right in front of you it's hard not to answer people's questions. With a few drinks and a beautiful girl staring into your eyes, well it's hard not to try to impress her. Just a little.

He drank the last of his coffee, leaned back in the booth and came clean. He told Woody about the success of the exahertz range, the breakthrough of twisting the helical wave and how he had unfettered access to unlimited information. Transparent to everyone. Anyone.

Woody shoved the last corner of his egg sandwich into his mouth. "I get it. Like that old guy in the first Matrix, right? At the end of the movie he sees green lines moving around, numbers scrolling all over the place. Is that how it is for you?"

"Not exactly."

"Oh, I know. More like that Terminator movie? The guy asks the Terminator, what's that smell? And the Terminator sees the multiple choice in his head? Chooses D. 'Fuck you, asshole'." Woody says the last sentence in a low robotic voice.

Mitch gave a little shrug. "That's actually more like it, now that you mention it. Maybe a combination of the two. I don't see a digital blueprint. Well, not automatically. But I can pretty much call one up at will. And I can cruise articles to get different answers to different questions. A philosopher answers a question differently than a scientist. That sort of thing."

Mitch turned toward the window and watched silent cars stream by on the busy street.

"Good one," Woody said.

"I'm not kidding. I still have to practice, work out a few glitches. But overall the endeavor has exceeded my expectations."

"Prove it."

Mitch turned back to face his friend. "Excuse me?"

"You heard me. Start talking."

Mitch sighed and tapped his resin finger once. The display in his mind's eye filled with data in response to audio streaming in from adjacent tables. "Bring it on."

"So I can Google something with you?" Woody asked.

"You can ask me any question on any subject. Come on, let's get this over with."

Woody thought for a moment. "What's the capital of Utah?"

"Salt Lake City."

"Capital of New Zealand?"

"Wellington."

"Yugoslavia? "

"There is no Yugoslavia, fool."

"No? What happened to it?"

"The Montenegrin vote in oh six dissolved the union. Serbia declared independence and presto. No more Yugoslavia."

"I knew that. Trick question for you, fool," Woody said.

"What is this, geography class? Why don't you ask me something I don't already know."

"Who won the academy award in 1975? Movie and actors."

"One Flew Over the Cuckoo's Nest swept it all. Best picture. Jack Nicholson and Louise Fletcher won best actor and actress. Say, did you know Nurse Ratched was a metaphor for the Soviet Union?"

Woody blinked in astonishment. "Well I'll be damned. How do I know you're not making this up as you go?"

"You have a micro. Check it out."

"This is too easy," Woody said. "Nothing but one word answers. Tell me something complicated."

"Ask me something complicated. You're in charge."

"What's the square root of seven thousand?"

"How many decimals would you like?"

"Three's fine."

"Eighty three point six six six."

"Cubed root?"

"Nineteen point one two nine."

"Natural log?"

"We still on seven thousand?"

"Yep."

"Eight point eight five three."

"World population?"

"Seven point five four six billion."

"Where does my dad live? What's his address?"

"I don't remember his first name. Always been Mr. Logan to me. Tell me his name and I can probably tell you where he lives."

"Dwight."

"There's more than one Dwight Logan living in this country."

"Philly."

"Then I'm guessing he lives at 1104 Cedarpoint Road."

"How much is his house worth?"

Mitch nodded. "Now you're thinking, Woody. Another question I can't answer. I could guess based on recent sales in his area, but it's not something I can answer quickly. That's a compound question, requires multiple steps."

"Can you record information between steps?"

"No. My program doesn't write results into device memory. On my to-do list."

"Can you bookmark where you've been? Set up favorites while you surf?"

"Sure. The micro itself does that. Remember, I'm just accessing the micro as though my head is an external monitor."

"What do you call the damn thing?"

"Call it?"

"Yeah. Everything needs a name. What do you call it?"

Mitch thought for a moment. "*InSyte*."

"In sight?" Woody brought an imaginary rifle to his shoulder and tilted his large head. "Like I got you in my sight?"

"One word. *InSyte*. With a 'y', like *byte*."

Woody bared his teeth and raised his eyebrows.

"No, asshole, not bite. Byte. Like bits and bytes. Are we through with the questions?"

"Just one more," Woody slowly dropped his hands and his eyes softened. "What are we talking about here, Mitch?"

"Instant access. To all mankind's knowledge. All the time."

Woody stared. "Sort of like God."

Mitch smiled at his friend. What a rush. "I wouldn't go that far," he said.

"No? Why not."

"Well, I can't see everything that's going on or know what'll happen next week. I can't see into men's hearts or be all places at all times. I just see what's happened in the past. As long as it's recorded."

"OK, sorta like a micro, then. A walking micro."

"Exactly like that, yes. It's not that complicated. First we digitize our entire collection of knowledge."

"Who's we?"

"Mankind. Stay with me."

"I'm trying."

"Then we develop these tiny devices that everybody carries to make phone calls. Then we create wireless networks that connect the devices to a collective database practically everywhere on the planet. The devices get smaller and smaller until we attach them to our bodies permanently. I happen to use e-resin."

"With you so far."

"Of course, you haven't gained anything if you're still using twentieth century interfaces like liquid displays and keyboards. As luck would have it, there are ways to connect to the optic nerve and software decodes speech, interprets dialect, you name it. Eventually the technology had to take us here. Maybe I'm the first to cobble it together. I won't be the last. Just a matter of time before everyone has this capability. Just a different way to interact with a micro. That's all it is."

"So you don't have to manually search for information? The software hears people and… just looks?"

"Sort of. The best way to describe it is to say I can search the Grid the way you search your memory."

"Man, I'm trying to get my head around it. What does this mean? For like, the social order? Does it mean everybody has all the answers and we're all brilliant? Or does it mean people stop learning and we're stupid?"

"Look at it this way. When calculators came out in the seventies, people asked the same questions. Would we forget how to do long division? Add and subtract?"

"I see where you're going with this."

"Yeah. Quite the opposite. The calculator and PC allowed us to focus on concepts." Mitch gazed through the window and thought about the people walking, riding, shaping the world moment by moment every day. "Do you know the most important metric in economics?"

"I been wondering."

"Productivity. Ratio of output over input. Even small improvements dramatically change our lives."

"OK. So?"

"In the seventies and eighties, productivity grew one and a half percent annually in the U.S. Then fourth gen computers and IT software hit the market and finally the technology was easy to use."

"Lemme guess," Woody said. "Everybody got a whole lot more productive."

"You got it. Over the next twenty years productivity rises two and a half percent per year. And that despite three wars, a dot com collapse, and the Great Recession."

Mitch lifted his coffee cup, felt it was empty, set it down.

"We sort of hit a wall over the past decade. Productivity's been flat. *InSyte* can change that. I'm not talking about turning a crank faster on a machine. I'm talking about fundamentally altering the way we all think and work. *InSyte* can do for the twenties what the computer and IT did for the nineties. Drive productivity gains off the scale."

Woody looked at him through the corners of his eyes. "That's a bit much, ain't it? All because of your invention?"

"Not because of my invention. Because of the overall improvement of knowledge." He thought for a moment, then corrected himself. "No, that's not right. Because of the improvement of access to information."

"Stop, stop, stop. Let me catch up with you. And you haven't answered my original question."

"Which was?"

"What are the implications? I mean, how do people interact with each another? You're not talking about using a calculator you keep in your shirt pocket, here. You're talking about giving people all the answers all the time. To any question. And it's impossible to tell if that person's smart as hell or just reading from the Grid. Or even paying attention? Christ!"

"I know. I've thought about it. Every civilization has a class system. Since the Greeks. Professor Martin was right about one thing. Today the classes are separated by education."

"Meaning knowledge."

"That's right. If suddenly everyone knows everything... well, that raises a lot of interesting questions."

"Damn right. How could people be satisfied with lower lots in life? Think about it. If you're better at searches you'll know more than your Doctor. You literally do a better, faster diagnosis."

"It's not enough to know something, Woody. Experience plays a huge role. It's not like I can read how to conduct open heart surgery and then go perform one. The how-to knowledge doesn't help if I faint at the sight of blood. Same applies to flying an airplane."

"OK. Good point."

"And personalities will always dominate. I might have access to the same information as a businessman, but if he reads people better he's going to close the sale and I'm not. A lot of factors differentiate people way beyond mere information. Sure, you've got to have the info to begin with. But how you deal with situations, interact with people, control emotion... those are real attributes that aren't going away."

"So we're Red Teaming, right?" Woody asked.

"Sure," Mitch said. In war gaming, Red Team activity was used to reveal weaknesses in military readiness.

"You've given me the strengths. Where are the weaknesses?"

"Well, I have some tweaks to make. Not one hundred percent there, yet."

"That's not what I mean, dude. I'm asking you what are the negatives of the concept. The enchilada. Not just the current rev."

"We just talked about this. What are the negatives of calculators?"

"Calculators don't hook into your brain, man."

Mitch shut his eyes and combed fingers through long hair. What happened in the ride to the fair with Kate? He had lost control for a moment, seriously disconnected from himself.

Had he *lost* control?

Or had something taken it? Something other than his own consciousness? Something selfish?

"Hey, I just thought of a good one," Woody said. "How 'bout meeting somebody at a bar? Let's say you're attracted to intelligent types. How do you know you're talking to someone who's actually smart or just logged on?"

Mitch hesitated. "That would be an interesting question for Kate, actually. Which is why I need to come clean with her."

Woody brought his hands together in a 'T'. "Whoa, whoa, time-out, Mitch. You don't want to do that."

"No? Why not?"

"Believe you me. Big mistake."

"It's a mistake not to tell her at this point."

"Hey, I know we had a lot of fun with those two but the fact is we don't know them. Not really. We met 'em Friday, remember? You wait all this time to tell me, your best friend. Now you want to rush out and tell some skirt you just met? Come on, man."

"Well---"

"Well nothing. Go meet your Buyer. Get some patents, first mover advantage. Cover your bases so no one steals your shit."

"That's true, I suppose."

"Hey, I appreciate how you feel about Kate. You're right, she's a keeper. I think we both know that. You need to let her know what you're tapping into, I get that. But before you spill your guts, give it a few more dates. That's all. And cool it on the know it all stuff."

"Maybe you're right."

"Damn right I'm right. Let's go to class."

23

Martin stared.

"Excuse me, Professor, could you repeat the question?"

"Mr. Logan, I am not in the habit of repeating myself," Professor Martin replied. "I will make an exception for you, however, since you are evidently in the habit of going through life a day late and an Amero short. Once more from the top. Please describe how Grid engines impact our society financially. Some would argue Grid engines are bad for business, auctioning search results to the highest bidder. Others argue the negatives affect only the weakest players. Do inspire the class with your thoughts."

"Well, I think it depends on the type of engine."

"Search. For our example, assume 'search'."

"OK. And what, exactly, is the question?"

"Good or bad?"

"For who?"

"For society as a whole."

Woody smiled. "I get it. Loaded question. You want me to say Grid engines are bad because they hurt people's ability to think."

"My, my, Mr. Logan, you are at last tuning into the political winds. Wonders never cease."

"But aren't there other things to consider?" Woody asked.

"What did you say?"

"Aren't there other considerations?"

"What?" Professor Martin leaned forward, eyebrows raised.

"Other considerations, sir," Woody said. "You know, other things to think about?"

"Three silly questions from a silly mind," Martin said. He stepped back and gazed across the auditorium. "Do not allow yourselves to be caught in analysis paralysis. Clearly the cons outweigh the pros and society would be much improved if we simply turn off the search engines. This is the first concept you must understand in order to move to the next level of your development. To become adults and leave childish things behind. You must learn to scotch emotion from your decision making. I realize this is a foreign concept and one you may not fully grasp. But I do hope you can store this wisdom in your small, under-developed minds. And one day many years from now perhaps some of you may mature to the point of understanding my concepts."

Professor Martin turned back to Woody. "You, Mr. Logan, will clearly NOT be in that group."

Mitch tapped his resin finger and it was suddenly clear that the real question was…

"What about Alexandria?" Mitch asked.

Professor Martin turned toward Mitch, brows knitting together. "If you have a point, Mr. Downing, please attempt to make it concisely. If not, then let us move on."

"Comes down to the City of Alexandria," Mitch said. "I have a point to make, Martin. See if you can stay with me here."

Martin had begun to turn away, now he paused. A murmur stirred the auditorium as the group consciousness became aware that an unusual event was transpiring.

"Young man, what could you possibly tell me about Alexandria that is remotely relevant to our discussion?"

"Alexandria represented a golden era of education and knowledge," Mitch said.

Martin slipped on a sneer and Mitch guessed it was something he practiced in front of his bathroom mirror.

"Alright, then. I'll play your game," Martin said. "Why does Alexandria stand out above other middle eastern cities of the time?"

"Alexandria melded the classical Greeks with the ancient wisdom of Egypt."

"I'm losing patience with you, dear boy. Tell me why I should care about---"

"Alexandria represented new and profound ideas. Professor Martin, PLEASE! Is this about losing and winning to you? Can you check your ego and concentrate on the discussion? Is that possible?"

The hall was dead silent, every eye on Mitch. He stared at Martin and the professor appeared slightly shaken. That was good. Mitch took a deep breath. "The Grid was never intended to improve our intelligence. It wasn't designed to make us more creative or rational."

"Yes, Mr. Downing, exactly my point. And here I thought for once you might have something original to contribute."

Mitch stared at Professor Martin. "But the Grid allows us to fly, Professor Martin. To soar. Don't you see that?"

"I don't see that at all."

"Then you're not looking! Open your eyes, Martin. If you were researching a paper fifty years ago, how many books would you open?"

"Three. Four. Several." Professor Martin was out of his comfort zone. He tried to take control through empty assertion. "Class, class, this is hardly a productive---"

But Mitch was having none of it. "The Grid allows you to open hundreds. Thousands."

"Mr. Downing, what in the world---"

"You're not cutting and pasting other people's analyses. You're exploring their thoughts and taking them to the next level. The standard for research isn't lowered. It's raised to the nth degree!"

"Mr. Downing, please," Professor Martin.

"Does the Grid sometimes fail us? Certainly Does it provide all the information we'll ever need? Of course not. The Grid may not turn us all into geniuses but it'll keep most of us from looking like assholes."

"Mr. Downing, I don't appreciate---"

"When a Grid search reveals something you haven't considered or undermines your basic ideas, it lets you know you haven't done enough work. So look again. And again. You'll find the facts."

"How? How do you separate fact from fiction?"

"As people we just do. We know how to separate truth from lies. It's in our nature. And you have a moral obligation to get to the facts of the matter. You can try to embed yourself in a fact free zone, but the Grid will catch you every time."

No comment from Martin.

"To claim Grid engines make us dumber implies that every project disseminating information should be criticized on the same grounds. Was that true of the Encyclopedia Britannica? The Human Genome Project? The Library of Alexandria?"

Silence in the auditorium.

Martin turned to look at Woody, attempting some measure of escape. His mouth opened and closed like a fish trying to breathe on land.

"So there you have it, buddy." Woody said.

Professor Martin dropped his jaw and the class erupted into applause.

"I suppose blowing a professor out of the water in front of a couple hundred students is your idea of laying low?" Woody and Mitch strode toward the parking lot across campus.

"I couldn't stand to see that prick patronize you."

"But I thought we just agreed you don't need the attention."

Mitch could only shrug.

"Well you got him pretty good. At the end he sort of looked like a bug wriggling around on his back up there."

Mitch felt an ache deep in his head. "You know what? I have to be somewhere. Catch you later."

Mitch rubbed his forehead and walked away. He started to turn off his micro then changed his mind. He glanced toward a building. Visual packets travelled to a server in Orlando that recognized the structure as the campus library and blueprints sprang into his mind with plans and drawings. He started to follow the plumbing schematics then his headache intensified and he decided to turn the micro off after all.

24   Monday March 9, 2020
Tampa, Florida

Mayor Delaney watched the catamaran race over angry water. Massive sails shimmered in salty spray. The huge carbon mast leaned away from the wind. Dual hulls cut through tall waves like they were soft goose shit and the Mayor imagined placing a full tumbler of scotch on that deck and not spilling a drop.

Phelps smiled at the YouTube video on the wall monitor. "Still dreaming about that yacht, Mr. Mayor?"

The Mayor snorted and killed the video. "Thanks for coming by, Paxton. Have a seat."

"So what is it that's got you so excited about this young man?" Phelps sunk low to the ground in an over-stuffed chair. The Mayoral office was large and chilly. The space was dark and aged and somehow out of touch. Phelps hated meeting here.

"I'm telling you the kid is brilliant," Mayor Delaney said.

Phelps drummed his fingers across the arm of his chair. "When do I get to meet this genius?"

"Right now. He's in the outer office. I see you're still not on board, Paxton. Tell you what. Hit him with your best shot. If the kid stands up to your heat and you're impressed, we move forward with my plan. If he folds then I fold and we forget about this whole thing."

"Sounds like a reasonable plan of attack," Phelps acknowledged.

"Amen. Let's settle it then." Mayor Delaney tapped his micro. "Janet, send in Mr. Downing."

Tapestry patterns wove blurry people Mitch assumed were relevant in some distant Florida past. Behind the Mayor's desk were two small frames. One proclaimed *The great day of the Lord is near*. The other stated *Mine is the power and the glory*. Mitch wondered to whom the personal pronoun referred.

A photograph on a side desk caught his eye. The photo stood in stark contrast to the rest of the dark décor. The frame was the color of beach sand. Three bright blue and yellow ceramic fish swam across the top and there might've been a fourth at one time but it had apparently broken off and swam away. The frame housed an actual print of a remarkably beautiful young woman who knelt on the sand in low surf with a puppy held across her lap. Golden Retriever. She wore sunglasses and her dark hair fell in front of her shoulders. Her smile was big and bright. She petted the dog's head and scratched his side. The retriever displayed a tongue-hanging grin. The ocean horizon was cocked at an angle behind her and Mitch thought whoever took that photo was a bit careless.

But still a great photo. And sad. Kate's late Mom.

Mayor Delaney stood and reached across the desk to shake Mitch's hand.

"Thank you for coming today, Mitch. I'd like to introduce you to Paxton Phelps, our Council Chair and Deputy Mayor for the City. Paxton, meet Mr. Downing."

"Hello, young man. Pleased to make your acquaintance. You have certainly made a strong impression on our Mayor."

"Nice to meet you, Mr. Phelps," Mitch replied. Shaking Paxton's hand was like holding a Christmas ornament. He had the sense he shouldn't squeeze too hard. The men took their seats.

The Mayor smiled broadly. "Mitch, I need a favor."

Mitch waited.

"We have a Council session scheduled for tomorrow evening. I expect it to be well attended by the public. The Council will hear any and all issues the people care to raise. Then we'll set aside time for the two final vendors to summarize their proposals for Wireless World."

Mitch nodded and reviewed the agenda posted on the City's gridsite. His micro resin was clear today, impossible to detect without close examination.

Mayor Delaney glanced at Phelps and pretended to hit a drum cymbal with his right index finger. A signal for Phelps to proceed.

"Mr. Downing, what do you know about the City's vision for Wireless World?" Phelps asked.

Here we go. "Where do you want to start?"

"What do you understand about the project's origins?"

"You're using a radio system purchased in the early nineties from Planetcom. Fully depreciated two decades ago so I'd say you got your money's worth. There are advantages to using a new network based on open standards. For one you could ditch your expensive walkie-talkies and use open micros that are essentially free. You know all this and that's why you issued an RFP."

"That's very good, Mr. Downing," Phelps said, honestly impressed. "Now, how would you quantify the pros of Wireless World?"

"Conventional wisdom says it's important to control your public safety systems. You have National Standards to address your ability to handle hurricanes, APCO tells you how to declare emergencies and so on."

"You haven't answered my question. What are the pros of the current Wireless World analysis as specified by the City's consultant?"

"Well that wasn't actually your question and I haven't read the consultant's report so I don't have that information." Mitch glanced on grid. The consultant had not released his report. Odd.

"I see. What's your understanding of the controversy surrounding Wireless World?"

"There are two planes to the controversy, both related to price. A billion is a hell of a lot for this City to spend on any project. There's an existing wireless network that's home grown. Expand it. Use it. Other large cities have done exactly that."

"Mexico City and Montreal. Hardly world-class," Paxton observed.

"That's just in the Union. Tokyo and Seoul have also moved to micros."

"You're talking about a 'poor man's network'," Paxton said. "Unacceptable for public safety applications."

"I think Tokyo and Seoul might disagree with you. Either way, consider the second plane of controversy. You're down to two bids. The New Light proposal costs five hundred million and the Planetcom proposal twice that. According to New Light, their proposal matches the competition in every specification. Beats them in some."

"Do you believe that?" Phelps asked.

"I believe that's the key question. Again, I haven't had an opportunity to study the consultant's report, I can't really say."

"Fair enough, Mr. Downing," Phelps conceded. "Let us assume for a moment that the consultant's report showed the New Light design cut corners to come in at half the Planetcom price. What messaging would you use to convince the public that the City should go with the more expensive proposal?"

Mitch stood and walked to the room's south wall. He looked at photographs of the Mayor with prominent national figures, most known for strong religious views. The electronic frames rotated through photos every few seconds. The Mayor appeared young and slim in each picture. No wrinkles, no shadows under the eyes. Obviously the frame's 'enhance' mode was enabled.

These men were glossing over something. Just like the electronic photo frames.

Mitch turned and said, "First, you have to consider your audience. If I lived in a combat zone and was afraid to tip-toe to my mailbox without getting fragged then there's not a lot you could do to convince me."

"Mr. Downing, please---" Phelps began.

"Face it, you've got certain sectors that have waited two years for up-armored patrols. Your consultant could try to explain the technical criteria for the City to spend a billion instead of five hundred million but if that message means I don't get troop protection then I'm not on board."

"Mr. Downing, it is unnecessary for you to explain the City's challenge. My question is how would you articulate the message to help the City achieve our goals?"

Mitch looked at the Mayor. Delaney stared impassively. Mitch turned back to Phelps and shrugged.

"A question of priorities, Mr. Phelps. What if you lived in a tent city near the beach? Or a shanty town on the river? You're willing to work but you don't have money for training."

"Mr. Downing, I hardly think---"

"What ad campaign would convince you to hop on this train when you wake up every morning with your face in the dirt and watch your wife bathe your children in a filthy river?"

Phelps threw up his hands.

"Has the consultant submitted his recommendation, Mr. Phelps?"

"No, he has not."

"Then how can you support your position when you don't yet have a position?" Mitch's narrowed his eyes. "Just what exactly is your goal here, Mr. Phelps?"

"Mr. Downing you are trying my patience. Can you please share with us what message might resonate with you as a personal citizen to support moving forward with the Planetcom proposal?"

Mitch looked again at the Mayor. Deadpan, not giving anything up. Were they both in on it? Probably.

"First of all, I wouldn't let on that I had a position prior to the consultant's report being released. *Once* the report is released, *if* it were to recommend the Planetcom proposal then I'd focus my message on the total cost of ownership over a five year horizon. The money you save on the radios could have a positive impact on the combat zones. There are some interesting studies with similar projects in Italy and Japan."

"I see." Phelps gazed at Mitch through tented fingers. "Mr. Mayor, I don't believe we'll benefit from discussion of text book approaches here. I'm sure this boy would receive a stellar grade if this were a schoolyard project. We are not, however, in a classroom."

Mitch continued. "Let me be candid with you, Mr. Phelps. From what I've read, New Light's not cutting any corners. They've got the public safety network for hundreds of major Cities. Globally. Cities much larger than Tampa. I mean, come on. Why would they come in and underbid? They have deep pockets. Plenty deep enough to go after in court if they really cut corners."

"Mr. Downing," Phelps said. "I appreciate your passion but do not appreciate your naiveté. If you think you can come in here and lecture me with your schoolboy perspective---"

Mitch smiled. "I see, Mr. Phelps."

"---then you're not as smart as you may appear based on your unique gift to regurgitate facts."

"Insult your opposition to avoid the debate. Classic. Frankly I wouldn't recommend you lead any discussion with Wanda Deter. She'll look like the victim and you'll come across, not inaccurately, as patronizing and disingenuous. But, hey, good luck with that."

"What are you trying to say?"

"I just said it. Wanda Deter's going to kick your ass."

"Gentlemen, gentlemen," Mayor Delaney interjected with a chuckle. "Back to your corners, please. Mitch, I think we can use you to help craft our message. Course, I don't want to ask you to take a position on anything you don't believe in one hundred and ten percent. So let me ask you straight up. Do you think the City should build a new wireless network and that doing so would benefit our citizens over the long term?"

Mitch thought fast. He needed more time to figure out how to play this. From the inside. "Yes," he said.

For now.

"That's great," the Mayor smiled. "Then it's settled. I'll ask our PR boys reach out to you and we'll look forward to your participation in tomorrow's meeting. God Bless you, son."

25   Sunday March 10, 1918
Rostov, Russia

He did not remember the rest of that day the way a person would not remember the day they were born. The process of coming into the world. But that was the day Cheslov indeed met his destiny.

He watched the bear lope across the frozen ground.

Fifty meters. Forty. Thirty.

Then a blur of motion and the bear was surrounded by whirling dark shapes.

The pack moved in a fast circle around their prey, lead by a large black male. The wolves darted in from behind to nip and rip, trying to panic the great animal.

The bear connected a massive swipe of his claws and an unfortunate wolf sailed away from the frenzy. The line immediately closed. Cheslov admired the lethal discipline of the pack, hunting their prey with many acting as one. The pack was a single elastic animal and Cheslov wondered what on earth could stand up to such a predator. The bear spun in circles, roaring and clawing at shadows, unable to focus on any one wolf. It finally faltered and broke toward the forest in a dead run.

Halfway to the tree line, the bear stumbled.

Wolves swarmed onto its arms and legs and head and the animal screamed in the pain of knowing what came next. Long teeth sliced through fur, ripped into organs. One wolf pulled away, head low with stretched intestines. The bear's scream climbed an octave and it tried to rise but couldn't shake the weight of the wolves.

Cheslov lay still but did not try to hide. The pack was downwind across the plain and wolves could smell prey from a thousand meters.

As if reading his mind the alpha turned and stared at Cheslov across the field. After a moment the black wolf trotted toward him with a gray at its side.

Cheslov crawled backward, dragging his splintered leg over frozen dirt. His head hit something hard. He rolled onto his back and looked up at a shining black wall of obsidian.

End of his world.

The wolves stopped in front of Cheslov. The black leader lowered its head, shoulders pushed toward the sky. Its face and bloody snout were gray. Traces of silver travelled from its forehead, slithered across its dark coat. Dark ears cocked and black eyes shined like curious dark pearls.

Cheslov stared into its eyes, mesmerized. The wolf looked like a statue, ancient but strong. Cheslov detected an odor of decay.

He tried to look away and realized with some fascination he was unable to do so. The wolf gazed with patient black eyes and somehow reached into his head. Young Cheslov felt a sensation like persistent leafy tendrils creeping into wet stone. His pain disappeared. The wolf opened its mouth and sunlight glinted off yellowed teeth, unnaturally long. The wolf appeared to be smiling at something of which Cheslov had no awareness. Something secret. Something protected. Something prehistoric.

The gray wolf snarled and lunged. His eyes never leaving the black, Cheslov whistled softly and Helsing struck from behind and downwind.

The gray wolf flew sideways, powerful jaws sunk into fur on its neck. The wolf was stunned but its winter mane was deep so Helsing did not reach flesh. The gray wriggled free and Helsing exploded forward, teeth gnashing at the wolf's hindquarter. This time the dog's sharp front teeth dug to bone.

The wolf yelped and the pack looked up in unison from their meal across the field. The black wolf snarled and the meaning was obvious.

Stay out of this!

The gray shook free, turned with head low, front paws spread wide. Snow and ice packed its brindled forehead and green eyes glared. Black lips pulled back from wicked teeth in a silent growl.

Not many domestic dogs could go one on one with a wild wolf. Different breeds were used to hunt wolves where dogs worked as a pack to corner the animal until humans could kill it. But wolves and German Shepherds were not that different. They could cross breed and were closely related. And Cheslov had not raised Helsing to guard sheep. He'd raised him from a pup to fight for survival.

Helsing had once tracked a pair of mammoth Russian Boar. Cheslov fired three shots from the Mosin to knock the smaller to the ground. Helsing took the larger down in less than a minute with such viciousness Cheslov had been overcome with emotion and pride.

Helsing lowered his domed head, long square muzzle growling, bushy tail raised. The wolf lunged and Helsing sprang into the animal's neck from below where its mane was ineffective. The big dog clamped his jaws with all his strength and sharp teeth sank into soft flesh.

The gray kicked and clawed furiously but the dog did not let go. The wolf twisted and turned but couldn't get any leverage against the Shepherd. Helsing jerked his colossal head back and forth and the wolf was dead.

The dog pulled away from the prone wolf and looked at Cheslov. Ears tall, Helsing opened his mouth in a bloody smile and Cheslov read the pride on his face. Helsing turned toward the black wolf, lowered his head and his smile turned to a snarl.

The black wolf looked away from Cheslov toward Helsing. Pain flooded Cheslov's leg and his head felt empty. Cheated.

When the alpha met Helsing's gaze the dog cocked his massive head sideways and widened his eyes. The wolf was inside Helsing's head and Cheslov did not think the outcome would be good for his dog. He whistled but it was too late. Helsing lowered his tail, curled it between his legs. Cheslov could see that his noble dog was no longer there. Helsing lurched toward the tree line and the black wolf attacked from behind like a storm on a meadow.

Eventually Cheslov watched the black wolf pull itself from Helsing. It turned and trotted forward and he watched it come with a sense of resignation.

The black wolf stopped with its bloody snout nearly touching Cheslov's face. Cheslov stared into black eyes and relief swept through his cold and injured body. He tasted coppery blood on the wolf's breath and was grateful as the pain retreated from his mind. Was he dreaming or moving between reality and a dream? His body was turning inside out. Color left his world, dark shadows everywhere. His eyes were open but he no longer saw the plain, one moment laying on cold ground the next running through trees low to the ground everything black and white and why wasn't the wolf attacking him?

The wolf was inside his head and Cheslov thought the wolf would never leave he didn't want the wolf to leave he wanted the wolf, welcomed the wolf.

Needed the wolf.

Something within him withered toward death while something new unfolded in black birth. Altering from one life form to another. Something other than human.

Something bigger.

Something stronger.

26

"Like to order a pizza," Woody said.

"I see your national ID number is 84930283748954903. Is that correct?" The voice sounded human but Woody knew it was a computer, one hundred percent software.

"I guess."

"Calling from latitude 27.967, longitude 82.461?"

"Sounds about right. I'd like to order an extra large Shameless Carnivore, delivered."

"Alright sir. Twenty plus the zone charge brings your total to thirty."

"Zone charge? What zone charge?"

"Sir, you're adjacent to Sector Four. Orange crime zone and we have to cover the liability for our delivery vehicle. I see you purchased five pitchers of beer Saturday night at the Undertow. Triggers another twenty for the health charge---"

"Excuse me?"

"---and you'll have to sign a liability waiver."

"A what?"

"You can sign the form online. Or when we deliver for an additional fee."

"No, no. I'll go online. How much do I owe you?"

"Twenty plus the zone plus health brings the total to fifty."

"Jesus Christ. Fifty Ameros for a freakin pizza?"

"You can save twelve if you change the pie to a Fruit Aficionado. You can save another ten if you pick up."

"Man, I *so* do not feel like driving." Woody said with a sigh.

"I'm sure you can afford the fifty. I see you spent three hundred at Mons Venus four nights ago. Lap dances. Plus an additional sixty-two on drinks."

Woody hung up. "We're going out."

They jogged through their neighborhood after dinner.

"What do you think's going on?" Woody asked.

"They're going with Planetcom. The Mayor believes it's the city's destiny."

"God Complex, eh?" Woody said.

"Or could be Dunning-Kruger." Mitch said, pulling ahead of Woody.

"Come again?" Woody pumped harder to catch Mitch.

"You know. The phenomenon wherein dumb-asses think they know more than smart people."

"Say, I've worked for people like that. And they don't realize this about themselves, do they?"

Mitch pulled farther ahead of his friend. "Ignorance begets confidence," he said over this shoulder.

"Bet your ass."

Mitch reached their pad and jogged in place waiting for Woody. Why should he care which vendor the Mayor selected? Just another run of the mill crooked political deal. Happens every day. As long as Mitch got his coverage, he should be cool either way.

Woody jogged into the yard and leaned heavily onto his knees.

"Well, you don't suffer from Dunning-Kruger," Woody said between deep breaths. "Maybe the God Complex part."

Mitch smiled. "Didn't we already have this conversation?"

"I suppose we did. So what's your next step, pardner?"

"I'll go to the City Council meeting."

"And what will you say?"

Why couldn't he let it go? And what was that crazy vision he saw driving to the fair? Something about a fire. A big one. The Mayor's fire.

"I'm still trying to figure that out," he said.

27

Located in northern Iran, Mount Damavand is the highest volcano in all of Asia. Also the Mount Olympus of Persian mythology. Mitch hiked the southern route to its summit in late spring when he was twenty-one years old. Rehabilitation.

Most of his two day journey was spent scaling steep rock cliffs but midway through his trip he walked through beautiful meadows near the southern face. Flowers that grew in the mountains flourished as they basked in the high altitude sun. He walked for miles through the fields and saw blossoms of many different colors but none as unique as a certain small blue flower. Blue petals surrounded pure black centers and stood out in the rich pastures over all other flora.

Kate's eyes bloomed the same shade.

She reached toward his face. He reached up to touch her hand and felt his fingers sink softly into the screen.

The diode matrix printed onto his bedroom wall provided incredible resolution. The visual effect was a seamless blend from his room to hers, as though the wall disappeared and her room became a virtual extension of his space. The experience was stunning and technically exceeded the acuity limits of the human eye. People often walked into walls when the screens were first released, so manufacturers responded by creating soft cushiony panels.

"What are you going to say?" Kate asked.

"I'm going to support the build-out," he said.

"Are you going to support the build-out with Planetcom?"

"Can't say that I am. I don't think they need me to go that far. I'd just come across as a shill. But I'll support the overall project."

"Mitch, do you honestly believe the city should spend this money?"

"I think the city has a responsibility to put the best system in place for firefighters and troopers."

"OK. And do you think they should spend five hundred million with New Light or twice that with Planetcom?"

"Didn't you just ask me that?"

"You're not answering my question. Which vendor?"

"That's the question, alright. The five hundred million Ameros question."

"And the answer…?"

"Kate, I honestly can't see why the city should spend twice as much with Planetcom. It's clear your Dad wants to go with the higher bid, but I can't figure out why. I know it sounds crazy but I think it has something to do with his religious beliefs."

"Don't be too hard on him. Yes, he has deep faith. Yes, a little overboard. Maybe a lot. Ever since Mom died. But he means well. Mostly."

Mitch thought about losing his own father. Does something to a kid. And to the surviving spouse. Maybe he should cut the Mayor some slack. "OK, Kate. So when am I going to get the chance to see you in real life?"

She pretended to browse through her calendar. Brought a hand to her chin, rubbed thoughtfully. "Let me see. I'm just not sure. Could we sync our calendars and allow them to auto-schedule a half hour slot?" she teased. "Then auto-select a Grid connection and send an alarm before the meeting to remind us?"

"Tell you what," he said. "Why don't I pick you up and we'll go to the Council meeting together?"

"Oh, Mitch," she sighed. "That sounds sooooo romantic."

Part 2

Trial by Fire

28   Tuesday March 10, 2020

Just inside the polycarbonate main doors a long hallway lead to a checkpoint staffed by armed personnel.

Mitch accessed the blueprints in his mind and knew they were walking through a full body scanning tunnel. According to records, the tunnel utilized proprietary amplifying polymers to detect trace levels of explosive materials in parts per quintillion resolution. That detection level exceeded the ability of trained dogs, the old gold standard in explosives detection. Exquisite sensitivity.

They were bombarded by low level neutrons and the subsequent gamma radiation signatures were being read to determine all chemical compositions. Explosive materials all have similar ratios of carbon, hydrogen, nitrogen and oxygen which are easily detectable.

Of course the densities of all items in his possession were being examined. Proprietary software on the Grid used axial tomography to compare all density patterns to a predefined -- and constantly updated -- threat library. Fast, clean, easy. No need for security eyeballs to get involved.

Nonetheless, there were plenty of security troopers and he noticed most were armed with incapacitance tasers. The troopers could either use electric batons or electrode pairs fired from pistols to interrupt the superficial muscle functions of any unruly individuals.

They also carried traditional MP7 submachine guns with extended one hundred round magazines and holographic sights. The MP7's combined the reliability of an AK-47 with the stopping power of an M-16 A1 at a fractional size and weight.

Of course, many soldiers carried old fashioned tactical infantry laser rifles that blasted simple, smoldering holes through people. No school like the old school.

Several guards stole glances at Kate's long legs. Mitch didn't blame them. She wore a short blue cargo skirt with faint tulip patterns. Her dark legs looked dynamite and that's one of the explosives guards are supposed to notice, right? In fact, you might say her outfit was arresting. Haha.

Mitch absently watched a short video clip that demonstrated how the entire area was equipped with a stasis field generator. The stasis fields could be invoked at any time and everyone in the sector would experience near infinite rigidity. Mass mob shutdown. Only used for extreme measures, of course, since prolonged exposure often resulted in suffocation.

Mitch and Kate finally entered the Council chamber and selected a seat toward the front so they could take in all the action, all the theater.

He gazed around the large, rather bland auditorium. The room held one thousand people and was nearing full capacity. Nice turn out for a City Council meeting where the average attendance was closer to one hundred. People spoke in hushed tones throughout the great hall which resulted in soft background noise. He checked the history. The municipal government used the chamber since the building was constructed in 1979. Of course there had been a number of modifications along the way.

Cameras were mounted in the ceiling, Las Vegas style. Not exactly hidden but definitely unobtrusive. A large platform dominated the front of the room where seven seats faced the audience behind a crescent table with black modesty panel. Liquid crystal plates displayed the name of each Council member. Phelps sat in the center with three seats to his left and three to his right. Beside the Council table was a single large seat behind a tall set-up that resembled a judge's bench. The Mayor's perch.

Surrounding the stage was a domed partition of transparent armor. The outer strike plate of aluminum oxynitride was lighter and stronger than traditional glass polymer laminates and could handle fifty caliber armor piercing rounds from several models of sniper rifles currently proliferating the civilian market. The dome also reflected magnetically charged particles, allowing its occupants to move about freely should the stasis field be brought into play.

Bright flags digitally waved on the wall behind the stage. One for the state of Florida, one for the old U.S., and a flag for the United States of the North American Union. The ole red, white and olive USNAU flag was displayed prominently above the others on the largest monitor. The displays could also be used for slideware to help illustrate discussion topics.

A dusty wooden plaque in the corner proudly proclaimed that the United States of the North American Union was founded July 4, 2013. The signatures were from the president of Mexico, Prime Minister of Canada, and then democratic president of the US.

He counted thirty armed troopers throughout the great hall. Not mere window dressing. They wore urban combat fatigues with body armor and battle helmets that hid faces. The soldiers scanned the crowds like robots. The helmets provided heads-up displays that detected body temperature and were set to alarm at predefined thresholds. Nervousness by any individual in the crowd would be quickly detected.

All soldiers carried taser pistols holstered at their hip. Many had MP7 submachine guns strapped over their shoulder.

A few carried Goodbye Guns on their belts in trademark orange, triangular holsters. Also referred to as Active Denial Systems or, simply, Ray Guns. The sensation from exposure to a Goodbye Gun was like standing in front of an oven, too hot to bear for even a few seconds without scrambling for cover. They used compact beam generators much like those found in microwaves and tended to result in prompt and highly motivated escape behavior. In rifle form the Goodbye Guns had a maximum range of five hundred meters making them excellent weapons for crowd control. Much more so than rubber bullets, which barely worked beyond rock throwing distance. The Goodbye pistols were effective to a hundred meters making them just the perfect handheld appliance for clearing a large room. They worked similar to early camera flash bulbs in that they delivered their payload for short bursts then needed a few minutes to develop the next charge. The maximum shot duration was thirty seconds though in practice they were rarely used beyond three to five second sprays.

A podium was located in front of the stage and positioned so citizens were forced to look up to address the Council. An obvious position of deference.

Mitch turned and watched more people file in. Most folks wore shorts, sandals, and short sleeved shirts like himself. The good people of Tampa, come to plead for their lives. He noticed two groups of men dressed in dark suits, the corporate teams representing New Light and Planetcom.

"That's gotta be her," Kate whispered.

He turned and recognized Wanda Deter walking through the aisle toward the front of the auditorium. She looked casual in flat heels, blue jeans, a white blouse. She was black, attractive with a piercing gaze. She did not look like a woman to be taken lightly.

Just past Wanda, staring directly at him stood a large, bald man. Mitch felt a sudden chill.

Who is that guy?

Something about him seemed familiar. He met the giant's gaze. The dark man grinned wolfishly and Mitch remembered exactly where he had seen that smile so many years ago.

29 Saturday April 10, 1999
Wolf Creek, Colorado

The year Mitch turned five his family camped outdoors for a full week in western Colorado. Bobby would turn ten that Summer. The trip occurred the year before the trouble began. The last year they were together as a young family, pure and undamaged.

Early Spring in an open plain, the night air was dense and cold and their roaring campfire felt like a furnace. They sat around the flames and roasted marshmallows and acted silly. Mom and Dad drank hot toddies from a thermos and laughed hilariously at their horrible singing.

Mitch and Bobby sat with backs to the fire and delighted in the warmth pressing through their jackets. They sat until they couldn't stand the heat then scurried around in circles until their backs cooled. The young boys did this over and over and laughed until they cried each time the heat forced them up.

Despite a full moon, the sky was cloudy so the campsite disappeared into blackness three meters from the blaze. Wind pushed broken cloud formations high overhead and the result on the ground was kaleidoscopic. Every few moments bright moonlight broke through the clouds and the plains lit for miles before descending again into blackness. Pitch black beyond the perimeter of the fire, then mild light for miles and miles. Like a celestial light switching on and off and on and off.

Mitch arched his back, closed his eyes and felt heat trickle through his jacket. The light flipped on and he first saw the reflection from so far away it looked like a single point of light. Then blackness.

"Bobby, did you see that?"

"I saw something," Bobby replied.

Mitch glanced at his older brother, reassured that Bobby was looking in the right direction.

"Probably a deer," Bobby said. He looked down at Mitch and smiled. "I'll bet I can stay here longer than you this time."

"No way," Mitch said, but it was hard to beat his older brother at anything. The heat in his back was already intense.

He listened to his mother and father's laughter. Such a beautiful sound. The light came on again and the reflection was much closer. Mitch made out two points of light. Then blackness.

"Bobby? A deer wouldn't come closer to us, would it?"

"I don't think that's a deer," Bobby said.

Mitch's back was hot. He wasn't sure how much longer he could sit here. His Mom and Dad sang a simple song about needing *Help* from somebody, but not just anybody.

Light flipped on and the reflections were close. Mitch could just make out eyes attached to a dark face before blackness fell again. Now the animal was close enough for its eyes to reflect the fire. He watched two points move closer through the darkness.

The heat in his back was almost unbearable. But he felt cold.

He looked wide eyed at his older brother whose little mouth formed a dark circle.

"Dad! It's a wolf!" Bobby cried.

"I see him," their father said. "Don't worry, boys. He won't come any closer."

"How do you know?" Mitch asked.

"Every animal's afraid of fire, son."

"Dad, I'm scared," Bobby said.

Then his Dad stood in front of them waving a big burning log toward the wolf. In the darkness it looked like a solid flaming wall.

And there, just a few paces from the fire, it stood.

Mitch had seen wolves at the zoo, but nothing like this. It looked like his neighbor's motorcycle, low and dark and full of muscle. His family had a big dog named Mickey when he was born. Mickey was a Doberman. He got hit by a car last year and Mom said the vet had to put him to sleep. Mitch knew that meant he could never wake up. Mickey seemed like he was just the biggest animal on the planet. Barrel chested with a bark that shook your bones. Mom was always yelling at Mickey to be quiet, saying that dog was such a nuisance. But Dad said Mickey only barked because he loved them and wanted to protect them. Dad said Mickey weighed over a hundred pounds and that was as big as a grown-up.

Mickey would have attacked the wolf in an instant. And Mickey would have been hurt. Ripped apart. Mitch didn't know what in the world could stand up to an animal like the one glaring from the darkness at the edge of the firelight. The wolf's face and long snout were as black as shadows on a dark road. Streaks of gray crawled from its forehead and seemed to slither across its body as the light from the fire shimmered and hissed.

"What a beauty," Dad said. "Look at the size of him."

"What kind is he, Dad?" Bobby asked.

"Black wolf. Must be more than three feet at the shoulder. Close to two hundred pounds, I'll bet. Never seen anything like it, not even close."

"Oh my God, Bill," Mom said and Mitch heard her voice crack the way Bobby's did sometimes because he was going through 'a change'. "Are we safe?"

"Perfectly. He won't come any closer to the flame. Trust me." Mitch watched his Dad look past the wolf into the darkness but Mitch could've told him there was nothing to see until the light came on. "Unusual to see one like this without his pack. Wolves are social creatures."

Mitch looked back at the wolf. *My, what big teeth you have.* But this was no kid's book this was a real monster and the monster had black eyes but the funny thing was the eyes didn't look like a monster's they actually looked like a person's those black eyes gleamed like dark pearls they were sort of beautiful and he didn't want to look away his back was on fire and his legs started to shiver and then it happened, for just a moment he felt the wolf moving around. Inside his head. And it felt… well, it felt good.

"Get out of here! GO ON!" Dad stepped forward and waved the torch in a wide arc.

Those black eyes twinkled and the dark mouth opened into a wide smile and long white teeth reflected the flames.

Dad rushed at the wolf. "I said get out of here, NOW!" The wolf's eyes darted to Dad and left his head and Mitch felt the way he did the time he dropped his ice cream cone at the beach after just one lick. Cheated.

The wolf sprang away and was gone.

Mitch whirled toward his father and glared. He opened his mouth in a snarl then his back felt like it really might be on fire so Mitch stumbled to his feet and ran toward his Mom. He unzipped his jacket and let it fall to the ground.

His Mom gave a high laugh that sounded weird and he didn't know why but then he didn't care because she rubbed his and Bobby's backs through their shirts.

"Did you get a good look at him, Dad?" Bobby asked. "Did you see the size of that big fella?"

"I sure did, son."

"He looked somehow... human," Mitch said.

Dad smiled. "Son, wolves are marvelous creatures."

"Like dogs." Bobby said.

Dad nodded. "Think of the smartest, most expressive dog you've ever known."

"Like Mickey?" Mitch asked.

"Yes, like Mickey. Mickey would've made an average wolf. Wolves are that smart."

"Why is that, Dad?" Bobby asked. "Aren't they related to dogs?"

"Sure. But wolves have to be smarter. They live in the wild. Everyday their survival depends on their smarts." Dad tossed the log back into the fire.

"Alright everybody, show's over. Just a big curious wolf. Pass the thermos, Laurie."

Mom passed the thermos and they acted like the whole thing was done. But Mitch knew better. He sat shoulder to shoulder with Bobby and scanned the horizon for reflections. Eventually he fell asleep with his head in Bobby's lap. Bobby absently rubbed Mitch's back and peered watchfully into the night. Soon after, Bobby fell asleep as well.

Around midnight Bill and Laurie carried their sleeping boys into the tent. Bill threw logs on the fire and looked toward the west. How odd that wolf came up to the fire like that. Well, the Ranger said animals were bold this spring. The drought had thinned the food chain. He judged how long the fire might continue to burn, decided to come out again in a few hours to throw wood on the hot coals.

Laurie felt her husband slip in behind her. He smelled of smoke and his face was rough on the back of her neck from his three day beard. She took his hand in both of hers and pushed back into him.

One year later Bill was dead from the cancer. Two years after that the family started to lose Bobby. Slowly at first, but gaining speed and crippling momentum as the drugs took absolute control. At Bobby's funeral six summers from the camping trip, his mother would remark that Bobby at sixteen had the body of a sixty year old man.

30   Tuesday March 10, 2020
Tampa, Florida

Whoa. What the hell just happened?

Man, it'd been a long time since he'd thought about that crazy old wolf. His head was numb his legs felt cold and his back tingled. So many years and why did it all come back just from looking across the room at that tall dude? He looked again but the man was gone.

"Where are you?" Kate's mouth pulled into a frown. "You look like you've seen a ghost... Mitch?"

He smiled at her. "Sorry, just thinking about a night I went camping with my family. A long, long time ago."

Kate gently bit her lower lip. "You were really back there, weren't you? What happened that night?"

"Music. My parents liked to sing, especially after they had a few. Loved that bubblegum music, I mean my Mom especially loved that simple stuff." Mitch pointed toward the stage. "Hey, here comes your father."

She reached over and playfully squeezed his fingers. The Mayor walked onto the stage, took his seat and the meeting was called to order.

31

"Good evening and God Bless. I want to thank each and every one of you for coming out here tonight. I know you all lead busy lives and I want you to know we appreciate your attendance and participation in your city's government." Mayor Delaney nodded appreciatively at the full house. "We have a lot on our agenda this evening so I want to outline the order in which we'll proceed. We start with an open forum, absolutely wide open. Any citizen can take the floor for a five full minutes to discuss anything that's on your mind. Anything at all. Nothing's off limits. Once everybody's had their say, then we'll move to discuss Wireless World. I'm certain our distinguished vendors don't mind going last tonight. In fact, since you're being paid by your firms and our citizens are here on their own, whether you mind or not doesn't concern me."

Appreciative laughter rippled through the hall.

"Mr. Phelps, please call our first citizen to the podium."

"Yes sir, Mr. Mayor," Phelps replied. He signaled the Master at Arms who spent the next several minutes directing and organizing a line of citizens to address the Council in sequence.

Finally, a senior citizen ambled to the stand and peered up at the Council. Her face was weathered and her eyes were milky but her voice was clear.

"Good evening," she said.

Multiple, simultaneous greetings back to her from the Council.

"My name is Jane Woodall. I was born in Tampa, Florida in 1940 and have lived here all my life. I live in the Seminole Heights area of our City." She looked at each of the Council members in turn as she spoke. They smiled encouragement.

"My husband of fifty years passed on six months ago."

"God Bless," Mayor Delaney said.

"He was murdered."

"Oh dear Lord."

"He was murdered because there is no police presence in my neighborhood and the gangs are out of control. I'm ashamed to say that since Burt passed, I'm frightened to go out after dusk. Afraid to go into my own front yard. The hoodlums roam the streets at night like packs of wolves. I simply cannot believe what goes on out there."

Her voice broke and she rubbed tears from her eyes.

"Almost every night my yard is invaded and vandalized. Why, just the other night my baby Jesus was kicked over, beaten and painted black."

"Oh, my," various murmurs of indignation from the Council.

"My son moved in with me, praise the Lord. He agreed to stay for just a little while so I could get some sleep. He sacrifices time with his family in order to provide an old woman with some peace of mind. Now I sleep a little bit but I worry about his safety. Ladies and Gentlemen I beg you, please give me some police presence in my neighborhood. I don't ask for much. Just send a car through our streets a couple times at night. I don't think that would cost a great deal of money. Surely would go a long way in helping my soul sleep at night. Sure go a long way to help all my friends sleep in peace."

"Mr. Jackson, I believe Mrs. Woodall lives in your district, does she not?" Phelps asked.

"Indeed she does, Mr. Phelps."

"Are you aware of the situation in her neighborhood?"

"Indeed I am."

"Have you considered increasing the trooper presence pursuant to her request?"

"Indeed we have. Our logistics programmers are currently developing an algorithm to increase the frequency of drive-throughs without impacting the minimum support requirements in the greater area."

Phelps could see confusion on Mrs. Woodall's face.

"I see," Phelps replied. "Mr. Jackson, are you saying that you're trying to figure out how to send a car through Mrs. Woodall's neighborhood more often without adverse effects on other neighborhoods?"

"Exactly so, Mr. Phelps," Jackson agreed.

"And how long have you studied this issue, Mr. Jackson?"

Mr. Jackson examined his notes. "Sir, I do not have that exact information."

"Please hazard a guess."

"Approximately six months."

"I see. And why can't we simply order a car to drive through her neighborhood a couple times a night? I mean, it makes sense to me that if her street needs to be cleaned then it needs to be cleaned. I don't understand how you can say that in order to clean her street another street might get dirty. Using that logic you'd never clean her street. That hardly seems fair."

Mrs. Woodall smiled at Phelps in appreciation.

"We can handle certain situations from a reactive standpoint. The problem, Mr. Phelps, is that to provide proactive trooper presence in her neighborhood is not in our budget. And a patrol car, of course, wouldn't stand a chance. Those boys'd get IED'd inside a minute. Mrs. Woodall's sector requires a Humvee with class four armor to FRAG 10. Simply not in the budget today."

"Drones?" Phelps asked.

"Not in the budget. Not by a long shot."

"I see. Let it be noted that we shall examine this issue more closely in chambers. Mr. Jackson, I want us to work on this one together." Phelps turned toward the waiting Mrs. Woodall. "Madam, I appreciate your coming here tonight to speak. We will take this request under advisement."

"Does that mean I get the extra patrols?"

"I'm sorry but we can't commit to anything at this time. We'll certainly take it under advisement but cannot, of course, make any changes til our next budget cycle. Thank you so much for coming here tonight."

Mitch watched citizen after citizen beg, plead and argue their case to the Council. He shook his head. How could the City in good conscience ignore all these people? Then award a contract to Planetcom that cost an extra five hundred million?

Finally, it was time for the vendors to present their designs for Wireless World.

The New Light team went first. Their leader was Larry Hendrix. He was middle-aged, attractive, articulate. Larry explained how his firm's bid exceeded the City's specifications in each key area – reliability, coverage, and emergency features. All at a fraction of the competitor's price. He said it was his firm's intention to offer predatory pricing to earn the City's business. New Light would do whatever it took to get a foothold in the southeast. Period. Time for the City to take advantage.

Larry presented articles from around the Union where the competition went back to multiple City budget committees to bleed funding for additional sites after awards were made. Classic bait and switch. He pointed out that by simply accepting New Light's fully compliant bid, the City could save enough money to fund all the civic issues raised over the previous two hours.

Finally it was Planetcom's turn at the plate. Their heavy hitter was Bud Colt. Where Larry spoke with a no-nonsense objectivity, Bud spoke with wide-eyed earnestness. Larry emphasized his points with educated articulation. Bud highlighted statements with cheesy winks and clown-like grins.

Bud knew the good folks at New Light loved their firm just like his good folks loved Planetcom. But boy did his team ever know how to design radio systems. Hell, that's what they lived for. Bud placed his hand over his heart and said if his team made a mistake and needed to add something in the future then God bless their hearts they would sure work out a fair price for any corrections.

Bud's presentation was followed by questions from members of Council. Most focused on New Light's proposal being half the price for more sites so how could the Planetcom bid be a better bargain for the City?

A young and nerdly Planetcom engineer went into way too much detail explaining the tools Planetcom used to predict coverage. Mitch knew the real intent was not clarity. The real intent was shock and awe, however irrelevant.

The Planetcom attorney pointed out the City's legal exposure in not following their own process since Planetcom's was the only fully compliant bid. He seemed to say they might sue not only if the City selected New Light but even if the City elected not to move forward at all. Pretty ballsy. The Mayor and most of the Council grinned at this poorly camouflaged and rather empty threat.

The Mayor called the city's consultant to the podium. "Sir, would you introduce yourself to the members of the Council? And please review your role and qualifications."

"Certainly Mr. Mayor. My name is Roger Taylor and I'm an independent consultant in the field of wide area wireless networks. My particular specialty is gov'ment. You hired me to develop and release a formal Request For Proposal for our distinguished vendors. Subsequently to review detailed responses and make a recommendation for final award."

"When did you release the RFP?" the Mayor asked.

"Last September."

"And who responded?"

"Three or four firms but only two were turn-key. New Light and Planetcom."

"And have you carefully studied their bids?"

"Indeed I have, Mr. Mayor."

"What makes you qualified to handle this responsibility?"

"Thirty years in the bidness says I'm qualified. On top of that I have a Masters in Electrical Engineering and a specialty in Information Technology."

"Alright, sir, those sound like acceptable qualifications to me." The Mayor turned his attention to the Council. "Do any of you have a question for Mr. Taylor pursuant to his qualifications?" No one responded. "Now, then, Mr. Taylor have you finished your analysis in accordance with your predefined metrics?"

"Indeed I have."

"And can you tell the good folks here tonight how the vendors scored?"

"Indeed, I can. In the category of coverage, the Planetcom design wins."

Loud moans erupted from the New Light team. Larry stood and shouted, "Mr. Taylor, how can that possibly be? We have more sites! There is no question but that our coverage exceeds---"

"Order!" shouted the Mayor. "Mr. Hendrix, we have a communication process here this evening and you damn well know it! I'll ask that you follow that process!"

Larry straightened his tie and sat.

"Please continue, Mr. Taylor," the Mayor instructed.

"In the area of Emergency Handling, the Planetcom design outperforms the New Light design."

"Oh come on!" Larry stood once more and shouted. "That's ludicrous. Our system is so much better at handling emergencies. Talk to the Police Department in Boston, for Chrissakes. When the explosives took out Fenway Park two years ago? Whose system do you think they used? Flawlessly!"

"Mr. Hendrix, sit down!", the Mayor roared. "If I hear one more outburst I'll have you tasered and removed from these proceedings." The mayor nodded at the consultant. "Please continue, Mr. Taylor."

"And in the category of price the New Light proposal is cheaper by half."

"Hell, I'm surprised you didn't give that one to Planetcom," Larry grumbled.

The Mayor pretended not to hear. "Thank you, Mr. Taylor. At this time I'll open it up for the public. If anyone would like to ask the consultant, myself, or any member of the Council a question, please select the number four and speak into your micro. Once you're recognized I want you to state your name, age, and occupation." The Mayor looked across the auditorium. "The floor recognizes the young man at the podium."

"Hello, my name is Mitch Downing. I'm twenty-eight, and a graduate student at USF."

"What do you study at the school, son?" the Mayor asked.

"Applied nanotechnology."

"Thank you, Mr. Downing. You may address the Council."

"Mr. Taylor, let me start by asking could you outline the key differences of a new system compared to the existing coverage the city has today?"

The consultant spent the next several minutes explaining how a brand new network would improve coverage, fall under complete city control, and provide better support of emergencies. Mitch asked leading questions so it was easy for the consultant to describe how the project would ultimately save lives.

The Mayor looked on with approval. Why not? Mitch was giving the politician what he needed by painting the project as a must-have. Then it was up to the Mayor to select his vendor.

As the consultant rambled on about group calls, Mitch's gaze fell on Jane Woodall. She removed her glasses, wiped her eyes and he thought of his mother. Who would ever watch out for someone like Mrs. Woodall?

Just like the picture frame in the Mayor's office. Something wasn't right. Just like the picture. Something was artificial. Wireless World. People living in poverty, begging for jobs, destroyed lives, rampant crime. How was it all connected? What did it all add up to?

He watched Mrs. Woodall squint at the Mayor and mouth the words, "I see you in there, fallen angel. You're going to burn us all to hell," then she burst into flame and Mitch was no longer in the auditorium, he was floating above. Just a passenger looking down at the images of his mind. He felt *inSyte* take over, crunching and chewing through calculations, regression analyses exploring causal relationships, independent and dependent variables in the room, in his mind, in his thoughts. Recent memories treated as random input to equations. An inflection point was reached, a positive feedback loop developed that spun out of his conscious control, a self amplifying chain reaction and his senses were overwhelmed by data flooding his head in a vision vivid and realistic as a high definition Quentin Tarantino movie.

A million jobless Nomads, mass demonstrations through dark streets. They march under banners reading "Abdicate The Theocracy!" and "Only Monarchs owe their Rule to the Will of God!"

Through a red haze the Mayor vows to quell the Godless rebellion, opens an offensive against the people that collapses, punitive actions further enrage the population. Southside trooper garrisons openly declare non-recognition of Mayoral authority and refuse to carry out commands.

Spontaneous revolution, Nomads march with Southside troopers, demand the Mayor's resignation, transfer of power to the Governor. The Mayor orders armed attacks, five hundred killed, three thousand wounded.

The great fire starts at a Southside bakery late on a Wednesday night in December 2021. Sirens sound, winds fan flames to a firestorm that rips, tears to the City's heart, no order in streets, rumors spread of government agents setting fires. Northside troopers become victims of violence.

Mitch fell to one knee.

He was in Hell, red and hot like the Hell of the ancients. Bodies hung by feet from a Chevron station at the corner of MLK and Nebraska, arms splayed toward earth like an inverted crucifixion. Piles of bodies beneath, captured and executed on the spot, crowds scratch and tear corpses in anger, troopers fire water canon and goodbye guns.

"Mr. Downing, are you alright?" Phelps was far away.

"Nowhere to run," Mitch mumbled over a thick tongue. "Don't shoot."

Explosion after explosion beyond belief, worse than the blackest nightmare, millions of Nomads horribly burnt. More difficult to breathe, people leaving shelters in dark inconceivable panic, dead and dying trampled, pushed by people behind into burning streets, falling ruins, cremated adults shrunk to the size of small children, pieces of arms and legs, whole families burnt to death, burning people running to and fro, dead rescuers, families calling and looking for children, fire everywhere, everywhere fire, and all the time the hot wind of the firestorm throws people back into burning pens from which they can't escape.

Mitch looked down to see his hands on fire. He watched skin blacken and separate around sizzling dark blood.

The pain of knowing the you you've always known will never be you again.

People scream, motion wildly, one after another faint to the ground, no oxygen, burning to cinders. A mother carries her infant on her back, both are burned to death but her back doesn't burn because the baby...

Mitch heard hazy voices. Hands gripped his arms, pulled him to his feet. He opened his eyes to anxious faces.

"Mitch!" Kate's voice faint as though calling from the entrance of a deep cave. "Are you alright?" *Alright, right, ite...*

"Yes, yes," Mitch's head was spinning. *Come on, get it together!* "I'm fine, please. Just need a minute to… I need some space." He shook himself free from the troopers who surrounded him. "Back-off," he snapped.

"Please get Mr. Downing some water," Phelps said to no one in particular.

Mitch spread his feet, willed himself to look at Mrs. Woodall. She sat quietly, a tiny woman drawn into herself. But alive and safe. She put her glasses on and gazed at him through watery eyes.

Mitch didn't know what just happened. He'd have to sort through it later. But he knew one thing with the utmost clarity.

An award to Planetcom would put into motion events that would result in the death of millions.

32

Everyone in the room was staring at Mitch. He felt the rush of the Grid through his mind and made his move.

"Mr. Taylor, let me ask you a question that I'm sure is on everybody's mind. These are two large firms, well established in providing networks across the world. Isn't that correct?"

"Yes," Mr. Taylor conceded. "That's correct,"

"Fair to say these vendors have been successful in the past responding to RFPs similar to what you released?"

Mr. Taylor nodded. "Fair to say, yes."

"You've been doing this for thirty years?"

"Yes, I have. Of course the technology has changed a bit in that time," Mr. Taylor said with a chuckle.

"But both vendors have stayed current with the new technology?"

"Yes."

"I see. So you've been doing this long enough to have a feel for the pros and cons of the each system."

"That's right."

"Is there much difference in the way the vendors handle emergencies?"

"There are technical differences, certainly."

"Allow me to rephrase the question. Are there substantive differences in how they handle emergencies."

Mitch caught the Mayor leaning forward in his seat.

"I'm not sure how to answer," said Taylor.

"On a scale of one to ten, could you quantify the differences in how vendors handle emergencies? Ten means a big difference, one means a slight difference."

"That's hard to say with precision."

"Closer to one or closer to ten," Mitch pressed, his voice becoming firm.

"Closer to one, but there are---"

"Thank you, Mr. Taylor. So I take that to mean the vendors have essentially tied on their score with respect to how they handle an emergency."

"Perhaps you could develop that conclusion," Taylor conceded.

"Interesting that you did not. As for coverage, I find it difficult to believe the Planetcom design provides better coverage than New Light with only sixty percent of the access points. Neat trick, huh, Mr. Taylor?"

"Site count is one variable in developing an overall coverage map."

"What are the other variables?"

"Transmit power, receiver sensitivity, antenna patterns, physical location of the sites. I could go on."

"I see," Mitch glanced at the Mayor who wore a look of impatience. Wanda Deter looked on with growing curiosity. Mitch glanced down for a moment as though he were flipping through mental papers. Then his eyebrows drew together. "Don't both firms use the same access points manufactured by the same third party?"

"Well, yes, but---"

"So doesn't that mean, Mr. Taylor, that both firms have identical transmit power, receiver sensitivity, antenna patterns?"

"Well, yes, that's true, but---"

"But what, Mr. Taylor? But what? How can you make an argument that the coverage is a factor of these things when both vendors use the exact same hardware?"

Taylor looked toward the Mayor.

"I'm asking the questions, Mr. Taylor," Mitch said. "Why are you looking over there? Look at me."

"Mr. Downing, well, I..." Mr. Taylor pretended to shuffle through his notes. "The final variable is the *location* of the sites. Where you actually mount the wireless access points. Planetcom spent more time doing their homework than New Light. They dug deeper and got better locations with building owners all across town. Hell, you could put four sites in poor locations and end up with less coverage than one site in a prime spot."

The Mayor's sudden smug smile infuriated Mitch. He glanced down. Then glared at the consultant.

"Mr. Taylor, doesn't the City have imminent domain when designing a public safety system? Can't the City dictate what goes where? If the City likes the Planetcom site locations, then doesn't the City have the right to use the same locations for New Light? And wouldn't that lower the New Light price even more?"

Mitch glanced around the room. Bud looked like someone had popped his balloon. Larry beamed and pumped his fist. The Mayor narrowed his eyes and frowned. The consultant said nothing.

"Let's talk about price, Mr. Taylor," Mitch said. "In working with these systems for the past thirty years, have you developed a feel for how much they cost?"

"Of course I have."

"How can both vendors come in here with similar designs, similar features, identical hardware in most cases. Yet, one's half the price of the other. How's that possible? Have you seen that before?"

Silence in the great hall. Much hinged on the credibility of Taylor's answer.

"Yes, I have."

"Oh?" Mitch was surprised.

"Means one vendor cut corners. That's the only way New Light's price is lower. And you can't do it in public safety, no place for it."

Mitch was incredulous. He didn't need to scour the Grid for a response this time. "Bullshit, Mr. Taylor. New Light didn't cut any corners. They have the same design as Planetcom except for one small fact. They have more sites."

Nervous laughter flowed through the hall. Taylor turned beet red then smiled as though he were in on the joke. A hammering noise. Mitch looked toward the stage. Mayor Delaney was actually banging a gavel. He only needed a gray wig and the picture would be complete.

"Thank you, Mr. Downing. You may take your seat!" Mayor Delaney banged until quiet was restored.

Mitch walked back to Kate. She took his hand and whispered, "Are you alright? My God, what happened?"

He didn't even know what the hell happened. How could he explain it to Kate? *No problem, darlin', I just had an epiphany that the world's going to end. Ever watch a City get firebombed? Fascinating stuff. There's some great footage out there on Tokyo and London. Of course, the real mack-daddy is Dresden, Germany. Like finding yourself in a giant fire pit, trying to swim through red-hot coals. If the smoke doesn't get you, there's always spontaneous combustion.*

He forced a weak smile and whispered, "I'm fine. Just a little woozy. You've been keeping me out too late."

"At this time we would like to hear from any other citizen who cares to comment or question this important initiative," Mayor Delaney stated. "The floor is open and you may direct questions to any Council member, either vendor, or our consultant. Anybody else care to come forth and address the Council?"

Wanda Deter stepped to the podium and the Mayor sighed so loudly it was amplified and heard by the entire assembly.

33

"I'm sorry if you find this tiring, Mr. Mayor," Wanda said. "But you have to understand something. Something important. My brothers and sisters are DYING OUT THERE!"

The hall was silent in the wake of her shout.

"Are you listening to what people are saying here tonight? We have war zones, Mayor Delaney. WAR ZONES! We cannot enter these areas unless we're in armored vehicles. What is wrong with that picture?" She shook her head in disbelief. "And that's just half the story. The other half is we have two hundred thousand people living in shanty towns, under bridges, on the front steps of our churches."

She made eye contact with Mrs. Woodall, gave her an encouraging smile, turned to the Mayor with a look of dead seriousness.

"Why do you suppose that is, Mr. Mayor? Because these people don't want to work? No. Suffer mental health issues? No. It's because their jobs have been replaced by machines. These people represent the blue collar of our society. The soul of our city. And they are ready, Mr. Mayor. Ready for an education. Ready to make something of themselves. Ready to become productive members of society again. Pay taxes again. Don't you see? Together we can all grow and become stronger."

She lifted her arms to shoulder height, palms up as though she were lifting a great weight. "Look around this room. The people you see are your constituents. These are the people who vote for you. At least, they did. But you sit there on your throne and reek of royalty and act like you couldn't care less."

"That's not true. I appreciate each and every one of you," the Mayor exercised his best smile.

"Do you really?" Wanda asked through wide eyes. "Because that's not what it feels like down here, Mr. Mayor. Down here it feels like you're in bed with somebody and it surely ain't the people."

"Please, Wanda. Nothing could be farther from the truth."

Mitch chuckled and Kate elbowed him in the ribs.

"Mr. Mayor, I hear you. I hear the things you say. We need a good communication system to support our police troopers. Our fire department. Our emergency medical teams. I get that. I really get that. I'm not here to argue with you today on whether we need a good communication system. I do not want that to become the central issue. If you try to make that the issue then I surrender." Wanda held up her hands with a large, bright smile.

Mitch saw exactly where she was going with this. Draining the current from the Mayor's gun before the first shot was fired.

"I listen patiently this evening, along with my friends and family. Along with your constituents, Mr. Mayor. I confess I am not a scientist. I am not a technologist. I do not pretend to understand the physics behind these systems. And yet, I am an intelligent woman, Mr. Mayor. An educated woman. And I understand one thing. I understand the need for fiscal responsibility in my own house."

She looked the Mayor straight in the eye. "And the need for even greater fiscal responsibility in my government."

Various murmurs of affirmation throughout the hall.

"What kind of car do you drive, Mr. Mayor?" Wanda asked.

"Excuse me?"

"Simple question, Mr. Mayor. What kind of car do you drive?"

"I drive a late model Toyota Starlight. Nothing fancy."

"Hydrogen?" she asked.

"You bet. Green as a turnip," the Mayor said with a grin.

"How wonderful for you. I drive an eight year old Avalon. Old fashioned hybrid motor gets me ten miles per liter from traditional gasoline."

"Oh, my," the Mayor said. "Carbon taxes must eat you alive."

"Not bad, Mr. Mayor. Not too bad. Of course, I would love a new car. The Avalon has been a great partner all these years. She's got over three hundred thousand kilometers. But it's time for something new, right?"

The Mayor narrowed his eyes.

"I don't think anyone would disagree it's time for something new?" Wanda looked around the room and was met with murmurs of agreement. "So I've made up my mind, I'm going to get a brand new car. I'm fired up about it. I mean, I am going to love my new car." Her eyes were wide and she spoke softly as though sharing a secret. "Do you know what I would love to get?"

"No, Miss Deter. Please tell me."

"Mr. Mayor, I would dearly love to drive over the Sunshine Skyway in a beautiful new, hydrogen Lexus. Convertible."

"*Cherry Red*," someone added. Mitch looked at Kate and they smiled. Kate mouthed the word "enthusiastic".

"You only live once," the Mayor said. "But you should consider North American. Tell you what – reach out to Janet, my admin? Bob's a friend of mine owns Jackson Chevrolet."

"I won't be doing that, Mr. Mayor," Wanda's smile faded. "I simply can't afford it. Oh, I want to. Believe me, I want that car. But I can only afford the Avalon. And, Mr. Mayor, the Avalon meets my needs just fine."

Mitch was amazed the Mayor hadn't seen that one coming.

"You see, Mr. Mayor, as the head of my household I have fiscal responsibilities. Yes, there's that word again. Sure I want that Lexus. But I can't feed my babies with that Lexus. I can keep the Avalon and still feed my babies. Do you see what I'm saying?"

"Indeed, Miss Deter, I get your point."

Wanda fixed her intense gaze on the Mayor.

"I'm not sure you do. You have the same responsibilities to your family. And to your flock here tonight. You've listened to them come before you this evening, one after another, telling you of their need for food. Your children are starving, Mr. Mayor. And I dearly pray you will not buy the Lexus when the Avalon will meet your needs and allow you to feed your children."

Wanda returned to her seat and the room erupted into thunderous applause with shouts of "Amen," "Hallelujah," and a lone, but heartfelt, "Tell us, sister, tell us."

The Mayor banged his gavel. "Order, order."

"He's stuck, isn't he?" Kate asked.

"I believe so," Mitch said.

"He has to award to New Light, right?"

"No other rational move. Except, of course, no award at all."

The Mayor looked out across the great hall. "The floor is open once more. Any other citizen care to step forth and address the Council?" No one opened their micro and the Mayor continued. "At this time the City Council will conduct their vote."

"Mayor Delaney!" Wanda stood. "This is outrageous! There's no vote scheduled this evening. What are you trying to pull?"

The Mayor motioned to security while he addressed the Council. Troopers positioned themselves in front of the stage and Mitch shook his head slowly at the unfolding madness.

Mitch watched Phelps's lips moving soundlessly in front of his microphone. Apparently only the Mayor's mic was live.

"You will submit a vote for two resolutions. Your vote for Resolution A is either yes or no to move forward with the contract. Your vote for Resolution B is either Planetcom or New Light. Questions?"

No questions from Council. At least none that could be heard over cut mics. Across the auditorium people stood and murmured angrily at the sudden turn of events.

"Ladies and Gentlemen of the Council, I ask you now to cast your votes electronically. I will read the results once your votes are tallied."

Several minutes passed as the Council voted. Voices grew louder and more furious throughout the hall. Mitch looked at Kate. Her mouth was a tight line.

At last the Mayor stood before the assembly. The hall quieted to hear the results.

"Good people of Tampa, I will read the votes. On the first resolution let it be so recorded that on this date of Tuesday, March 10, 2020, the City Council has voted five to two to move forward with full funding release for Wireless World."

Low murmurs throughout the auditorium.

No big surprise.

"On the second resolution let it be so recorded that on this date the City Council has voted four to three to move forward with an award to Planetcom to provide and build the City's next generation Wireless World!"

Pandemonium exploded in the great hall.

34

Mitch heard shouts of indignation followed by screams of pain from several areas as citizens were tasered. This was escalating into mass chaos.

"Let's get the hell out of here," he said to Kate. He took her hand and they made their way toward the exit at the back of the hall.

The Mayor, to his credit, pressed on. "This is a great day in our City's history. An important step in bringing our fine City firmly into the twenty first century! Thank you to the consultant and to the Council..."

Mitch couldn't believe it. People were actually trying to work their way *toward* the stage. It was only a matter of time before the troopers upped the ante beyond tasers. Since San Francisco's thermochemical assassinations in 2015, governments had zero tolerance for civil disobedience of any kind.

"Get behind me!" he shouted to Kate. "Put your arms around my waist!"

A head ache roared into his mind like a freight train.

She hugged him tight and he doggedly pushed his way through the shouting throng. He tried to sidestep a fat man wearing red camouflage pants and unlaced tennis shoes. The man leered at Kate and ran a meaty hand up her thigh.

"Out of the way, boy," the oaf said. He put a ham hock sized arm against Mitch's chest and shoved hard.

Mitch easily sidestepped the sweaty arm and as the man's momentum carried him forward Mitch slammed his elbow sideways into the exposed larynx. The fat man grunted but stayed on his feet. He sneered at Mitch, drew back a fist. Mitch hit him again and crushed his trachea. The man fell to his knees and Mitch saw that his bright blue ball cap bragged *Catfish Fear Me*.

"You alright?" he shouted at Kate.

"What did you just do?"

"Later!"

The scuffle produced a hole in the crowd and Mitch pushed forward through the exit while troopers fired Goodbye Guns into the people behind. *InSyte* triggered video of a scene from the old Poseidon Adventure movie. Cold seawater bursting through bulkheads to drown the foolish crowd that elected not to escape with Gene Hackman toward the surface. Mitch wanted to turn his Grid connection off and realized with mounting dismay that he could not actually bring himself to do so.

35

They met at a diner in South Tampa just before midnight. Woody and Molly shared a tall beer. Mitch and Kate drank strong coffee.

Mitch absently analyzed conversations from surrounding tables. Teenagers in an adjacent booth replaying their night of partying. An elderly couple sharing a soft conversation in a corner. A cook telling dirty jokes to a short waitress with a pretty smile. Words triggered searches in Mitch's head that ran in new directions like cracks in a windshield. He wanted to turn *inSyte* off.

Yeah, right. Add it to the list of things he wanted to do and couldn't.

"The public is shut out from the political process," Woody said. "It ain't right."

"How did it come to this?" Molly asked.

Her question triggered a new crack. *Natural consequence of competition. Google IPO'd in oh four and what was their first move? Hired a fleet of Washington legal reps.*

"Ain't no telling," Woody said.

The Jimi Hendrix Experience released January 1, 1970 ... well the sunrise is burnin' my eyes baby. There ain't no telling baby when you're gonna see me 'cause I really hope that uh, it'll be tomorrow..."

"So your Dad's mind was made up, eh?" Woody said. "Little dog and pony for the people to make it look good but that's all it was. A show."

Mitch disabled *inSyte's* automatic voice response and silence descended like a soft blanket over his mind. Ahhhh. Free to ride the light on his thoughts alone.

"That certainly appears to be the case," Kate said.

"Oh well. Life in the big city," Molly offered.

Let's start with what he knew. *InSyte* had conducted multiple unsolicited regression analysis. Apparently the data mining started with Martin's lectures and continued with his meeting in the Mayor's office. The Commissioner's meeting provided the final inputs.

"Gee, Molly, that's insightful," Kate said.

Mitch looked at Kate.

Molly glanced up from an examination of her blackberry-purple nails. "Get with it, Katie. That's the way the world works."

And the survey says? Giving the award to Planetcom will be a tipping point that plunges millions into poverty over the next two years.

"Guys, obviously I love my Dad," Kate said. "But I can't believe he'd ram this contract through the system and hand all that money to Planetcom."

Mass anarchy. The city will burn to the ground and millions will die. Ninety-nine percent certainty.

"I hate to say it," Molly drank from her beer. "But there's gotta be a personal payday for your Dad in all this."

Initial efforts to contain the fire will be met with violence. By the time people realize a monster is loosed, it's beyond containment. Way beyond. Everyone caught in a great oven. Like Dresden in forty-nine.

"What do we do now?" Kate asked. "I mean, when I think of those poor people tonight begging for their lives … it makes me sick to my stomach."

"We find the paper trail and blow him out of the water," Mitch said softly.

Kate turned and faced him. "How?"

"Find a link between Planetcom and your Dad."

"You mean communication with Planetcom? Aren't there legitimate reasons for their team to talk to my Dad?"

Mitch frowned and shook his head. "Bud Colt's a junior woodchuck. I'm talking about somebody behind the curtain. Nothing you'll find on the public record."

"How do we flush something like that out?" Kate asked. "I mean, if there's no record then how do you find it?"

Mitch said nothing. The table grew quiet as the night wore heavily on their minds.

Mitch shut his eyes and felt a sense of motion as though he were riding a roller coaster. He opened his eyes to stop the wave. Could he ever unplug *inSyte* again? At last a question he couldn't answer.

36   Wednesday March 11, 2020

Mitch knew sleep wasn't coming so he opened his mind to the Grid. Spread your little wings and fly away. Fly away, far away.

I need warp speed, Scotty, and I need it now!

He'd told Woody he couldn't see into men's hearts or be all places at all times. But that wasn't true. Not exactly. He could tap into camera feeds and blogospheres and eyes and ears and he clenched his fists into the sheets because now he was tripping, *really* cruising, wandering the earth like Kwai Chang Caine in a rocket ship.

Times Square, the Vegas Palazzo, McKenna Beach, Midtown Tower Tokyo, One Churchill Place, he was in the stratosphere, the exosphere, one camera feed to the next to the next, he tore across stepping stones like a *presence*, like a true *being* that was *being* everywhere at the same time, a part of all things. He sailed oceans climbed mountains scaled buildings ducked through tunnels bounced into satellites above the planet holy crap through a dorm room *are those real* and people were in every position on everything everywhere doing working playing *thinking* and it turns out he did know their thoughts after all.

Slammey28 screamed in a tweet that his next move was to pocket his baby Glock and hunt down the ex. The forty caliber knew how to get a bitch's attention and she ought to know better than to fuck with a man's truck come on, who *does* that? TheBiffer18 slipped silk boxers inside out so his member would be caressed by only the finest material during his lap dance in the city and BarbE-Dahl69 said *Hallelujah Brother*, she loved to see a man have a good time in this world. HarryPitts41 had a rotting cat in his kitchen and was there anyone else out there who had to kill their feline cuz it wouldn't stop pissin in the sink and if so, how did they get rid of the carcass in an apartment community? DangerWillRobinson suggested a contractor-grade lawn bag, you could get 'em at the local Home Depot. madEllen19 sobbed, how could bubbuh26 leave her in second life after the adventures they shared, what kindda man just up and runs off after slaying dragons together and making love at the Lost Gardens of Apollo? mamapower58 toyed with the idea of suicide since the C took her son she just couldn't stand it, oh Lord did anyone out there hear her, please God anyone at all, oh please, oh please, I'm begging---

Captain! She can't take much more of this!

Mitch squeezed his head to stop the pain. *Focus! Come on, man. FOCUS!*

He folded his imagination down to the ocean and soon he was floating in dark water and that was OK, that was his happy place. After a few minutes of gentle rocking he regained control of his thoughts. Rationality from chaos.

Jesus, what is it with this thing?

Realistically there were two ways to reverse the award. Option One? Expose the Mayor's corruption. Doesn't matter if the son of a bitch is actually prosecuted. The suggestion of impropriety would hang the award for years.

Option Two? Take the Mayor out in a covert and the award goes away. At least for now. The problem with Option Two was the potential for backfire. Could trigger a martyrdom effect, propelling the contract forward on sympathetic legs. Oh yeah, Option Two could also assassinate any feelings Kate might have for him. Way too much collateral damage.

So for now he liked Option One. High enough odds. Speaking of Kate, how much should he share with her? The answer was … nothing. She didn't know about *inSyte*, so how could he tell her about his vision? The only person he could confide in was Woody. Next time he saw him.

No question that the Mayor was taking a pay-off. Mitch just needed evidence. Where to find it? Unlikely the Mayor would be foolish enough to store anything in public areas of the Grid. So he'd have to look in restricted areas.

The term 'firewall' dated back to the early nineteenth century. Houses were constructed with bricks inside inner walls to stop the spread of a fire. A firewall's function within a network was similar, primarily used to prevent unauthorized movement from one area into another.

Without thoughtfully planned configuration the value of a firewall was just about zilch. The larger the business, the tougher to implement. So most large networks allowed all traffic through unless something was identified as a threat.

City governments tended to have huge networks with relatively unsophisticated users. He pulled the covers over his head and went to work.

He located the IP address for the City's storage array and he was in. He found the sub network for corporate contracts, entered a character search for any file related to Planetcom, then scanned through seventeen hits. All harmless, technical, boring. No smoking gun. Then again, why would anyone hide files on storage servers available to city staff?

He changed gears and after negotiating two default-allow firewalls he found a virtual array partitioned exclusively for the Mayor. He used 'Planetcom' and 'Wireless World' as search criteria and read through the resulting documentation. Nothing incriminating.

OK. Let's try something a little closer to home. Most government workers used private email accounts to conduct personal business away from prying eyes. Private accounts were generally with one of the large experience providers like AT&T or Verizon. These mammoth corporations always used open rule sets. Relatively simple to find the Mayor's personal IP address and follow it to his home network.

Mitch let out a low whistle. Well, well. What have we here?

The Mayor's private network was intercepting and dropping his packets. This occurred transparently, with no acknowledgement of any kind back to Mitch. So the Mayor had an application-aware firewall to protect his home network. So called AA firewalls inspect every bit and byte for proper content and restrict outright any intrusion.

When Mitch was a young boy in Summer Camp his counselors played a game. Bastards taped a twenty dollar bill to the top of a metal flagpole. All you had to do was climb the pole and the money was there for the taking. What ten year old boy couldn't shimmy a flagpole? Only one problem. The pole was greased top to bottom with thick silicone gel. No matter how hard you tried, it was impossible to get traction.

He was climbing the same damn pole while the counselors snickered. Security of the AA variety was certainly effective. And definitely rare. Because packet diversity made AA complex and difficult to configure. Mitch could not remember seeing one on a home network. He drummed fingers on his chest beneath the covers.

"What are you hiding?" he said out loud to the darkness.

37

In Kate's dream she was back in the auditorium of the Municipal Government Building. The mood was light and festive and the large crowd beautifully dressed. She gazed around the room and smiled at tuxedoed men, ladies in formal evening gowns, long stemmed drinks held in elegant, white gloves. Everyone appeared relaxed and in wonderfully good cheer. Soft music radiated from everywhere and ladies smiled demurely as men told their tales.

Motion at the front of the hall. Kate turned to see Cameron Diaz on the Council table looking younger and softer then her forty seven years should allow. She was decked out like ten million in a short, hip cocktail dress with a Burberry check pattern. Justin Timberlake sat in the Mayor's bench and a hidden orchestra played an extended introduction to something that sounded familiar but Kate couldn't put her finger on it until Cameron started to sing.

"Just sit right back and you'll hear a tale, a tale of a fateful trip, that started from this tropic port aboard this tiny ship."

Gilligan's Island, the old syndicated show that still garnered decent streams from young audiences across the union.

Kate was amazed at the intensity with which the room responded. Ladies hiked their skirts and boogied with eyes squeezed shut. Men screamed to the music, dancing hard and fast, almost violently.

Cameron threw her dopey smile at Justin, surprised at the reaction to the ridiculous song. Her unbelieving eyes asked Justin *can you believe this crazy shit*? Justin tilted his head and shrugged to reply that no, he most certainly could not.

"The mate was a mighty sailing man, the skipper brave and sure…"

Kate turned and across the room spotted the oaf who groped her yesterday. His filthy tank top and red camo pants stood in stark contrast to the dark tuxedoes all around. He danced in a rapid circle by pivoting his body around and around on whirling, fat legs. Whenever his feet touched the floor he slapped his right buttock hard and leapt again, as though spurring a reluctant horse to carry an unwanted load.

He spotted her and stopped, staring with wide eyes. His lips moved but there wasn't any sound. She could see why. His neck was swollen and black. She remembered the sound of Mitch's elbow hitting the man's throat. The first strike made a popping sound like a breaking seal. The second strike sounded gooey like someone crushing an orange.

She stared at his lips and tried to make out what he was saying.

"Your boyfriend …"

She moved closer.

"… is not..."

She moved closer still.

"Your boyfriend is not what he seems." Fear pinched the oaf's eyes like a pig at slaughter.

"THE WEATHER STARTED GETTING ROUGH,
THE TINY SHIP WAS TOSSED---"

She heard a thunderclap then the music ended and she was swinging in her backyard in her four year old body with a feeling of total and complete relaxation.

She shut her little girl eyes and lost all worry because she couldn't possibly understand there were risks and perils and tough choices and bad things that could happen if you didn't watch your step in the world. All of that was ahead of her. For now she lived only in the moment.

Besides, parents did all the worrying. Her four year old world contained play time and meal time and play time and sleep time and play time and two colorful, lovable, all-powerful, huge warm people who tended to every need. They were always there to return a smile or understand and reflect a frown.

She opened her eyes and swung toward an impossibly blue sky. She fell backwards and watched thick grass run past her feet. Her father's soft hands pushed her gently forward in another journey through green and blue, up and down, over and over, crimson and clover. Her twenty-four year old mind luxuriated in the tranquility of the perfect moment.

"Higher, Daddy," she said. "I want to go super high!"

She stole a glance over her shoulder into the lean face of her Daddy. So young and handsome. Why, he looked like one of the boys in her chemistry class. Someone called from the house that lunch was ready and Kate fought back a sob to realize that on this sunny day her Mama was alive and breathing just inside those walls.

"Wait, Daddy, wait. I want to go inside!"

"Hold on, baby," her Dad said in his soft easy voice.

He pushed hard and she swung until her feet were as high as her head and she squealed with delight.

"Did you say push harder?" her Daddy asked and his voice changed ever so slightly. She heard a roughness as though he were swallowing crumbs.

"No, Daddy." she shouted. "I want to get down."

He pushed harder and his hands weren't gentle at all.

"Owwww." She started to cry. "You're hurting me."

The yard darkened. She looked up and saw heavy black clouds block the sun.

Where did this come from?

Her feet flew higher than her head and she gripped the chains with small hands to keep from falling. She shrieked in her little girl voice and sailed backward toward her Daddy.

His cold hands nearly shoved her off the seat. She didn't fall because luckily she wasn't a little girl anymore, she was a grown woman. And of course she swung in slow motion. At the top of her arc she again squeezed the chains tight to keep from falling. She swung back toward the man and wanted to drag her feet but couldn't move her legs. She managed to twist her head to steal a glance and now she screamed in her grown up voice.

A young man no longer stood behind her. He'd been infested by something old and grizzled. Something stooped with age and a filth she didn't understand.

She was at last able to move her legs so she dug her heels into the dead grass to stop her descent. She leapt from the swing and whirled to face the creature that her father had become.

"What have you done?" she demanded. "What have you done with my father?"

It stepped forward and its skin was mottled and brown. Its hair was gray and swarmed with tiny, dirty insects. Hands reached toward her with black fingernails. A cracked smile revealed yellowed, rotted teeth.

The eyes were vivid blue.

"Why, Angel," it said through a throat clotted with dirt. "I *am* your father."

She wanted to run but willed herself not to move.

"Come to me now," it said.

No, no, no, no, no. This is a dream.

"Come to me now, God Bless, or I'll split you from your pie hole to your asshole and lay you in the grass to bleed."

Wake up, wake up, WAKE UP!

A drum beat in a neighbor's yard.

What the fuck?

"Kate and Chase?" Mom called from the kitchen. "Come inside it's time to eat!"

The ominous drum beat louder.

She awoke to staccato sound. Her ring tone. She opened her eyes. Looked at her clock. Seven am. Shut her eyes. Opened them and looked at the monitor on her desk. Someone calling. She flicked her finger and

Mitch appeared on her display. He looked disheveled. Like he hadn't slept.

"I need to get on your network," he said.

"My network." She was confused.

"Your home network."

She stared at Mitch, regaining her senses. She wanted to come awake to get as far from her dream as she could. But a part of her wanted to go back and confront her father and demand to know why he had … *deteriorated*. She closed her eyes and attempted to reach in and pull her young Dad back to the swing. She thought she had one chance to save him but needed to act quickly.

"Why," she said thickly.

"I think your Dad's hiding something there. Something important."

Then she remembered the City Council meeting. The vote. The conversation in the diner.

"Come on over." Her mouth was dry.

"I don't think that's a good idea."

"Why not."

"Is your Dad there?"

"Not sure. Just woke up. Probably."

"Well, first I'm not so sure he'd appreciate my company after the position I took with his consultant. Second, I'm not sure he'd appreciate us snooping around on his home network. Not to mention hanging out in your room with the door closed."

"OK. I get it. I'll come over and we can get on my network from my micro. I need to shower."

38

Kate's micro provided turn by turn directions and soon she arrived at Mitch's apartment in South Tampa. She parked and hopped out of her hydrogen coupe. The morning was clear and the cool breeze felt clean.

She was a little nervous, her first visit to Mitch's home. His space. His crib. The neighborhood wasn't bad. The apartment community looked nice. Not far from Bayshore. Good restaurants in the area.

I could fuck him here, she thought with a wry smile.

Then again, that might depend. You could tell a lot about a man by venturing into his castle. She had dated guys who looked put-together. The whole package. Or so she thought until she saw how they lived. Not that she was a total neat freak. She just appreciated a little cleanliness.

OK, so she was a complete germaphobe. Cross contamination was no laughing matter. She pinged Mitch from her micro to answer the door and mentally steeled herself for the worst. Please God, don't let him be a total slob.

The door opened and there he was. She slipped into his arms and they walked inside. She looked down and they kissed.

"Where's Woody?" she asked, glancing around.

The apartment wasn't cluttered. In fact, she couldn't remember seeing a man's space that was so clear of stuff. Just a few essentials. A sofa, a chair, a shelf with a few books neatly arranged. The shelf also contained a simple vase with real flowers and a framed picture. She walked forward to get a closer look at the photograph.

"Spent the night with Molly," Mitch said. "Can I get you a cup of coffee?"

"Sounds wonderful."

"Hungry?"

"Not after the late meal last night."

"Same here. Coffee'll be ready in a minute."

She glanced down the hallway and noticed a wood frame surrounding a doorway marred with dents and small cracks. Like someone had pummeled it. Repeatedly. She'd have to ask Mitch about that.

She looked at a metal frame that held an actual photograph. Like one of those family pictures taken at a photo shop in the mall. Generic brushed blue background, the kind that brought out the best color from people in the foreground. She scanned the photo from left to right, one face at a time. First was a man, mid-thirties and handsome. Strong face and a proud smile. Soft brown eyes. His arm was around a beautiful woman who appeared to be in her early thirties. She had a warm face with a big smile and bright, lively eyes. Next was a young boy, eight or nine. Dark hair, dark eyes. He looked shy. Catching a glimpse of how difficult the world could be but no clue how to deal with it. He had his father's strong, handsome face, though, and a boy with a face like that would develop confidence soon enough.

She saw the last face and her eyes widened. A little boy, no more than five. The smile is what got her. The photographer had caught something special. That little boy with the dark mop of hair, dark eyes and an absolutely radiant smile, one that told the world how proud he was to be with his family that day. One little arm was over his older brother's shoulder. His other arm reached across and held his brother's hand.

She moved her fingers across the little boy's face. He looked somehow more vulnerable than his older brother. She didn't get the same vibe that the little face would develop a strong confidence in life. He looked more... exposed? She pulled her gaze away.

All horizontal surfaces were clean with hardly any knick knacks. No food spills that she could see. No foul and mysterious odors. So far so good.

The entire wall opposite the kitchen looked down a snow covered mountain on a sunny day with a large blue lake at the base. She felt a slight perception of motion, gently rocking above the mountain. She put a hand on the bookcase to steady herself.

The resolution was so crisp, like looking through a big window. She walked closer to the wall and looked down. She loved doing this. Her body reacted with a slight sense of vertigo. She watched the tree tops pass by, small pines barely peeking through snow. Tough to see where the room ended and the wall began. She reached down to brush a branch and smiled when her fingertips sunk into the screen.

She joined Mitch in the kitchen and was delighted to see that everything was clean and tidy. She was impressed with the minimalist arrangements.

"Do you eat out a lot, Mitch?"

"Not too often. Love to cook actually."

"How intriguing." She said with a smile. "And what do you like to cook?"

"Oh, I have a few specialties. Nothing too exotic."

She nodded. That was the key to being a good cook. Understand a few basics about heat application and have a few meals you can throw together without a recipe.

"Your place is nice, Mitch. I'm impressed. Clean. No clutter."

"Cream and sugar?" he asked.

"Cream. Thanks,"

"Clutter's a form of visual distraction I don't need." Mitch handed her a cup then poured one for himself. "Everything pulls at your attention. Less clutter, less stress."

"I think your place is charming." She leaned against the counter and cupped the warm mug in her hands.

Mitch flipped the kitchen wall screen and they saw her father proclaiming a great day for the citizens of Tampa moving one step closer to the future. No mention of the riot or the resultant decision to invoke the stasis field. Some elder people had suffocated, including Jane Woodall. No mention on the opinion channel. But Kate had read it on the blogs and twitter feeds.

She sipped her coffee. The video changed and Wanda Deter promised to appeal the Council vote. The ballot was unscheduled and the Mayor had executed an end run around due process. Wanda would fight this decision all the way to Tallahassee, she wouldn't stop until the vote was repealed and the Mayor put in jail. A beautiful opinion journalist asked how the Deter woman COULD DARE QUESTION CITY LEADERS DURING THE CURRENT WAR ON POVERTY, then compared Wanda's position to the one Hitler took during the great civil war between the states and the euro-trash Nazis. Her rant was followed by a short blurb on a nurse missing since Friday.

Mitch turned it off.

"Where did you learn to fight?" Kate asked.

"Learned a few moves in the Navy. Got lucky yesterday, that's all."

Kate nodded. Obviously he wasn't telling her everything. The man on the beach. Robbie at the bar. The redneck last night.

Your boyfriend is not what he seems...

They had nothing to do with luck. But she didn't have the energy to pursue it any further. She looked back at the mountain scene. Now the perspective was from a skier slaloming back and forth down a wide, steep snow trail. The visual was delicious.

"Where is that?" she asked.

"Heavenly. Lake Tahoe."

"Have you been there?"

"Couple times. I took that from my flip camera quite a few years ago. Nice, huh?"

"Man, oh, man. That's a long way from Tampa." She set her mug on the counter and closed her eyes. "A long way from Tampa sounds really good right now. I feel like I want to grow a set of wings and just fly away. Miles and miles away."

Mitch looked at her. "I know exactly what you mean." He took Kate's hand and lead her into the family room. They sat on the sofa and she leaned into him. He put an arm around her and lightly kissed her hair.

"I'm still trying to make sense of it all," she said.

"I know. Me too."

"Do you think my father's dirty?" She tried not to think about her dream.

Mitch paused. "I do," he said finally.

"We have to find out the truth, don't we?"

"We do." No hesitation this time.

She turned and kissed him tenderly on the lips. Lightly stroked his hair, the back of his neck. Kissing him was like skiing down quiet, cool powder toward a still, blue lake.

Without a word she stood, took his hand, lead him to the bedroom.

Nothing else in her mind. Her senses were numbly focused on *him*. *His* hair, *his* eyes, *his* smile, *his* laugh. *His* essence. Just *him* and she wasn't exactly sure who *he* was but she was falling in love with *him* so she stopped thinking about it and just flowed down the waterfall into a pool of warmth that engulfed her senses until there was room for nothing else. No need.

She met his passion fiercely at every bend and curve, returned every touch. She kissed his face hungrily and held his body close to hers. She guided him, pushed him, pulled him. Then it changed and they moved as one, smiling into each other's eyes, building to and sharing together in the soft release.

After, they lay under covers, naked bodies pressed together.

She ran a hand across his chest. She felt traces of a scar from some long ago accident.

"What happened, here?" she asked, peering closer. "Were you shot?"

"Yes," he said with a small smile. "Fleeing the scene."

"Oh my. What were you stealing?"

"Time," he said.

"Hmmm. What really happened?" The room was dark but she could tell he had experienced a serious injury from rubbing her fingers across the area.

"Just told you. I'll tell you again. But right now there's something I'd rather show you."

Then he moved against her and she kissed him and stirred the cool warmth. He opened his dark eyes and they made love a second time, more slowly but with the same sense of shared astonishment and release. For the rest of the morning nothing else mattered.

39

His face looked peaceful in the shadowy light. He rested one hand on his chest, the other tucked beneath his pillow. She thought about the photograph on the bookshelf. She could just make out that little boy, asleep and defenseless. She knew that once he awoke the boy's face would be gone.

He opened his eyes and smiled and sure enough, it was.

That's OK. I'm not here for the boy. I'm here for the man.

They kissed and moved closer, enjoying the warmth and softness of each other.

40

Kate sat and rose shakily to her feet. Mitch watched from the bed. She was achingly beautiful. Her nakedness almost too perfect. Her long, graceful movements were accentuated by shadows in the room. His eyes were drawn to the darkness of her hair and he just wanted to watch her move around his room forever.

She disappeared into the kitchen but soon returned with a treat. Peach ice cream in a small cup with a single spoon. She cuddled next to him and fed them both in silence. He kissed her again and savored the cool, sweet taste of her lips. She painted e-resin onto his left index finger. She insisted on sea foam. He playfully objected, to no avail. They slept again.

Later they awoke. He wanted nothing more than to forget about everything and lay with her all day. But they had something to take care of, something they needed to do together. Reluctantly, they dressed.

41

"OK, Kate. Let's get to work."

She flicked her micro and logged onto her home network through a virtual private connection using Mitch's bedroom wall as the monitor. Her home page contained photos and links for music and school.

"I'll have to explore this in more detail when I have time," he said.

"Don't you think that might be a bit personal?" she teased.

"You're right. How presumptuous of me," he said and they both laughed.

He followed her network places and found her father's personal subnet.

"Good news is we're on the other side of that damn firewall. Bad news is your father's personal subnet is password protected." He raised his eyebrows. "Any ideas?"

"How many characters?" she asked.

"Let me see." He examined the properties for a moment. "Looks like eight."

"Alphanumeric?"

"Yeah. Could be letters, numbers or a combination. No requirements for special characters. So it depends on your father."

"How do you mean?"

"The best passwords are random sets of letters and numbers. Some letters capital and others lower case. Sixty-one possible entries for each of eight characters. Two point three times ten to the eighteenth possible passwords. Unbreakable."

"Passwords like that are hard to remember," she said. "My Dad's not that kindda guy."

"Good. So he'd use a name or maybe a special number? Like a date?"

"Exactly."

He nodded. "Let's break his code."

"First of all, my Dad's a name guy. Not a numbers guy."

"That helps. You just saved a lot of time."

"He'd use a word that was easy to remember. A name, maybe. Or something about his life. He wouldn't use a random eight letter word."

"Something religious?"

"Probably not. He set it up when Mom was alive so I doubt it would be religious. She wasn't really into religion."

"He may have changed his password."

"Mmmm, he's more the 'if it ain't broke don't fix it' type."

"OK. Let's start in the usual places. What was your Mom's name?"

"Lauren."

"That would have been too easy. What about your Dad's parents? Brother? Sister? Anybody in the family with an eight letter name that you can think of?"

She thought for a moment. "He has a brother named Clifford."

He typed c-l-i-f-f-o-r-d in various combinations of capital and lower case letters. No luck.

"Does your Dad have any big toys that might have names?"

"Excuse me?" she said, laughing. "My Dad's a grown man. Do you think he has a stuffed bear named Chestnut?"

"Does he?"

"Well, as a matter of fact..." she opened her eyes wide as though they had stumbled onto something. They both laughed some more.

"Thinking more like a boat," he finally said.

"I wish. No, my Dad doesn't own a boat."

"What kind of car does he drive?"

"2015 Corvette."

"He told Wanda he drives a Starlight."

"Pure bullshit."

"I see. What color's the 'vette?"

"Black."

He nodded appreciatively. "Great car. The last year Detroit made a real performer, before the bailouts and the gas guzzler taxes."

"My Dad says that all the time. He freakin' loves that car. Of course, I won't comment on how wasteful it is to drive a hog like that."

He entered c-o-r-v-e-t-t-e in various case combinations. No dice.

"OK, let's take it up a notch. What are his favorite activities? Hobbies?"

"He plays a lot of tennis. Loves golf. He does love the water, just doesn't own a boat. Oh, and he used to be into skydiving."

"Lots of interesting stuff there," he said. "Let's start with boats. Your Dad doesn't have one?"

"No but he wants one real bad."

"Kind of a shame to live in that beautiful mansion on the bay and not have a boat."

"The mansion comes with the job. But my Dad can't afford the boat he wants."

"Which is?"

Kate smiled. "A Catana."

Mitch gave a low whistle. "No lie? Which one?"

"Orion."

"Your Dad aims high. Twenty five meter custom catamaran. You could take that baby through some massive seas. Boat like that's built for sailing around the world."

"It's been his dream for quite some time. Well, ever since Mom died."

"Kate, do you know how much a boat like that costs?"

"I know they're expensive."

"Yeah. About five million."

"Like I said, it's a pipe dream. I think in his mind that boat represents something beautiful he can never have."

Like his wife. "I see. Well, we all need our dreams. So how does he get out on the water without a boat?"

"The smart way. Goes out on other people's boats."

"Anyone in particular?"

"He's been hanging with one guy a lot. I haven't met him, but my Dad talks about the guy's yacht. Has a funny name, like a cartoon character. Let me think. Oh yeah. *Chorny Volk*."

Mitch frowned. "Black Wolf."

"That's good," Kate said. "Do you speak Russian?"

"Who owns that boat, Kate?"

"Like I said, I haven't met him. Some business associate of my Dad's. He talks about him and the guy sounds creepy. But his boat sounds really cool."

"Do you know his name?"

"Noooo, I don't recall that my Dad ever mentioned his name."

"I think I saw him at the Council meeting."

Kate's turn to frown. "How would you know that?"

Mitch thought about the camping trip. "Hard to explain. But I think he's bad news. Real bad. And somehow I think he's connected to all this. In a big way."

"You think he's our missing link?"

"I do. Just don't ask me how. Yet. Maybe when we break your Dad's password we'll figure something out. What kind of clubs does he own?"

"Calloway."

Mitch tried several combinations of c-a-l-l-o-w-a-y to no avail.

"What's his favorite course?"

"Let me think. I'd say World of Woods up near Spring Hill."

"Well, nothing there so far. Who's his favorite pro?"

"El Tigre. Can you believe he's still number one in the world at forty four?"

"And happily remarried," Mitch smiled and nodded. "How about tennis?"

"He plays with a Wilson racket and mostly Penn balls. His favorite player is probably that old dude, McEnroe," Kate said with a sigh. "This is harder than I thought."

"Patience, my dear." Mitch grinned. "This work requires a tremendous amount of patience."

"Say, isn't that an eight letter word?" she asked.

He tried every combination of p-a-t-i-e-n-c-e. No match. "You mentioned skydiving."

"He used to jump when I was a baby. Hasn't been for a long time. That's a young man's game."

"For sure. Have you ever been?"

"No. But I'd like to. How about you?"

"Once or twice." Something tugged at his mind. Something just out of reach. "Tell me more. What got him into skydiving? It's one of those things a lot of people talk about but not many give it a go."

"He was a paratrooper in the Army," Kate said. "Never saw action in Iraq. But he jumped a lot up at Benning."

Something here but he just couldn't get his arms around it. He needed more information. "How many times did he jump?"

"Enough to earn his Snow Cone. He's proud of his cones."

Mitch closed his eyes and thought. 'Snow Cone' was slang for an army parachute badge. Depicted an old World War Two style parachute, taut ropes descended from an open chute to a single point.

"What degree? Did he make it to Senior? Master?"

"Senior," Kate said.

He was close. "That's at least thirty jumps."

"That's right. He had thirty three, I think. Why's the number of jumps important?"

"The first five are static line. Cord fixed to a runner inside the plane so the chute opens without you having to worry about it."

"Yeah, so?"

"After that you pull your own cord. Which means you also jump out of the plane on your own. As opposed to being pushed out the hatch by a jump master."

"And?"

Mitch smiled. He had it.

"So what do you say right before you jump?"

"Oh Mitch, that's positively brilliant."

They were in with their first try of g-e-r-o-n-i-m-o, all lower case.

42

"Now what?" Kate asked.

"Now we officially begin to snoop."

"I know that, silly. But what are we snooping for?"

"We'll know it when we see it. Something personal between your Dad and somebody at Planetcom. Could be anything. Email record, document, maybe a voicemail."

Together Kate and Mitch combed through her Dad's subnetwork checking all directories, visible and hidden.

They found it in a file named fu.wav. Her Dad had recorded a conversation and stored it in a hidden directory. They listened to the message and he watched Kate's face fall in the final knowledge that her father was corrupt. Up to now it was a little game, an adventure they shared. The wave file made it real.

"Are you alright?" he asked.

Kate turned to him. Her gaze was steady, beautiful eyes determined.

"Let's hear it again."

He clicked the arrow on the electronic dashboard.

A few seconds of light static, then a deep voice with a thick accent.

"We shall discuss that topic on our next outing, Mayor Delaney."

"We'll discuss it right now."

"Nyet. You know better than to have such discussions that are not face to face."

"I'll tell you exactly what we're going to do. We're going to talk about it now. Don't worry about this connection, I've got so much encryption on this channel it'd take the CIA fifty years and they still couldn't break it. I know who you are. And I know what you are. Let me tell you something, Mr. Kee-reel. You don't scare me. Not one bit. I have the divine power and I'm holding the cards. Do you know what that means?"

The deep voice said nothing.

"It means you'd best get your head out of your ass, stop fucking with my staff, and do your job. Planetcom's gonna get the contract and you're gonna get paid just like we all agreed. Your job is not to worry about that. Your job is simple. Make sure nobody around here gets in the way."

The deep voice chuckled. "Do not pretend I am the only benefactor from our arrangement. You shall have your payday, also. You shall have your dream vessel. Is that not correct?"

"Goddamn right that's correct. Let's not play games with respect to who gets what out of this. We're all winners. But I'll be damned if I'm going to sit back and let some low life Russian scumbag run around my City with guns blazing. Acting like a

cowboy. Without my permission. Do you think this is a movie, son?"

Another low, deep chuckle. "I know what this is. This is how I live. It is others who sometimes do not live so well."

"Are you threatening me?"

Dead silence. Someone terminated the connection and the wave file ended.

He stared at Kate. "That's the Russian from the Council meeting yesterday. He owns that boat. I knew he was involved."

"Why would my Dad record that and hold on to it? The file implicates him just as much as the Russian."

"Recrimination." He saw *Chorny Volk* registered at a slip in Bull Pier to a man named Cheslov Kirill. "Your Dad probably has another version with just the last line from the Russian. The edited version publishes automatically if Kirill makes any unexpected moves."

"I can't believe my father has done this." Kate rocked on the edge of her seat. "What a bastard. Will he know we copied that file?"

"I don't think so. We didn't leave any trace of intrusion."

"What do we do now, Mitch?"

"Call Wanda Deter."

"Let's do it."

"Not we. Me."

"What do you mean?"

"There's no need for you to be involved with the call. I'm not saying things will, but I'm saying things *might* get dangerous. We're talking about a lot of money. Let's keep you off screen for this one."

"Don't be ridiculous. We're in this together."

"You have to trust me on this. We're in it together but we also need to be careful."

"But, Mitch---"

"Please don't argue with me. This is non-negotiable. I need you to stand over there, away from the camera. Say absolutely nothing. Don't try to get my attention. I don't want Wanda or somebody watching this later to figure out there's someone else in the room during the call. Wouldn't be hard to figure out who it is. Everybody saw us at the Council meeting."

"You're referring to the Russian."

"Just stand over there for me, OK?"

43

"You're the man who grilled the consultant yesterday," Wanda said. Her camera was in a tight zoom and her eyes looked tired.

"Glad to see you made it out of there in one piece," he said. "I need to talk to you about something important. Related to Wireless World."

"I'm listening."

He relayed the events of the past several hours, leaving Kate out of the picture. Finally he played the audio file and watched energy return to her eyes.

"I knew the son of a bitch was dirty," Wanda said. "He thinks he can get away with it since we don't get the media coverage you'd see in Miami or New York. There's no impartial reporting around here. Hell, the Trib and the Times were harvested years ago. Nobody's watching local political news."

"Guess he doesn't know about the blogosphere," Mitch said. "Incredible how he lives in the last century."

Wanda stared at him. "Let's be clear about something, Mr. Downing. There are people who will do anything to prevent that file from reaching the wrong hands. Five hundred million is worth killing over. You understand what I'm saying?"

"Yes."

"You can tell no one about this. Absolutely no one. Do you understand me?"

"Yes."

"Good. I want that file."

"I can email it."

She shook her head. "Not unless you're using military grade encryption. I have no doubt the City monitors everything going into and out of my account. Been that way for the past several months. We need to meet live for this one."

Mitch frowned. "If they filter your attachments then don't you think they monitor your calls? Won't they hear everything we're saying right now?"

"I don't think they're monitoring real time. But yes, eventually they'll hear it. We have to move fast."

"OK, where do you want to meet?"

"Where are you?"

"South Tampa."

"I'm just north of the City. Let's meet at the parking garage across from the Aquarium. Easy access in and out. I'll be there in one hour. I'll add you to my buddy list and we can track each other."

"Perfect. See you in an hour."

"Thanks," Wanda said with a grateful smile. "Repealing that award will mean a lot to a lot of good folks." She reached forward to end the connection, then stopped. "Oh, and Mitch?"

"Yes?"

"Weren't you with the Mayor's daughter at the meeting, yesterday?"

Fuck.

"Yes."

"Does she know?"

"She doesn't know anything. I haven't seen her since the meeting."

"She will, eventually. This'll all come out. Are you two close?"

"Yeah." Mitch forced himself not to look at Kate.

"Tell her not to be too hard on her father. We can't always understand why people make the decisions they do. Tell her things get complicated. Forces come into play that are difficult to understand unless you've walked in that person's shoes. And tell her we'll have this behind us soon. I promise."

"I appreciate that, Wanda. Now let's get going."

He ended the connection and turned to face Kate.

"What do you think, oh wise one?" she asked.

"She's right. At the end of the day your father's got this whole thing fucked up beyond all repair. But he is your Dad and one day soon all this will be behind us and he'll still be your Dad. He'll admit his mistake and he'll need your love and support. I hope you can be there for him."

"Could you be there for a loved one who lied to you and violated your trust?"

"I understand," Mitch said carefully, "that it is easier to forgive an enemy than a friend. I understand you can't simply flip a switch and stop feeling the anger. But I also know that emotion will wear you down unless you let it go."

"I need to address this. I need to talk to him."

"Kate, you heard her. We can't let your Dad know we have this file."

"What do you think he's going to do, Mitch? Kill us? Come on. This isn't New York. This is Tampa Bay. Besides, I won't tell him we have the file."

"Then what will you tell him?"

"I'm not sure. I want him to admit he screwed up. I want to give him the chance to tell the truth. To me. That'll go a long way toward helping me forgive."

Mitch nodded. "Alright, Kate. Go talk to your father and I'll take the file to Wanda."

44

Cheslov removed his headphones and started to whistle. He watched a flock of seagulls move across the sky. A dirty gull in the lead carried some morsel in its mouth that the others wanted. They swooped and turned and pecked at his tail until he dropped the scrap. It landed in the water and was devoured from below by a school of pinfish.

He smiled at the silly selfish birds. They were like people in their behavior and conviction that the entire group should starve before merely the strong should eat. Responsibility therefore fell upon the truly bold to take what they deserved. Any real mother and, indeed, true creator would be pleased to observe the strongest of her children satisfying their appetites.

Predation, after all, is not violence. Merely the act of survival. To filter sick, weak animals from the herd is a vital part of any healthy ecosystem.

He shook his head at the peasants who wandered around confused, unable to follow their true nature.

He chuckled and it sounded like a soft snarl.

The Deter bitch was wrong on two accounts. The City was not spying on her. He considered himself a private citizen. He had programmed the intercept software to alarm his micro at any mention of key words on any call to her. Wireless World being chief among them.

He watched the shrieking seagulls protest in vain as he considered the best way to proceed. After a few moments he went below deck to gather the proper tools.

Part 3

Happiness is a Warm Gun

Greg Kiser

45

Kate walked into the kitchen and found her father pouring Scotch over ice. She watched him fill his drink and thought about her nightmare. She had seen her father as a young man and as something beyond an old man. She paused a moment to make sure he was just her Dad now, a man nearing fifty with a few wrinkles around his eyes.

He turned. "Hi, Angel."

And he was.

"Hello, Daddy."

She heard the sadness in her tone and knew her Dad heard it too.

"What's the matter?"

She chose her words carefully. "Daddy, I want to ask you something. And I want you to give me a straight answer."

"Of course."

He spoke too quickly.

She held up her hand. "Please slow down and listen. Please."

"Alright, Kate," A long swallow. "Tell me what's on your mind."

Kate stared into blue eyes she had seen since she was a baby and watched them become guarded. She swallowed and now her voice was as clear and calm as the water beyond the picture window.

"I want you to tell me the truth about the Planetcom award."

"The truth? What do you mean, Angel?"

"I was at the Council meeting yesterday."

"I know. You were with Downing." He tried to smile, seemed to struggle with it, shrugged instead. "That's good, though, right? I mean, you saw what happened."

"I saw quite a show. I watched people ask for help, beg for their lives. Saw a consultant lie through his teeth. Saw a kangaroo court with you at the head of it. Yes. I saw everything."

Her Dad fabricated a smile as guarded as his eyes. "Is there a question in there somewhere?"

"I want you to tell me the truth. Did you get yourself in trouble somehow? Please. Be honest with me."

"Katie, come on, there's no---".

"Daddy STOP IT," she shouted and the silence that followed rang in their ears. She continued again softly. "Please, stop it. I need to hear reality from you. The next words you speak need to be the truth. If you can't be honest with me then I guess we're no different than two strangers passing on the street." She looked into her father's eyes. "Please be careful and understand me. I need to hear truth. Right now."

He looked at her and his guarded smile was down. At least she had that. She saw that his glass was empty.

"Alright, Kate. Listen to me carefully. We're not two strangers on the street. You're my daughter and I love you. We stood in this very kitchen not one week ago and we had this conversation."

He walked to the freezer and tumbled two ice cubes into his glass. Returned to the counter and poured four fingers of Scotch. Another long swallow. Two fingers remained in the glass.

"Kate there's something here you don't understand. I…" Another swallow. His eyes were red. Wet.

"Go on."

"I'm not free to make all the decisions. Even as Mayor … there are certain powers that I answer to."

"What kind of powers?"

"Kate, I'm elected to this office by millions of people."

"Meaning you have obligations."

"Powerful forces are at play. Do you have any idea what I'm saying?"

"Yes. You're supposed to take care of them."

"Katie, honey, it means more than that. Much more than that." He looked like a small boy cornered by a bully.

Her right hand went to her mouth.

"Oh, I see, Daddy. Now I get it. You're saying you have obligations to certain groups, big business. I understand that, I do." She felt a weight lift as her father told her the truth at last. "Somebody's blackmailing you."

"No, Katie."

"Who, Daddy? Who's blackmailing you?

He shook his head. "Katie, you don't understand."

"We can fix this together. Wanda Deter can help, she knows somebody in Tallahassee who can---"

"Kate, listen to me. I'm trying to tell you something here. The only reason I could get to the top of this mountain, the only reason I was elected and put in this position by millions of His servants is because it's the Lord's work."

Kate stared, incredulous. Her face flushed and she struggled to keep her hands from shaking. "Don't be RIDICULOUS!" she shouted.

"He put me in charge and now He speaks through me."

"Ever since Momma died you have gone farther and farther into the DEEP END with your religious nonsense. What is WRONG with you?"

"It's not my will, these aren't my decisions. That's what I'm trying to say, honey, don't you see?"

"You're supposed to use religion like a blanket. To comfort people, make them feel better."

He tipped his glass upright and ice slid past his mouth onto the floor. He pulled the empty tumbler away and his face was wet. "Blankets also suffocate. You don't understand and you never will. But that's OK. You don't need to."

"But you, you carry it around like some kind of shield. You beat people over the head and then you hide behind it."

"But it's God's truth." He wouldn't look in her eyes.

"Daddy, you are DANGEROUSLY close to madness. Did God tell you to give the contract to Planetcom? Did He speak to you?

"Kate, come on."

"Did he say, hey if you do this little favor for me I'll buy you a boat?

"KATE!" He raised his voice. "Enough!"

"Is THAT the way the Lord is working, here? Is THAT what you believe?"

"Washur tongue, girl." He sounded like he had mud in his mouth.

"I will NOT. If you're going to stand there and hide behind God to rationalize corruption then I'll have nothing more to do with you. Not now, NOT EVER."

He stepped forward and slapped her face hard with his open palm. She saw it coming but made no move to block it. She wanted him to hit her, wanted to feel the pain and know it was real. Wanted him to hammer the final nail home so she couldn't blame herself later.

"Lauren, please...," he began. He shook his head and leaned down with his hands on his knees. His damp eyes were unfocused, his voice trembling. "You talk to me that way?"

Tears filled her eyes and her ears rung and it took a moment for her to accept what had actually happened. Her father had never raised his hand to her before this moment. She felt the sting on her cheek. Watched condensation sweat down his empty glass. Looked at the stranger across the room. Thought about hitting him back. He was strong but she could hit him hard if she moved fast.

Instead she turned her face and offered the other cheek. "Sermon on the Mount, Dad?"

He opened and closed his mouth. She watched saliva stretch between his lips. She stood motionless and couldn't help it, a little tear trickled down her face. She knew in that moment she'd lost her Dad. Her best friend who always took her side even when she was a little monster and taught her how to swim in waves and find hermit crabs and draw butterflies and pulled teeny tiny splinters out of her toes and always, to this day held her hand in parking lots which was a little embarrassing but so sweet and she always had a mental image of him as young and funny and all-intelligent, just a perfect man and now he was gone. She silently cursed whatever God was out there who would take her Momma then banish her Daddy into … *this*.

She turned and walked from the kitchen all alone.

46

Mitch tracked Wanda's approach in his mind's eye using satellite data transmitted over the Grid from the GPS receiver in her micro.

He watched her Avalon enter the garage in real time from cameras mounted at the entrance. Followed its progress through camera arrays on each level. Watched her pull in beside him with his eyes. He continued monitoring the video feed from the cameras.

She got out of her car and walked toward him with long strides, hand outstretched.

He took her hand and was struck again by how attractive she was. And he was pleased to see how relaxed she appeared considering the stakes. Her long dark hair blew slightly in the breeze from an electric luxury sedan that rolled by in silence.

"What will you do with this file?" he asked.

"Give it to a friend of mine in Tallahassee. Bob Calley, state representative. He'll nail the Mayor to a fucking cross." She smiled and it filled her entire face. "Of course, knowing our Mayor, he might like that."

He guessed her to be in her mid twenties. His own age. He was surprised. The way she spoke and presented herself, she seemed older. Smooth dark skin, soft hair, long delicate features. Only her eyes hinted at the depth of her intensity.

"I thought you were impressive yesterday, slapping around the Mayor's consultant like that," she said.

"Not that it did any good."

"Why were you there, Mitch?" Her face looked curious, not at all un-friendly.

"Believe it or not, the Mayor asked me to attend."

"Why in the world would he do that?"

He raised his eyebrows and smiled. "Well, he wanted me to promote his agenda. As an unbiased casual observer."

"I see. And why didn't you?"

"I thought I'd support the idea of a new network. Never intended to promote an award to Planetcom. When I saw how things were going … I don't know. Just couldn't help it. Everything seemed so obviously wrong."

She nodded. "How's Kate taking it?"

He hesitated. "Too early to tell. She wants to do the right thing, but it'll take time to sink in."

"I thought she might come with you."

"She went to talk to her Dad," he finally said.

She nodded again. "I really appreciate what you're both doing. I have family and friends who need more help than they've been getting. A lot more." She took his hand in her two smaller ones. "Thanks to you and Kate, I think they'll get more help now. This will make a tremendous difference in their lives. I want you to know how much it means to me."

The camera video went black in his mind.

"Something's wrong," he said.

He flicked his left index finger to begin the transfer. Flicked it again. Then again.

"Is your wireless enabled?" he asked.

"Of course. What's the problem?"

"Not sure. I can't get a lock on your phone." He tried to look on Grid and realized he had no connection whatsoever.

What the hell's going on?

47

Cheslov made a slow drive-by to ensure they were alone. They were. He parked a few rows down and turned on the broadband spectral generator in his shirt pocket. The device transmitted powerful waves throughout micro and Bluetooth frequency bands. The spectrum was broad jammed and no one could use a micro for Grid connection or local file transfer within five hundred meters of his car. The waves also prevented the charged couple devices in the garage's video cameras from capturing any images.

Cheslov got out of the car.

48

When Mitch was a boy he had a friend named Steve who kept a spotted python in a forty gallon aquarium in his bedroom. He never bothered to name the snake. The snake already had a Latin name, Steve said. *Antaresia Maculosa.* At one and a half meters, Mitch knew the snake was small by python standards. Even so, it was a pretty damn big snake. It hardly ever moved. It seemed to enjoy laying motionless, content to live in the pleasure of the warmth provided by its heat lamp.

Steve kept new-born mice in his freezer. They were aptly called pinkies. He would thaw a pinkie for one minute in the microwave, then toss it into the snake's tank. This was a highly efficient and convenient process that Steve was forced to abandon after his Mom found the pinkie stash in her freezer next to the chocolate mint ice cream. She was most upset. Irrationally, according to Steve. The pinkies were sealed tight in a zip lock bag and it's not like bacteria are active in a freezer for shit's sake. From that point forward Steve had to use adult mice. But that was OK. The python had outgrown pinkies.

Steve fed the python once a week and preferred dead prey. A live mouse could bite or scratch, damaging the snake's exotic skin. At twelve, Steve was already an accomplished herpetologist. He easily killed the mice by hand, separating their vertebrae at the neck just below the skull. Scientific and humane.

Steve dropped the dead mice into the snake's tank. The snake slowly lifted its head with that rapidly flicking tongue. Steve explained that a snake's forked tongue was a sensory organ. Each time the snake flicked out its wet tongue it snared chemical particles in the air. Then the snake inserted the forked tips into two awaiting openings of the Jacobson's organ strategically located in the front roof of its mouth. The organ's chemical receptors analyzed and identified the particles. Mitch thought the odor analysis on dead mice must have been boring to Steve's snake. He never saw the python react beyond a few initial flicks of its tongue. It must have sensed no need to hurry, this particular prey wasn't going anywhere. The boys watched until they got bored then went back to their video games. When they returned the mouse was always gone. Well, not exactly. Mitch saw a big lump in the snake so he knew where the mouse was.

One day Steve offered his snake a special treat. Three live mice.

"Aren't you going to kill them?" Mitch asked.

"No," Steve said with a devilish grin. "I always wanted to observe him with live prey. Let's see what happens."

The snake was long and its coiled body traversed the entire aquarium. The head was at one end and its body wove through shredded newspaper and small decorative branches. The tail snuggled against the glass at the far end.

Mitch watched Steve drop the three mice simultaneously into the tank. They landed and the snake's tongue flicked rapidly.

Mitch remembered thinking the mice must not have the same sensory organ in their tongues because they seemed oblivious to their predicament. They separated and began to explore their new home. The first mouse scampered unwittingly toward the python's head. The second mouse scuttled around the center of the tank. The third mouse scurried to the opposite side near the snake's tail.

Mitch noticed the snake tighten almost imperceptibly, like a powerful spring compressing upon itself.

Only now did the mice sense something amiss. Their legs froze, little snouts pointed upward carefully sniffing. For one brief moment all motion ceased.

The snake struck with astonishing coordination and speed never demonstrated or even hinted. The python seized the first mouse in its jaws and sank needle sharp teeth to bone. In the same motion the snake coiled its large mid-section around the second mouse and constricted the noose in a blur, fating the creature to slow suffocation.

The third mouse, horrified, leapt halfway up the smooth wall of glass. The snake slammed its tail into the little white body, killing it instantly. The awe-struck boys recoiled at the loud slap.

Two seconds. Maybe three. Then it was over and the snake had won. The head and front legs of the first mouse disappeared into the snake's extended jaws. Rear legs backpedalled in futility. The second mouse lay looped in several coils of the snake's mid-section unable to move and unable to breath, as though in a coffin. Mitch looked into its doomed pink eyes. They seemed strangely resigned. The snake pinned the third mouse against the front glass as if in warning to all. Its diminutive legs were spread, head cocked sideways, small bloody mouth jacked open. Somehow the sightless eyes of the third mouse looked angrier than the dying eyes of the second mouse.

Mitch wondered if the snake felt pride or exhilaration. It didn't seem to. The python's unblinking black eyes were emotionless.

The two boys stood with their jaws on the floor and stared at the killing machine they'd been unaware of to that point.

Steve finally turned and clapped his hands with a huge grin. "God-*damn*. Did you see that?" He laughed the contagious chortle he used whenever Mitch thought it more appropriate to be appalled. That laugh always made Mitch feel a little less afraid, a little cooler. Mitch smiled through his shock and tried to laugh too.

Mitch looked up just as the dark giant from yesterday's meeting approached. Wanda turned and a flash of metal sliced her right eye, through her nose, past her lips. The blade caught in her teeth and jerked her head downward forcefully, at an unnatural angle. The sudden motion looked strange and felt bizarre since she still held onto Mitch's hand.

Mitch tried to let go so he could defend himself but her hands tightened into a death grip over his. He was in real trouble. He recognized and was actually a little impressed by the professional execution stroke that made it impossible for her to scream. Impractical to utter any sound when a blade is pushed through the roof of your mouth and into your throat. Most people went for the neck, of course. Ultimately effective, but required a few minutes to bleed out. And a lot can happen in a few minutes. Coming in through the face resulted in immediate incapacitation and was therefore regarded as the superior killing thrust but you'd better have the brute strength to back it up. This giant apparently did because his next move was to coil a large paw around the front of Mitch's neck and lift him off the ground. Something wet and medicinal was shoved into his mouth.

He thought about Steve's python and that seemed funny somehow as his body went into shock and his world went dark.

49

Mayor Delaney sipped twelve year old whisky and emptied the contents of a small amber vial onto his desk.

Machiavelli said there is nothing more difficult to plan, more dangerous to manage, than the creation of a new system. The initiator has the enmity of all who would profit by the preservation of the old institutions.

Lauren, please help me find my way.

He sorted through the little violet pills strewn across his desk. He started taking them soon after his wife died. He had so many responsibilities and was under a tremendous amount of stress. Then the Lord threw him a curve ball with Lauren's death. A real humdinger.

The dose was fine-tuned for his particular metabolism, weight, and endorphin levels. Initially a single pill each day created a strong sense of well being. Soon two pills were required to achieve the same effect. Before long five pills daily did the job.

He damn well knew it was dangerous to continue to increase his medication without consulting his physician so he had drawn the line at six.

No reason, fortunately, to go beyond six once he found that mixing the pills with Scotch increased their effectiveness several fold.

Oh, Lauren, I wish you were here to help me.

God knows he tried to be a good father to Kate after Lauren's death. Tough act to follow, though. Damn tough act. But just how in the hell could his own daughter accuse him of taking a bribe in return for the award of a contract? Was it a bribe to accept rewards for doing the Lord's work?

God had given him a heavy, heavy burden. Yet another test. How could his daughter not see what was obvious and true? It was as though the Lord had placed a great rock upon his back. But could God create a rock so heavy that even He couldn't lift it? The Mayor didn't think so.

He counted pills on his desk. *One, two, three, four.*

Power is influence, and perfect power is perfect influence and he now had perfect power. Because he was chosen. He knew this to be true just as he knew all of his actions were simply flows of divine energy. This wasn't vanity, it was destiny.

Five, six.

There were those who would take his power away. The Cretins were always liars. Was it wrong to do the Lord's will? Was it better that a man shun His will if it happened to bring Earthly rewards? The Mayor did not think that was true. Many people would oppose him. Devils who would resist and deceive and accuse and worm into his head to stop the Lord's work. He must be strong. He must be stalwart in his quest. He must stand above the fray and continue His work at all costs.

The time was at hand and he needed a little extra push to continue God's work. Just a little extra fuel.

Seven, eight, nine.

There, that should do it. It's OK. This, too, was His will. The Mayor placed the pills on his tongue three at a time and chased them with smooth Scotch whisky.

Please, Lord, this is too much. Please don't ask me to do this.

He shut his eyes and pushed his fists against his forehead. His head felt empty, without sensation. He clenched his hair and pulled. He needed to make sure he could feel something and he grinned as pain flooded his senses to fill the blankness.

(The Lord helps those who help themselves, little buddy. You know that.)

Physical matter will fracture when pushed beyond its ability to cope and so a tipping point was reached in the Mayor's mind. Cracks formed slowly at first then cascaded like millions, billions of tiny dead limbs in a powerful storm, destruction rolling like a tidal wave through wicked streets.

When the convulsions came the Mayor's eyes rotated into darkness and his chin dropped to his chest. He entered a cave and it was dark, but not black. A tiny beam of light filtered in from somewhere above. The air was damp and heavy but the Mayor could walk upright so it wasn't all bad. He heard running water and *just what in the fuck was he doing walking in a cavern*? He banged his head and the rock ceiling didn't have any give so it felt like somebody'd tapped his forehead with a Louisville

Slugger. Blue aluminum. He saw stars and he knew where that light came from. He crouched and carefully felt his way as the path grew ever tighter. Soon he crawled along on all fours and that's when he first heard it.

A scraping sound like an animal with long claws scampering across hard rock and it was tough to tell from which direction with all the goddamn echoes. Maybe if he wore his Bose acoustic headset he could figure out where the noise came from. Eventually he crawled on his belly across wet rock and hoped he was in a connecting tunnel so he could stand again. The scraping sound became a slither and he wondered was there a big snake around somewhere and he was not a happy caver because the one way you did not want to run into a snake is when you're crawling along on your goddamn stomach so he moved faster but the slithering sound grew loud as if to keep pace. He sloshed through deep water and the slither sounded wet and then he knew it was he who made the sound, it was he who was the reptile and for the first time he wondered… just whose side was he on? Would God devolve him to this sorry state? Would *God* do that?

(Do you want to know the answer, little buddy? Do you really?)

He cried and slithered faster and at last he came to a vertical fork in the wet tunnel. Upwards lead to light. Dim, but light nonetheless streaming in from an aperture high, high above. But reaching that light was one hell of a climb. He thought about pulling his fat ass through tight spaces over sharp, dry rock and it was a bitch of an idea. A real whore.

Another path lead down into soft darkness. Water trickled over flat, smooth rock and the Mayor imagined sliding down a Calypso mat slide, like the Wahoo Run at Adventure Island and that sounded like just the ticket. Who knows? The slide might lead to an exit. Could in fact lead to the same point as the more difficult path. Who's to say?

"Chase, come on up!" Lauren said.

He squinted and saw the light above came from Lauren. He was not surprised because she was an angel and

(he always knew he was the one who killed her)

everyone knows angels radiate beautiful light.

"Chase, take this path," Lauren said. "I'll help you. The climb's not as hard as it looks."

"Darlin', that climb may not be hard for you," the Mayor said. "But I'm not so sure I can make it."

"Chase, come this way," something else said. The Mayor looked down and spotted his wife's dark face in the shadows below. "You have to lead the flock. I know that now. You have to lead the flock. Can't let those sheep tell you where they want to go. Shit, man, you'd never get anywhere. Let's face it. Everybody's not worth saving."

"I always tried to tell you but you never wanted to listen," he said.

"Honey, I learned my lesson," the Lauren-thing said through dark teeth. "Come down with me now, I *miss* you."

"Chase, don't listen to it. You know which way is right," said Lauren's beautiful voice. "Listen to me. Come up to me. You must. You simply must."

"Repent, my love, repent," said the dark Lauren. "Come down and sail with me. We'll have *such* great fun."

And there it was. Orion Catana fait accompli. Attainment achieved. Achievement attained.

Whatevah, whatevah, the contract was signed, sealed and dee-livered. As promised. The Planetcom execs would conduct the wire transfer and the USS Lauren Delaney was about to set sail. Life in this shitty little burg was over. He and Kate were free to hit the high seas on a big beautiful cat sprinting over water so deep and blue it doesn't look real. Just watch the dolphins come along side and try to keep up, half playing and half thinking this big fella's looking for food and when it finds something there should be plenty for all the friends, the pack of sea wolves following along, sun glinting off their teeth and black eyes. The Planetcom execs were adamant, Cheslov was the man for the job. Zero margin for error and he might be an overkiller but after all it's all about execution in the big leagues where dogs eat dogs and wolves eat lambs and men eat boys and---

"Chase, come *up* to me! Please!"

He blinked and slapped wet hands over his ears. He had a choice, and somehow he knew this was the last time he would have it.

And as he had his entire life, he chose the easy path.

Without another thought he pushed over the wet rock and slid down into the depths.

At first the ride felt cool and mossy-smooth. Then the air grew hot and wicked like an overheated outhouse and he screamed because he had taken the wrong path after all but it didn't matter, he was committed. And let's face it, did he ever really have a choice? Maybe at some point, but not today. He knew in his heart he'd chosen the wrong path years ago.

The Mayor sat in the dark for an hour and let his eyes regain most of their focus.

Enough to see the sins of his daughter were now evident.

She, too, had chosen the wrong path. He had spared the rod and she'd taken an unrighteous path. One that could interfere with the Lord's plan. Yes, he could finally see that he had to reign her in. For her own good.

God's will.

50

Molly was sweating profusely.

"Do you know what would taste great about now?" Woody asked.

She turned to face him, reached out and lightly stroked his arm. She couldn't believe how wonderful he was in bed. So tender for such a large man. She looked down the length of his body, stopped at his midsection. He was... *magnificent*.

"Besides me?" she asked.

He propped up on an elbow and grinned. "A cigarette," he said.

"Absolutely. I would die for a menthol. Hey, better watch out for the health police and the political gentry. It's out of control, you know."

"Ain't that the truth. Can't even talk about Santa anymore. Don't want to mislead the young children." Woody squinted and shook his head. "Not even supposed to mention the stork. That's what people said in the old days when I was a kid. Babies were delivered by the stork. Funny, right? Now everybody says no, no, don't say that, it'll mess with their heads. So when a little kid asks you where babies come from, you know what you're supposed to say?"

"From God?"

"That's funny. You thought that? No, you're supposed to say from a good screw."

"You're a freak," she said with a chuckle. She rose naked from the bed, walked across the room, leaned over to open a drawer in a small corner table. "I'm fresh out of cigs but might have something else."

"You're right," he said.

"About what?"

"Your butt is the same color as your arm."

"Told you." She wriggled for effect.

She turned around and wondered which view Woody preferred. Hoped it was a toss-up. She sat on the bed beside him and lit a thin, crooked joint. Took a deep drag and enjoyed the sensation of smoke expanding in her lungs. Exhaled quietly.

"So why do you fight people in cages? What's that all about?" she asked.

He smiled. "Simple. It's about understanding how to control my body. Then proving it by engaging in a controlled manner."

"Engaging?"

"In conflict. With some other asshole."

"Silly me. Here I thought it was the male imperative to dominate."

"OK, that's where it starts, I'll grant you. Then it's up to me to see how far I can take it. How deep is my faith. In me. What am I willing to sacrifice."

Molly smiled and lightly rubbed his chest. "Hey, that's not about control. That's about heart."

He nodded. "That's it. Heart. I always wonder about the next fight. I always wonder if I'm going to be good enough to get to the next level." He looked at her for just a moment then looked away. "I'll tell you something else. To get in that cage? You drive your body to its limit. Then past. And when I step out of that cage, when I do that? I got nothing to prove to anybody. Man, that's freedom."

She passed the joint and Woody pointed to her nails, painted a glittery red.

"What color's that resin?"

"Ape-ricot."

"Too much," he said with a laugh. "So tell me, darlin'. How'd you meet Kate?"

He took a long drag then closed his eyes and held still. She watched him trying not to cough.

"We had a class together. Freshman year."

"What class?" he asked in the silly whisper of a man trying to speak without exhaling.

"Expository writing. We had to write something like every week. I loved to listen to Katie read her stories in class." Molly smiled, a little stoned and a little self conscious. "I mean, I was really mesmerized. I remember thinking wow she just has this wonderful grasp of human nature. She tunes into a plane that I just don't catch at all. I mean, nobody does besides Katie."

"That's really schweet." He nodded and passed the joint.

"How did you meet Mitch?"

"In the Navy. Boot camp."

"What year was that?"

"Twenty twelve."

"Oh cool. You've known him a long time. What did you guys do after boot camp?" She flicked ashes into a cup of water on her bedside table.

"Studied electronics."

"Were you stationed together on a ship?"

"Eventually."

"Which one?"

"The numb-nutz."

"The numb-nutz? Is that a ship?"

"Sorry, that was our pet name. But hey, that's all we ever called it. I mean the USS Nimitz."

"Carrier, right?"

"That's right."

Molly shook her head. "Couldn't be much fun. Did you go there straight from boot camp?"

"Noooo, like I said we studied electronics right outta boot," Woody smiled and gently rubbed her forearm and she laughed out loud.

"Duh. Let me try again. I promise to pay attention. I really want to understand this." Now they both laughed. "OK. What did you do after electronics school?"

"Went to California. Coronado."

She took a slow drag and her face lit into a big grin. "Oh, I *love* that place. The Hotel Del. Some Like It Hot. Marilyn played Sugar Kane. Don't you just *love* that name?" She put her right hand over her heart and pointed to the ceiling with her left. She turned her head slightly and gently rocked her shoulders. She started to sing in a soft voice, "*I want to be loved by you, by you and nobody else but you,*" but then she couldn't help it she burst out laughing. "Sorry, there I go again." She shrugged apologetically. "OK, Daddy-O. What the hell did you guys do at the Hotel Del?"

"BUD/S."

"Buds?"

"Basic Underwater Demolition. SEAL School."

Molly dropped what was left of the tiny roach. She leaned down to find it before it lit her sheets on fire. She found the tiny spec and it burned her index finger so she dropped it into the cup of water and stuck her finger in her mouth. She whirled and stared at Woody and she hoped her eyes were stern because it was all his fault.

"What? You guys were fucking SEALs? Navy SEALs?"

Woody nodded and smiled. "They pinned that Trident on my chest in thirteen. Proudest day of my life. Honest to shit."

She fanned her face with both hands for a moment and tried to process this information. Calm down, calm down.

She thought the SEALs were just the most bad-ass boys on the planet.

"Where did they send you?" she asked slowly.

"We deployed to Iran."

"You were stationed in Iran? Special ops? Holy crap! I mean, I guess it doesn't surprise me that you're special ops. I should've known. But Mitch? Wow, I didn't see that one coming. What did you do in Iran?"

"We spent time in Bushehr. Little seaside village on the Persian Gulf."

"How'd you like it?" She broke into a huge smile and slowly shook her head.

"Loved it. The Iranian's are great. I'd go back in a heartbeat."

"They're OK with Americans?"

"Are you kidding? They love Americans. They have burbs just like we have burbs. Maybe our governments don't get along. But hey, people are people."

She lowered her chin to her shoulder and gave him a sideways smile. "Did you get into any trouble?"

"Mitch did a good job keeping us out of trouble. For the most part."

"He seems level headed to me."

"Let me tell you something. Mitch is the most level headed man you'll ever meet. All the guys in our squad felt that way. But you don't want to piss him off. Because if you do he won't back off. We called him Mitch 'Double' Downing."

"Why?"

"You could fuck with him all you wanted, til you just got tired and quit. But fuck with his friends? He'll come after you. Double Down." Woody gave her a wry smile. "And trust me you do not want him coming after you. He doesn't look like the fighter. I know, I know. I look like the fighter."

"Come on. You *are* the fighter."

"Don't underestimate him's all I'm saying."

She laced her fingers through his and squeezed.

"Oh my God. I can't believe this. I bet you've got some *hellacious* stories."

"One or two," Woody's eyes sparkled.

"Come on, Woody. Give."

"Oh, Molly. Boring stuff. Ain't nothing like the movies."

"Oh, no you don't. Fess up. Tell me, tell me, tell me!"

"Sweet Jesus. OK, just one. Ummm. One time we were playing pool in some little dive. I was drinking Fanta laced with vodka. And I mean *laced*."

"Where'd you get the vodka? I thought those Muslims don't drink."

"Yeah, that's what a lot of people think. Not the case. Booze over there's older than Islam. Most of the folks I met would rather party than pray. They get the beer from Holland and Australia, vodka from Azerbaijan. Not to mention opium from Afghanistan."

"You are just a fountain of knowledge, my Wood-man. Now, what about that dive?"

"So it's just me and Mitch and six Iranians. Big boys. We play eight ball and me and Mitch keep winning. Mostly it's cool, but there's this one dickhead in their group. I try to be nice, you know, complement his good shots, encourage him when he misses. That sort of thing." His eyes roamed the room.

"What are you looking for?" she asked.

"What happened to that jay?"

"Floating in the cup, man. You didn't see me burn my finger?"

"Oh yeah, sorry." Woody smiled and shrugged.

"Come on, Redneck. Get on with your story."

"Where was I? OK, I was shit-faced. And that's a problem because if these boys start any trouble, I'm a sitting duck in my condition. Dee-dee just keeps sinking shots. Steady and quiet, just like always."

She gazed into his eyes. He was really back there.

"So I'm sitting on a stool, having about my tenth drink and a smoke. Dee-dee calls eight ball in the corner. Bank shot across the entire table. Prick bets him a hundred US on the spot he can't make the shot. Mitch steps up and drains it. Nothing but net, as they say."

She smiled and shook her head.

"Of course now the prick doesn't want to pay. He's getting agitated, raising his voice. I'm pretty sure he's cussing us out but we don't speak Persian so how do we know what the fuck he's saying. But I'm getting concerned because now it looks like the son of a bitch is trying to incite his buddies. Dee-dee looks at me and says let's go. I take a sip of my drink and the prick has a knife to my throat and he's yelling at his pack and now he's pointing at Mitch."

Molly brought her hands to her mouth and her eyes were wide.

"Before I can decide to piss or go blind, Mitch walks up and swings his pool stick in a big old arc right into the guy's skull. That shut the prick up. He dropped to the floor like a sack of camel shit. I'm thinking we should adios before his buddies decide to organize against us. But that's not enough for Dee-dee. Like the guy crossed a line and Mitch couldn't let it go. He kicked the prick in the face til I pulled him off."

She was stunned. "Then what did you do?"

"We ran like hell."

"And the guy on the floor?"

"What about him? I counted about six teeth scattered around his head, if that's what you mean."

"What I mean is … did Mitch kill him?"

Woody stared at her evenly. "No question about it."

"Oh. My. God," she looked down as she absorbed his words. "What about the prick's friends?" she asked in a low voice.

"They didn't want no part of Mitch. They stayed in their corner, away from us. They pointed at him and kept saying something over and over."

"What did they keep saying?"

"*Gorg Kouchak.*"

"What the hell's that mean?"

"I didn't know at the time but I looked it up later. It's Persian for *Little Wolf.*"

She thought about Woody, who stood a head taller than Mitch. But it was Mitch they didn't want any part of. Mitch is the one they called a wolf.

"But you're enormous," she shut her eyes and tried to get her head around it. "I just can't imagine him saving you. In a bar fight."

"There's something to be said for size and strength, sure. And speed. But the SEALs place a premium on speed of thought. It's all about how well you hold up under stress. Extreme stress. By that standard? Mitch is the picture of an elite warrior. In combat? He's one cool and dangerous cat."

She nodded. "Mitch 'Double-Downing'? Dee-dee for short? I like that." She rubbed her foot along Woody's inner thigh. "Maybe I'll call you Wood 'All-in' Logan. What do you think of that?"

"Actually, they called me Woodman. But that don't matter. Either way, I think it's time to go all in," Woody leaned forward.

She leaned back and playfully pushed him away with a bare leg. "Wait a minute. I want to hear the rest of the story. What did you do when you ran out of the bar? Did they chase you? Did you have guns?"

He hesitated and she could tell he was holding out on her. "What do I need, a security clearance? Tell me what happened. I mean it. Tell me the rest of the story."

"Jesus, Molly," he said with a sigh. "OK, there is another, how should I say … dimension to the story. After we left the bar---"

"What was it called? The bar?"

"The Samshiri something or other, I forget. So we hustled out of there and cut through an alley to get to our---"

Her micro chimed. She glanced at the wall screen, surprised. It was Kate. Molly pulled up the sheet and turned on the video.

Kate saw them in bed. Molly on her back beneath a sheet. Woody on his stomach nude, making no effort to cover up.

"Will you pull up the blanket, please?" Kate asked.

"What do you expect, Katie, when you call us at … what the hell time is it, anyway?" Molly glanced to the corner of the display. "Jesus, it's three in the morning." She rearranged the sheet to cover Woody, then saw Kate's expression. "Kate, what is it?"

"Have you seen Mitch?"

"Not since last night," Woody said. "Thought he was with you."

"He's not with me. I've been trying to reach him all night but he's been dark the whole time."

"Off the Grid? Are you serious?" Woody asked.

"Of course I'm serious, Woody. Don't I look serious to you?"

"I've never known him to go dark like that," Woody said.

"I've never known anyone to go dark like that," Molly said.

"Guys, I'm worried." Kate's eyes were red and her cheeks were wet.

"Let me think," Woody said. "He's in your buddy list, right? You can track his beacon?"

"Yeah, but like I said he's dark."

"Duh," Molly smacked his forehead. "Pay attention you big dumb ass."

"Oh man, I totally spaced" Woody smiled and reached for Molly's breast. "That's some seriously good shit."

"Guys, hey!" Kate said. "Stay with me, here. I said he's off Grid. But if he's not with you … I may know where he is."

Molly and Woody looked at the camera and simultaneously asked, "Where?"

Kate told them about the audio file incriminating her father. She told them Mitch left to meet Wanda Deter near the aquarium. She told them about the Russian and his boat, she thought he was somehow involved with Mitch's disappearance.

Woody grabbed his micro and Grid-searched *Chorny Volk*. The boat was registered at Bull Pier in the downtown Marina. He leapt from the bed and pulled on his jeans.

"I'm on my way. Kate, come over here and keep Molly company. I'll call you ladies when I find Mitch."

51

Mitch could tell he was on the water. He felt the boat sway in relatively small waves. Every now and again, the boat rocked on a larger arc. OK, he was in the lower hold of a moored boat. Felt like a good sized boat. Maybe two meter draft. Maybe thirty thousand kilos displacement.

The space was dark. So dark he would not have seen his hands in front of his face. But he couldn't move his hands. His neck felt stiff and wooden. He was restrained, laid out on a bed with his arms and legs tied securely to posts.

His head ached. Dull pain. Chemically induced. Probably methyl chloride or some derivative. But there was something else. He felt nauseous and cramped, beyond the chemical haze. He felt... *unplugged.*

In order to be this damn dark the port holes must be blocked. Not just curtains or wooden blinds. Something solid.

The compartment's unnatural quiet added to his profound feeling of emptiness. Non-existence. As though he had entered a dreamless sleep but he was still awake and---

OK, Downing. Snap out of it! Where am I and how do I get out of here?

He was in a lower cabin that was sealed tight. This room had been specially constructed. Reinforced with something to keep out light and sound. Or keep it in.

Sometimes compartments were reinforced in this fashion to act as freezers. More common with commercial vessels, but he'd heard of personal craft that occasionally had this done.

No signal. He couldn't believe it. The metal reinforcement blocked communication with the outside world.

A cabin door opened and a bright light shone on his face. Then the door shut and a small light was turned on. It took a moment for his eyes to adjust.

Then he looked into the dark face of the wolf.

He recoiled and shut his eyes. Whatever drug the Russian used was still affecting his nervous system. He shook his head and opened his eyes and saw that it was just a man who sat on a stool beside his bed. The man's face was dark and his eyes were solid black.

"Hello, Mitch," the dark man's voice was incredibly low.

"Who are you? How do you know my name?" he needed time to think.

"I am Cheslov. I know much about you. And you know a lot about many things, I am told."

He didn't bother to ask about Wanda. She was dead. This man killed her. That's OK. He'd return the favor.

In conflict, direct confrontation lead to engagement and surprise lead to victory. Sun Tzu's Art of War. He forced himself to relax. Cheslov held all the cards at the moment. Very frustrating.

"OK, I know a lot about a lot of things. So why am I tied to a bed on the *Chorny Volk*?"

Momentary surprise flickered through Cheslov's black eyes. Stupid thing to say but he couldn't help it. *Come on, Mitch!* Reign it in and calm it down. He forced himself to abandon emotion and focus with the logical side of his brain.

Cheslov smiled and, surprisingly, he had one of those smiles that consumed his entire face. From across the Council Chamber the man looked evil with dark amusement. Up close, his smile was harmless, charming. Mitch didn't have to try very hard to smile back.

"You know my secrets," Cheslov said. He gestured around, expansively. "She is my pride and joy, young friend. My pride and joy. We did not have vessels like this in Rostov, I can assure you."

"Why am I here?" Mitch asked again.

"You are a most impressive young man. Of course, they told me you have this ability. Somehow you know things you are not supposed to know, yes?" Cheslov's eyes widened in reproach. He reached beneath his coat and removed a long cigar. Snipped the tip using a guillotine cutter that looked like a worn, hungry mouth. Lit it up with a battered, gunmetal Zippo. Leaned back in his chair, took a deep drag. Exhaled a thick, hot, blue stream of smoke.

"Which is why you find yourself here. In my home." Cheslov's face saddened. Then he continued, as if explaining to a child. "I am sorry, young friend, to have to say this to you. That this is not a place a man wishes to find himself. This is not a room from which people live to see a new day. No, my friend, this is a room in which people take their last breath, see their last light. Hear their last sound."

Mitch remembered a long ago camping trip.

Cheslov smiled warmly down at him. "Why were you meeting the Deter bitch?"

Mitch said nothing.

Cheslov raised the cigar cutter to his face and a raven eye peered through the opening. He smiled as he slid the blades together. "What was your intention?"

Mitch started the process of extracting himself mentally from his surroundings. He ran number patterns through his head to take his mind beyond the pain and the possibility of what the lunatic might do next. There was only one place this was heading.

Of course he wouldn't answer any of the lunatic's questions. The best strategy to resisting interrogation is to simply not provide any information at all.

"Where is the file?"

Once you start to give up information, even about minor unrelated topics, it's hard to stop and easier to give up important information. The answers to the current questions didn't matter in the least. The only thing that mattered was to protect Kate. At any cost.

"With whom have you shared it?"

Mitch said nothing.

Cheslov walked to the head of the bed and slowly examined Mitch's fingertips.

"You wear your micro on your index finger. Painted with green resin. Quite the fashion statement. To whom have you sent the file?"

Mitch said nothing.

Cheslov grasped Mitch's left hand and held it the way a man might hold the hand of his son. Mitch felt a softness to the giant's touch.

"Why do you not answer? Are you afraid?" Cheslov gazed down at him with a not unkind expression. The giant's thick, dark eyebrows rose as if trying to coax Mitch to speak.

Mitch said nothing.

"I'll ask you once more," Cheslov said and a note of sadness crept into his voice. The hesitant father who does not wish to punish but is left no choice. "You have nothing to gain by continuing your silence. And quite a bit to lose. Yes, quite a bit."

Mitch stared at the overhead ceiling. Focused on the intricate wood carving.

Cheslov spread Mitch's fingers.

Mitch said nothing.

"Tell me. With whom have you shared the file?"

Mitch said nothing.

"Enough of these games," Cheslov said.

Using the guillotine cutter Cheslov severed the full tip of Mitch's left index finger in a cut that surgically sliced through the cartilage and capsule of the distal joint. He held onto the fingertip and dropped Mitch's hand. The open finger spewed bright blood across Mitch's head and his arms. Cheslov was not concerned. His mattress was sealed in a plastic liner for just such contingencies. He would dispose of the sheets at sea. Still, he decided to move the boy to the master bathroom's garden tub if the interrogation required migration to the next phase.

Cheslov returned to his seat at the side of the bed. He narrowed his eyes and studied the green fingertip as though he were inspecting an old coin.

He was surprised that Mitch had not uttered a word. The boy must be terrified. Scared speechless.

"Do not fight the fear, young friend. It is still possible that fear can help you," Cheslov said. "Fear evolved as a mechanism to protect us all. Evolutionarily speaking, nothing is more important."

Mitch pushed his finger hard into the pillow to stop the bleeding. He shut his eyes and pulled his body away from Cheslov the way a man shrinks from an intense flame.

"Fear is more powerful than reason," Cheslov continued. "Much more powerful. Of course, by definition fear is not reason and can be quite irrational. Are you familiar with your litigator Louis Brandeis?"

Mitch said nothing.

"Supreme Court Justice in the 1920's. The power of fear to overrule reason was greatly understood by your Justice Brandeis. 'When men feared witches'," Cheslov's dark smile widened and showed rather large teeth, "'they burned women'. Justice Brandeis wrote this in 1927. Pity that I cannot say with certainty where I was at that time. I would have enjoyed meeting him, I think. We would share a drink and talk of worldly things like men, no?"

Mitch was in SERE training as a young SEAL in San Diego. Survival, Evasion, Resistance, Escape.

There were two teams.

The Training Team were the interrogators. Five perverse freaks who chose to do this sort of thing for a living.

The Blue Team were the prisoners. A dozen young SEALs ranging in age from nineteen to twenty three.

Mitch and Woody were on the Blue Team.

The Training Team interrogated the prisoners on the first day. They used physical techniques to extract information. Most everyone was punched in the face and kicked in the stomach. Several prisoners were electrocuted with low level current across sensitive regions of the body. The Training Team initially targeted the insides of thighs and arms. Eventually ran light current through the groin.

Though painful, physical techniques were designed to avoid 'persistent' physical damage. 'Persistent' physical damage was defined as any injury visible longer than ten days. Mitch watched one of his friends suffer a broken nose and lose a tooth and thought her damage might qualify as 'persistent'.

Still, the physical techniques of the first day were child's play. The psychological techniques came next. The prisoners were kept awake and beaten during the first forty eight hours. On the third day they were allowed to fall asleep, only to be abruptly awakened and questioned. By the fifth day the body did its best to shut down and your will was not your own. Mitch's head was in a thick haze as though he were on some severe and horrible drug. Hunger and thirst could not compare to his body's overwhelming and sole desire to sleep.

To make things interesting, each man from both teams contributed fifty dollars to a pot. The Training Teams were highly motivated to earn this pot. To do so required that they obtain all information at one hundred percent accuracy from each man on the blue team. If they were unable to extract full and accurate information from one or more men, the pot would be split by any Blue Teamers who hadn't broken. Of course, any Blue team member who provided any accurate information at all was ineligible to receive a portion of the pot.

Once the Training Team extracted what they believed to be full and accurate data from all members of Blue Team, they presented what they'd learned to an Observer. The Observer only let them know if the information was one hundred percent complete and correct.

Until it was, the Training Team went back to interrogating all members of Blue Team.

The Training Team had no way of knowing which man provided incomplete or inaccurate information. So even Blue Teamers who had broken and spilled their guts continued to be interrogated. Mitch had listened abstractly to broken prisoners alternately shouting and begging for non-broken members to come clean.

Woody broke on the sixth day.

After seven days Mitch was awarded the entire pot.

"Tell me, my young friend, to whom you have sent the file," Cheslov said. "Why do you play this game? Simply tell me what I need to know and this will all be over."

Mitch said nothing.

Cheslov frowned and narrowed his eyes. No one had ever stayed silent. Everyone babbled by now. Lied. Made noise. Cheslov was impressed.

"Perhaps you did not send it to anyone. Perhaps you intended to give it only to the Deter bitch."

Cheslov rolled the green fingertip idly between his index finger and thumb. He squeezed and a few drops of blood spattered onto the floor. He stared at

Mitch for several minutes, gauging his reaction. Fear, Cheslov thought. Definitely fear. Yet, the boy's fright showed a certain strength. He was terrified and yet somehow managed not to beg.

Cheslov smiled warmly. "You are a good boy, Mitch Downing, a nice young man. I wish we had met under different circumstances. I think we would have been friends. I think we would fish together for tuna and get high on my vodka in the sun of the Gulf. Perhaps in a different life. But not in this one, I am afraid."

Cheslov opened a drawer and removed a roll of aluminum foil. He dispensed a small sheet and carefully wrapped the fingertip then dropped it into his shirt pocket. The foil prevented the micro from getting onto the Grid, a distinct possibility even severed as long as it was in its owner's vicinity.

It was safe to remove Downing from the smaller stateroom's metal chamber now that the boy no longer had control of his micro. How long would the boy hold out? In many similar examinations no one lasted more than one minute. No one fully sober had lasted more than thirty seconds. Cheslov thought it was possible for Mitch to greatly exceed those records.

"It is time to transfer you someplace that is more, shall we say, *conducive* to the next phase of our discussion. You are hiding now but will soon rejoin me and we shall continue our conversation," Cheslov's dead eyes gleamed. "You will tell me what I want to know."

Abruptly Mitch heard a change in the man's tone. The joviality disappeared like something tumbling into a dark pit. The playful cadence was gone, replaced by a menace conveyed through an utter lack of emotion.

"Yes, you will tell me."

And suddenly Mitch knew that he would.

This man was not part of a training exercise. This man would kill him slowly. Maybe skin him alive.

This man was perhaps not really a man at all.

"Don't." Mitch had one chance to keep Kate out of this. One moment. "Please, don't."

Cheslov reached forward and sliced through the knots that bound Mitch's arms and legs. Cheslov could see the terror controlled the boy. The boy's will to fight was gone. The boy would lay still like a petrified log.

Cheslov was wrong on all accounts.

The instant his bonds were cut Mitch exploded toward Cheslov. He shoved his arms against the bulkhead and simultaneously kicked both feet into the dark man's face with all his strength.

What happened next was due as much to surprise as to actual physical force. Mitch's feet connected squarely and loudly against Cheslov's jaw. Cheslov tumbled backward and Mitch was up and out of the bed. He opened the cabin door and sprinted through the hatch.

He bounded up the ladder to the top deck and looked around wildly into the night.

The boat was moored on its starboard side. A ladder lead to the dock more than two meters below. Mitch heard Cheslov coming up behind. No time for the ladder. He leapt toward the dock. Landed wrong. Fell on his side. Pain detonated up his right arm.

He struggled to his knees and looked into the smiling face of Mayor Delaney. Then Cheslov was beside him and kicked him hard in the ribs. Once. Twice. Thrice.

Mitch's world went black.

52

Cheslov turned to face Mayor Delaney and Phelps.

"God damn, Kirill. I thought you had the situation under control," Mayor Delaney said, looking at Mitch's prone body.

Cheslov smiled. "The situation is under control, is it not?"

"Only because we showed up," the Mayor said. "Otherwise this kid's long gone."

Cheslov pulled a nine millimeter Makarov from his coat pocket. Cold sodium light reflected off the blued barrel and was absorbed by the crosshatched pattern of the silencer. He aimed it at Mayor Delaney's face.

"Do you believe that?" Cheslov asked.

The Mayor stared, eyes wide.

"Gentlemen, please!" Phelps said. "Now is not the time nor the place. Let's remember we are on the same side, here."

Cheslov slowly slid the pistol into his coat pocket.

"Gentlemen!" Phelps continued. "What are our next steps?"

"Kill him," the Mayor said.

"What?" Phelps cried.

"Too much exposure. Clearly. He could bring down the Lord's plan."

"Whose plan? What are you *talking* about, Chase?" Phelps looked from the Mayor to the Russian. Cheslov shrugged and nodded. Phelps couldn't believe it. "Are you deluded? The Lord has nothing to do with this, you clueless numbskull! This is *Planetcom's* plan. They bought the three of us---"

"Shut up you naïve fool!" the Mayor said.

"The Lord doesn't have a dog in this fight," Phelps continued. "Just who are you trying to convince? Gentlemen, we are talking about a *contract*, here.

"Don't go soft on me," the Mayor said. "Don't you do it."

"This is *business*. How can that possibly be worth a young man's life?"

"You know how much money we're talking about, Paxton. I will *not* jeopardize my family's welfare for this punk."

"Jeopardize your family's welfare? How in God's name is this boy going to jeopardize your family's welfare?"

"That's just it," the Mayor hissed. "He's not. *Kill* him."

Phelps turned to Cheslov. Searched for any trace to show that he, too, saw this as ludicrous.

He saw nothing. Nothing at all.

The Mayor turned to Cheslov. "How do you plan to accomplish this?"

Cheslov lifted Mitch and slung him over his shoulder in a single motion. He reached beneath his coat, pulled out a long bayonet and held it up in the light.

Phelps looked at the dark, mottled blade. The edge was reflective as though recently honed.

"I will take him through the Skyway Pass into the Gulf. Ten leagues, maybe fifteen. I know where the bull sharks pool this time of year. He is a decent boy. I will show him mercy. I will cut his throat before I feed him to the shiver."

Cheslov turned toward his boat's ladder.

"What the *FUCK*!"

A new voice. The three men turned at once and there, striding rapidly down the dock, came a very big man looking very pissed off.

"You better put him down right *NOW* you ball-headed bitch!" Woody shouted, then sprinted toward Cheslov.

53

The Mayor and Phelps backed up. Cheslov held his ground.

Woody squared off in front of Cheslov. He was not so much angry as he was utterly astonished. That's good. Angry didn't win the fight. Tension was a loser. He closed his mouth and breathed through his nose. His eyes were narrow slits.

The two men studied one another.

Cheslov was a big man. Well over six feet. Heavy. Solid. His face was like an oak that has weathered storms over the years. Overall the impression was one of strength. Quiet, dark strength.

Woody Logan was bigger. Broad shoulders, deep chest, huge arms, long legs. His was the younger form, athletic, muscular and confident. Very confident.

"I said let him go," Woody said. He saw the large knife in the Russian's left hand. Ridiculous fingernails.

"This is not your fight, boy," The Mayor said. "In the name of God, son, listen to me. This is not your fight."

"It is now, Rev'rund," Woody didn't even glance at the Mayor.

Cheslov smiled, black eyes dancing with delight.

"My friend is hurt and you're... *amused?*" Woody asked. He stared at the man's face and started tuning out. This was a technique he'd learned as a SEAL and developed over years of cage fighting. The fight came from within. It wasn't about the outside. Fighters who tuned to the external world were fighters who lost.

Way too many distractions in the external. Men on the side shouted and taunted. Lesser opponents, externals, tried to intimidate. So much energy wasted. Pull it in and get ready. In the fight pain was immediate, constant, irrelevant.

He found his internal world where there were no distractions. Let the body take control, give command to the subconscious mind. Like when your eyes aren't really on the road and someone pulls in front of you and your subconscious slams your foot on the brake before you know what happened. Pure survival – yours, no one else's. The subconscious was an animal. Focused, patient, watchful. No distractions related to fear or pain or guilt. Just get out of its way.

His peripheral vision was going dark.

"This has gotten out of control." Phelps said. "Mr. Mayor, you have got to shut this down right now."

"Cheslov, shoot the stupid son of a bitch," Mayor Delaney said.

"We cannot go any farther," Phelps continued. "We are already way over the line! I will not stand by and watch an innocent boy get killed here."

The Mayor pointed toward Woody and raised his voice. "Strike him down, NOW, Cheslov!"

Woody heard none of it. "I said you're hurting my friend." He lifted his chin and gazed at Cheslov through slits. "Let him go."

Cheslov smiled wider. "Make me."

Woody looked deeper into Cheslov's eyes. Past the cheery amusement. He didn't like what he saw. Something in there. Something he couldn't identify. Just below the surface something bubbled and threatened.

He looked away. He'd been going external, now he pulled back in and moved toward Cheslov. This was no tournament match. No holding back. He needed to make this man fear him, understand his supremacy. That's what he'd learned on the front lines in Iran.

Cheslov dropped Mitch's body and it hit the dock like a dead shark and lay still. Cheslov tossed the bayonet into the dock and moved toward Woody.

"I said SHOOT HIM!" Mayor Delaney shouted. Then he realized that wasn't going to happen. These two men were going to fight. And there was nothing he could do about it. Good Lord.

The Mayor and Phelps stepped back to give the two men room.

54

Woody exploded toward Cheslov.

What most people noticed right away about Woody was his size. What they failed to consider was his speed. He had Olympic caliber speed, particularly from a stand still.

He was on Cheslov before the older man had any chance to react and connected squarely with his right elbow against the center of Cheslov's chest. Woody hit him hard, with all the momentum of his two hundred thirty five pounds driven forward by powerful legs. Everyone has reasonably strong elbows since they're practically all bone. Woody's were stronger than most. Every morning he slammed his elbows into the door jamb of his bedroom, leaving noticeable cracks in the frame. Over time the bone had built up like armor. Woody's elbows were formidable weapons indeed, ideal for the close strike.

Cheslov fell backwards and Woody pushed forward, swung his massive shoulders and whipped his left elbow savagely toward Cheslov's face.

Cheslov saw it coming and dropped to his knees just enough to allow the elbow to glance off the side of his head. Then Cheslov lunged forward and slammed his fist into the younger man's groin before pushing back up onto his feet, away from Woody.

Cheslov's chest ached deeply. If the boy had landed that second elbow Cheslov's cheek bone would have shattered. He had underestimated the boy's speed, but would not make that mistake again, could not let the boy get that close again.

Woody danced lightly from foot to foot. His face was calm, relaxed, emotionless. Cheslov's blow to the groin hurt, but pain was an external. Woody looked toward the sky and his subconscious mind mapped moves in advance, like a chess game. His speed surprised people. But his best opponents were surprised only once. The second time he came forward, his best opponents came at him to stifle his ability to gain momentum and avoid fighting from their heels.

Woody exploded forward again.

Cheslov rushed toward the boy, reached toward his collar with curved claws. He would use the boy's own momentum against him. Like running full speed into barbed wire with your neck.

Woody expected precisely that move. He dropped low and raised his legs as though sliding into home plate with cleats held high. He hit Cheslov's mid-section with his full weight, perfectly timed, both legs springing forward to add momentum. He would never do this in a tournament. This move would permanently cripple a man.

Woody bounced back as though he'd hit a tree. He hadn't expected that. But it didn't matter. He absorbed the fact that Cheslov had not gone down, that his full frame had essentially bounced off. But he had felt some give. A hell of a lot of force had been delivered to a focused point on the other man's body. Cheslov sure as hell felt that one. May not have cracked, but sure as hell strained. Sure as shit stressed the foundation. Woody thought this as his subconscious rolled him over and attacked while the other man's bones were still ringing. This time Woody came in sideways and hit Cheslov with a jack knifing double kick.

The first kick landed low on Cheslov's right thigh. The jack knife's subsequent hook kick caught Cheslov squarely on his floating ribs. The men on the dock heard a crack like a thick limb breaking.

Woody scrambled back onto his feet and resumed dancing, head back, eyes nearly shut.

They'd been fighting for two minutes.

Cheslov had landed one blow that the boy had apparently not even felt. The boy had landed three blows and Cheslov was in very serious condition. His entire chest ached as though he had been hit by a log. His right thigh felt like it had been kicked by a horse. He could barely support his weight on the leg and had lost the ability to push off to his left. Severe loss of mobility.

The real damage had come with the last kick. His lower ribs were definitely cracked. Every breath was like twisting a knife in his side. Cheslov had no ability to stabilize his right side. No ability to kick with his left leg or land a serious blow with his left arm. This could be over quickly.

"God damn it, Kirill. Get your gun and SHOOT him!" Mayor Delaney shouted in outrage. Spittle flew from his mouth and every cord and muscle stood out on his face and neck.

Cheslov didn't hear. His subconscious was in control too. And he relished the pain. Welcomed the proven life. The boy was a fighter and Cheslov applauded the young man in his mind.

55

Woody came out of his zone, just slightly. This fight was over. He'd done exactly what he'd intended. Taken out the man's left side. His dominant side. Amazing the guy was still on his feet at all but it didn't really matter. He no longer posed a serious threat. He had no offense. Woody let his subconscious slip away and looked at his surroundings, seeing them for the first time since the fight began.

The little man looked terrified.

The preacher pissed off.

Mitch lay in a heap, unconscious and oblivious.

He looked at the Russian. The old fuck was smiling. He was broken, that was clear. But smiling. And he still had that creepy light in his dark eyes.

Cheslov jumped forward and Woody elbowed him in the throat. Cheslov went down and Woody dropped on top of him. He put his hands around Cheslov's throat and the old fuck could only grab weakly at Woody's sides and Woody squeezed his thick neck to extinguish the life. He had to kill the son of a bitch. He didn't know how he knew, he just did. The way you'd know to put down a rabid dog.

He lowered his face and detected light hidden in the black holes of the Russian's eyes. He had to turn it off. "So long, you fuck," he whispered. "Time to burn with Shaytan."

Cheslov's eyes shifted as though something were moving around, trying to escape. What was in there? Some kind of animal? Then Cheslov's smile disappeared and his teeth, Woody swore to God, *creaked* into a line of jagged fangs and something was going on with those fingernails because they felt like claws in his side and then Cheslov's feral eyes slotted sideways.

Like a goat's eyes.

Woody froze. The way one might freeze upon the sudden realization he were face to face with a snarling wolf. Or a werewolf.

Woody looked into a dark tunnel in a dream, a nightmare where he couldn't make out the monster but knows there's something in the shadows, he can feel it slouching forward with sharp teeth and dirty fur and eyes flashing dark merriment. Coming faster and faster. A rush of wind. Filthy breath. Woody couldn't move his legs.

His mistake was coming out of the zone before the fight was truly over. He knew better. But it had been so long since he'd been in a fight like this one. A fight for keeps where you honestly tried to maim your opponent. Then kill him.

Now that he was out, now that he was external, he finally saw inside to Cheslov's dead soul and realized the man was not alone in there. Woody had started the fight against a man. Somewhere along the line he thought the man wore a wolf's mask. But now, past the man and past the mask, Woody met the beast and understood at last that there was no mask. He loosened his grip for just a moment and that was the only opening Cheslov needed.

Cheslov swiped claws across Woody's exposed throat in a blur.

The other men watched Woody leap away from Cheslov, moving with the urgency of a man who'd stumbled onto a bed of deep, hot coals.

Woody stepped toward Phelps with both hands pressed against his neck and his arms looked inky in the sodium light. He stumbled and Phelps saw the boy was drenched and for a moment wondered *how in the hell* before realizing red looked black in this light. Woody's head twisted and slid forward and Phelps caught the unnatural movement and realized with a shudder that the boy had nearly been decapitated. Phelps whimpered like a wounded dog and thought about medieval France, the person to be executed was advised to give a gold coin to the headsman to ensure he sharpened his axe. Relatively painless if you could avoid multiple strokes. The boy's eyes fixed on Phelps and his pupils were focused and Phelps remembered something else. A severed head could see for up to ten seconds.

The Mayor began to pray in a desperate tone. *"Yea though I walk through the valley of death,"*

"It is you who shall smolder with Chert." Cheslov snarled in a hoarse whisper.

"I will fear no evil."

Cheslov's voice contained none of his usual joviality and Phelps had the impression somehow that Cheslov was gone.

"For Thou art with me; Thy rod and Thy staff they comfort me."

Cheslov's body slowly rose from the dock.

"The Lord is my shepherd."

Cheslov attacked.

56

Phelps vomited violently on his legs and shoes.

He turned to look at the Mayor in the desperation one feels when witnessing an atrocity of mind blowing proportion. He wanted to hold the Mayor's hand. His knees were weak and his head was spinning.

The Mayor refused to meet his eyes.

Cheslov lifted his head from the slaughter. His features had changed, somehow blurred. Then the shadow was gone and it was just Cheslov.

The Russian appeared puzzled. He looked down and searched around the corpse as though he had dropped something. He finally shrugged and stepped toward the two men. They took an involuntary step backward.

"Please," Phelps said softly. "Please don't."

"I regret very much the necessity of my action," Cheslov's voice was hoarse and his mouth was wet.

Neither man could look directly at the Russian as he wiped his arm across his mouth then examined the blood that covered his sleeve. They missed another look of surprise.

"That boy had more courage than you two women combined. I hope you learned something here tonight. Something in the way of men. How men fight. How men die. It is something you may witness. But never participate in."

What Phelps had just seen did not remind him of how men fought and died at all. More like how one man may fight an animal, only to lose and be viciously mauled. He continued to look at his feet.

Then the Mayor shouted, "Where's Downing?"

They turned to see an empty dock.

57

Mitch awoke as the Russian climbed off Woody's corpse. While the other men watched Cheslov stagger from the butchered body, Mitch slipped silently into the water.

The water chilled him to his bones in an instant. His right arm was weak. His body was an aching mass of knots. He had at least two cracked ribs. Not to mention the tip of his finger was gone. White specks of light danced across his vision. He wanted to curl up and vomit.

Instead he forced his arms out one after another and willed his legs to kick. He could not quit. Could not resign himself to capture. Once away from the light perimeter, Mitch dog-paddled long enough to kick off his shoes and remove his shirt.

His only hope lay in getting out to open water. He was betting they wouldn't immediately think to search for him using the Carver. They'd do what anyone else would do in their situation. Assume he was hiding under the dock. They'd waste time before realizing their next choice was to search by land or sea. Mitch hoped they decided to search the shoreline by car. But he didn't count on it.

The shortest path to land took him slightly northwest to a finger where Bayshore Boulevard jutted into the bay. Mitch set a course ten degrees farther north than the shortest path to land. This took his total distance in the water from a thousand to maybe fifteen hundred meters. The longer swim was necessary to separate from the most direct vector in case they came across the water sooner. Every minute that passed moved the odds in his favor.

The northern tip of the bay was calm with seas less than half a meter. Good and bad. On the plus side, the low chop helped his speed. He could normally cross fifteen hundred meters in about thirty minutes moving at two kilometers per hour. In his injured state it could take forty minutes. On the minus side, he didn't have forty minutes. He did not have thirty minutes. He had to cross the open water in twenty. Because the calmer waters also made him easier to spot from a distance.

And if he stayed in the water more than twenty minutes there'd be other problems. He'd spent a lot of time in the cold Pacific, swimming through fifty degree waves in full combat fatigues and boots. The instructors pulled them out after fifteen minutes, the maximum time a man could remain in the water before hypothermia set in.

Mitch thought fast and hard. *Can I make this swim in twenty minutes? I'll have to. Is this the right decision, militarily? I think so. Do I have any other options? Not so you'd notice.*

58

Mayor Delaney and Phelps searched the water in the dock's immediate area. They came up empty, expanded their circle and became more frantic with each passing moment.

"He's got to be right underneath us," Phelps cried. "He swam under the dock and he's right beneath us. We have to find him. He can't survive in that water in his condition. Who has a flashlight?"

"Don't just stand there, you fool!" Mayor Delaney shouted at Cheslov. "Help us look, goddamnit. If that boy gets away we are all going to see the inside of the jail house!"

But Cheslov was not just standing there. He was looking out over the water. He tuned out the two men on the dock. He raised his chin, closed his eyes and listened intently. Felt the breeze blow in from the water. Sniffed the air.

Phelps risked a glance at the Russian's dark face. Cheslov's head was back, dark eyes closed to slits. He looked like a wolf tasting the wind. Phelps watched a facial tic dart stealthily across the man's shadowy face.

Cheslov's black eyes opened wide.

Phelps closed his eyes and groaned again.

Without a word Cheslov picked up his coat, retrieved his knife and walked toward the Carver.

"Where the hell do you think you're going?" Mayor Delaney stepped in front of Cheslov.

"I am going to get him back." Cheslov continued to look toward the water, slightly northwest.

"Listen to me, Kirill. He is not in open water. That boy did not have the strength to swim into open water. He is around the dock. We have to focus and we will find him. He's right around here."

The Mayor stared at Cheslov, but the giant continued to look northwest, oblivious to the Mayor's presence.

"Are you listening to me?" the Mayor shouted.

Cheslov moved his head until his black eyes looked down at the Mayor.

"You waste my time, little man. Go and drink your dark whisky and drape yourself in a warm shawl and I shall conduct the work of men. Do not trouble yourself with my tasks."

Cheslov pushed past the Mayor toward the yacht.

The Mayor grabbed Cheslov's arm from behind and attempted to spin him around. Cheslov whirled and shoved the Mayor. His body flew threw the air, fell and scraped across aged wooden planks. Deep splinters tore through his pants into his buttocks and legs.

Cheslov climbed aboard the yacht and revved the large motors.

The Mayor pushed himself up and staggered toward *Chorny Volk*, arms raised, hands waving wildly. "Get off that boat and help us look for the boy!"

But Cheslov was gone.

59

Mitch heard the motor fifteen minutes into his swim. He didn't bother to look. Light could reflect from his eyes and he'd be caught. Either the boat was on a heading south of him or it was not. Either he had put enough distance into his current heading or he had not. Either way, his only recourse was to continue to swim hard and fast toward his goal. He pushed northwest.

The sound of the motor grew louder. He pushed northwest. He had about two hundred meters to go. Fifty meters from shore the water would grow shallow as mounds of rubble formed a foreshore. The boat could not follow him beyond that point.

His arms and legs were enormously heavy. His upper chest screamed with the labor.

He pushed northwest.

Mitch could tell the boat was south of his heading. If he had not taken the northern track, he'd be dead right now.

The motor revved and the pitch changed and he could tell it was coming directly toward him. The Russian must have figured out his strategy. The boat had to get within thirty meters to spot him. Rocks scraped against his thighs and chest. He was safe from the boat, anyway. If that lunatic used a gun, then all bets were off.

He was forced to crawl the last few meters, then scramble up the slippery rocks along the bank. Now he was at his most exposed. He waited for the light to illuminate him from the yacht. The light would be followed by a bullet. Bullets from high powered rifles traveled four hundred meters per second. Faster than the speed of sound. A head shot and he wouldn't hear a thing. He would simply turn off.

But the light never came. Mitch made it up and over the seawall and jumped down onto the illuminated sidewalk of Bayshore. He landed in front of a startled young roller-blader. She appeared to be about twenty years old. Her hazel eyes were wide and she skidded hard using the rubber brakes on the back of her cinnabar boots.

Mitch crouched and wheeled back toward the water just as the yacht veered sharply fifty meters out. He glared at the boat. No search light. The son of a bitch was using night vision. He didn't try to make out Cheslov, did not wait to see if Cheslov would try to get off a shot. Instead he ran like hell across Bayshore and through the streets beyond.

No micro, no identification, no shirt, no shoes. No connection to the Grid. His lifeline was gone and he was as defenseless as the day he was born. He felt nauseous but he was alive and he was free and his head felt clear for the first time in days.

60 Thursday March 12, 2020

"What are you doing down here?"

A bright light shined in his eyes.

"I said what are you doing down here?" the voice was louder.

"Trying to sleep," Mitch said. He was shivering.

"You'll be dead before you wake up."

He had fallen asleep in the woods near the Hillsborough River. He'd picked a secluded spot in the brush several meters off the dirt road. He opened his eyes and looked into the unshaven face of a middle-aged trooper.

"Lemme see some ID," the trooper said.

"That's OK. I was just leaving." If the cop hauled him in the Mayor would track him down.

The trooper hesitated, considered rousting the bum further, decided to let it go. Goddamn junkies. Showing up all over the City. What's the use? He could spend all day every day on electronic paperwork.

"On your way, then." The trooper turned and walked back to his cruiser.

Mitch stood, hugged himself, hopped from one foot to the other to get warm. He grimaced at the sharp pain in his side, brushed off dirt and leaves, then limped up the trail toward the main road. The trooper stared darkly from his cruiser.

Mitch walked half a kilometer. Then his stomach coiled in a knot and he fell to his knees. He leaned forward and tried to vomit but his abdomen was empty so he only managed to dry heave. Several contractions passed, then he pushed himself to his feet and walked north along the blacktop.

He looked east and judged it to be around seven. *Let's see. Met Wanda late afternoon. Woke on the madman's boat around ten. Fell asleep in the woods around midnight. Supposed to meet the Buyer in an hour and here I am wandering through the woods like a wild man. Jesus Christ. I need a reboot. And how the fuck am I supposed to type now?*

Mitch couldn't believe the pesky cop had found him. Was he getting too old for this shit? Come on, he'd blended into open fields an arm's length from Taliban goat herders. His eyes watered as cramps again squeezed his body. What did that lunatic drug him with, anyway?

Maybe it wasn't the drug. There was another possibility. An idea lurked in the shadows of his mind like a disease. The nausea coincided with being cut off from *inSyte*. Quite literally, *ha-ha*. For every action there is an equal and opposite overdose. He'd have to address this later. He had something else to deal with at the moment.

Option One had left the building, what with the file being officially attached to his missing fingertip.

On to Option Two. Losing Woody was definitely a setback to planning a covert, but not a show stopper. He couldn't think about Woody, wouldn't allow the distraction of emotion. He forced himself to plan how he would take out the Mayor and the mad Russian.

A McDonalds up ahead. Back to civilization. Mitch ducked into the men's room to wash his hands and face. Looked in the mirror. A wild man stared at him through the glass. His right side was deep blue. At least his swim washed away the blood. And the salt water helped to heal his fingertip. Even so, it throbbed miserably.

Jesus, I need a reboot.

Mitch stuck his head under the faucet and washed his hair with liquid from the dispenser. He combed it the best he could with his right hand. He wanted to wrap his finger in a paper towel but the men's room only had an annoying hand dryer on the wall.

He hadn't eaten since he and Kate shared the peach ice cream. When was that, exactly? He wasn't sure. He walked out of the men's room and approached a teenage boy behind the counter.

"I can't serve you without a shirt, sir," the boy said.

Mitch pulled a napkin from a dispenser and wrapped it carefully around the end of his finger. Reading the teenager's name tag, he guessed *Carlton* made ten bucks an hour at this shit job. Something ceramic clipped to the kid's belt. Bingo.

"Sure you can," Mitch said. "I'll transfer one hundred Ameros to your personal micro."

"What?" Carlton asked through narrow eyes.

"Soon as I get my shit together. As you can see, I'm in a bit of a bind."

"What are you, a Nomad?"

Mitch smiled. "I'm a graduate student at USF. I'm in trouble and you're going to help me."

"What's in it for me?"

"I just told you what's in it for you. Give me two sausage egg McMuffins and a coffee. Super-size it. Let me use your micro to call my girlfriend. When she gets here I'll pay you. Capiche?"

Mitch figured a kid with this job would gladly take a chance on a potential pay off.

Carlton smiled. "Would you like fries with that?"

"I'll pass. But do you have any scotch tape?"

Mitch taped the napkin around his finger the best he could with what he had. He hungrily wolfed down the sandwiches, drank half the coffee and started to feel human again. His mind was clear, empty. Sort of like a reboot. He walked to the back of the store and called Kate.

"Oh my God! I've been so *worried!* Where are you, Mitch? I'm with Molly and we're both so worried! First we lose you then Woody goes looking for you and we lose him! What's going on?"

"Listen to me carefully, Kate. Woody's dead."

Silence.

"What did you say?"

"Woody is dead. I saw it happen. The Russian killed him. Your Dad was there. Do not go anywhere near your father. He is a very sick and dangerous fuck."

Silence.

"Where's Wanda? Did she get the file?"

"Wanda's dead too. Cheslov has the file. Stumbled onto some real bad shit here, honey. *Real* bad. I need you to pick me up. Bring a first aid kit. We need time to think. Plan our next move." He beamed the address from the micro's GPS sensor. "And Kate?"

"Yes?"

"Go off Grid right now and make sure you're not followed. If that sick Russian bastard can't find me then sooner or later he's going to come looking for you."

61

Chorny Volk's propulsion system harmonized like the Eagles on Hotel California. The inboard propulsion provided sedan-like maneuvering. She purred along at a mere thirty two hundred rpm to maintain forty knots. Her onboard micro steered the craft toward Cheslov's initial coordinates. Her steering system interfaced with the craft's sonar to acoustically detect and measure fish school densities at various depths. The yacht was currently searching for a density commensurate with a large shiver of sharks.

Cheslov reclined in his captain's chair. A tall crystal of chilled Stoli rattled in the cup holder. He enjoyed laying motionless, content to live in the pleasure of the warmth provided by the sun, already hot at eight in the morning.

Last night had been a debacle. If the Mayor and his rat mascot had not interfered then the swimmer's body would be on Cheslov's boat in place of the fighter's. Politicians. Scavengers who survive only on leftovers from the hunt.

He shook his head in amazement that the swimmer had deceived him. Twice. First the boy feigned fear. Then swam a northern heading to a point of land that added five hundred meters to his journey. Swam extraordinarily fast. After a significant beating.

Cheslov had a clean shot when the swimmer climbed out of the water. The Groza's holographic scope lit the boy's chest. He could not say precisely why he let the swimmer go. The girl who roller bladed into the picture was a factor. Cheslov did not like witnesses.

But there was something else. The look on the young man's face caused him to pause. For a moment the boy seemed to stare directly into his eyes. He wore a look of utter defiance. Hatred.

Cheslov had seen many final expressions. But he could not recall having witnessed such purity. Such beauty. Only a Higher Being could paint so perfectly upon the canvas of human expression.

He may yet kill the swimmer but did not want to do so with an impersonal shot from fifty meters. He shook his head slowly and admitted to himself the boy had been defiant all along. He had simply hidden his true expressions in the stateroom. Unusually resourceful prey.

Then again Cheslov had the file. He knew it was on the boy's severed micro. He did not think the swimmer had transferred the file to anyone else. Perhaps there was no longer a reason to kill him. Of course there was another person in the room during the conversation with the Deter bitch.

Surely the Mayor's daughter knew everything.

Still, without the file what could be done? Nothing from a legal perspective. The Planetcom award would not be reversed based on hearsay.

Murder charges were not filed without bodies. No mounted cameras were operational in the vicinity of the garage or the docks. Both areas had been bleached and thoroughly remediated of all blood and biological fluids. Cheslov would shortly conduct the proper microbial remediation on his yacht.

He did not look forward to seeing the Mayor when *Chorny Volk* returned from her current task. The Mayor would want the swimmer hunted and killed. The daughter was a question mark. Surely the man would spare his own blood.

Cheslov made a decision. He had no intention of going after the boy or the girl. The Mayor would react predictably with a tantrum. He was not actually certain if he could tolerate the Mayor's whines and cries.

There would be fallout from letting the swimmer and the daughter live. They would most certainly embarrass the Mayor politically. Cost the man his reelection. But Cheslov did not concern himself with such events. The contract award had occurred as promised, he had secured the file and should be paid in full. Perhaps there were loose ends, true. He normally did not depart until all business was final, all parties one hundred percent satisfied. But something was different about this situation. He could not define the difference but it was time to collect payment and move up the coast. The feeling was irrational but he couldn't shake it.

Chorny Volk's motors throttled down. He opened black eyes and looked west over the jeweled water. His chest ached and his thigh throbbed. The vodka helped. He pushed himself out of the chair and smiled down at the large dark shapes. He was back among his friends.

He reached into his pocket, removed the small package and unwrapped the foil. He sniffed the little fingertip, inhaled the strong odor. Of course, the odor was not as strong as that which emanated from the two bodies wrapped next to one another on the port deck. He flipped the fingertip and watched it sail through the air and splash lightly into the gulf. The green mass floated gently on top of the blue water. The flipping motion turned the micro on. Then it was devoured by a small, quick female bull shark and disappeared forever.

The first body was wrapped in a cobalt tarp. The Deter bitch's dark hair spiked through the top fold.

He had wrapped the fighter's body using the sheets from his bed. The blood was a mix from the two boys. He pulled back the sheet and looked at the young dead face. The right eye was twisted severely sideways in its socket. The unnatural sight line emphasized its deadness.

So did the fact that the left eye and most of the nose had been chewed away from what was essentially a severed head.

He fondled a dead ear, bewildered as to how this had occurred. He knew, of course, that he had caused the fighter's death. But he could not remember the exact moment of killing the boy. The boy was calm, composed, strong and incredibly fast. Cheslov thought he had lost. Then he was on top of the boy and a hot, coppery taste filled his mouth. He looked for but had been unable to find the fighter's eye or nose afterwards. He didn't want to think about what that meant.

He was sorry to have killed the young man. Certainly he did not mind a righteous kill. In fact he enjoyed killing those who did not deserve to live. But he did not so much enjoy killing people who shared his own spirit. That was a sorry business.

He rubbed the dead face. The fighter's blood was dry. It was necessary to excite the sharks to ensure a complete and efficient feeding frenzy. He went below deck and pulled the Groza from its rack. He would not need the scope.

62

Mitch melted into the branches of a live oak. He watched Kate and Molly arrive, glad to see the top was closed on Kate's coupe. He re-conned up and down the street. Ten minutes passed with no additional activity.

The local City government lacked real surveillance sophistication. He would have detected any tails. She was clean. The parking lot cameras were a different story. Important to get back to the lab as soon as possible. He climbed down the tree and approached the car.

Kate gasped when she saw him. He looked like a refugee. He wore ragged shorts and nothing else. His hair had a life of its own. His entire right side was black and blue, and one of the fingers on his left hand was wrapped tightly in a recycled napkin. Blood seeped through the beige paper.

She looked into his eyes. He smiled.

"Jesus, Mitch" She wanted to cry. Instead she forced a smile. "You look like shit. Get in the car."

"I need you to come inside and pay this kid first."

"Excuse me?"

63

Come on, come on, stay green for me. Come on. The traffic light turned yellow. Kate hit her brakes and mumbled, "Fuck, fuck, fuck."

The interior of her car was onyx with charcoal accents. Warm, wet air trickled steadily from dark vents. Kate drove west across the Courtney Campbell Parkway.

They had no destination.

Molly sat in the passenger seat. Mitch lay across the rear bench. Four aspirin helped settle the throb from his finger that was now disinfected and field bandaged. Kate had wrapped his ribs with heavy duct tape from Wal-Mart. The tape made it possible for Mitch to move without vomiting. As long as he didn't breathe too hard he should be fine for the next few hours. That's all he needed.

Mitch relayed the story of everything that happened since he and Kate split up the day before. He also explained his invention, coming clean with his ability to tap into the Grid transparent to those around him.

Molly cried softly. Kate was sad, numb. She couldn't get her head around the fact such a large, animated and incredibly vital man was gone from this Earth. Seemingly in an instant.

At the same time she felt deceived. And more than a little pissed. First her father. Now Mitch. "Why didn't you tell me sooner? No wonder you always knew just what to say."

Mitch wanted to tell her he had tried. He wanted to tell her it was all new and he was just figuring it out himself. He wanted to explain how all of his reasons were altruistic. But he didn't want to lie anymore.

"I'm sorry. I should have told you."

Kate couldn't shake a feeling of disappointment on a fundamental level. Like she met some amazing guy with a brilliant personality only to realize he's outgoing and funny because he's out of his mind on drugs.

"Silly me, I thought I was talking to you. I didn't realize I was having a conversation with the computer who wore Birkenstocks."

She glanced into the rear seat. Mitch lay on his back in an oversized T-shirt, flowered swim trunks and salmon flip flops. A perfect outfit for blending into the south Florida environment, courtesy of a quick stop into Island Tropics beachwear. His right arm covered his eyes. His chin was clean. Freshly shaven in the bathroom of the souvenir shop. He looked young. Vulnerable. Exhausted.

Large sunglasses lay on a dark ball cap on the floor board. The hat had a hideous plum lobster stitched onto the bill.

And yet, here was this man who risked his life to protect her. She had known him for less than a week and he had shown more courage and selflessness than any man she'd ever met.

"Did you talk to your father?" he asked.

"Yes. Complete waste of time. He lied to me too. What's our next step? *Goddamn it*!" Kate slapped the horn as a little white Honda darted in front of her then hit its brakes. "Fucking asshole."

"I need to get back on the Grid. I need to figure out how to track your father and the Russian. I need a micro. I can get one at my lab."

"Won't they see you as soon as you activate?"

"I'll hack in under the radar. Nobody's going to track me."

"What if they're watching your lab?"

"First they'll watch my apartment. We should have some time before they get around to the lab. Risk I have to take. Since it's a public space I don't think the lunatic will be there. Drop me off in the Sun Dome parking lot. I'll head to the lab and be back in half an hour."

"You son of a *bitch*," Kate said to the pick-up turning left at the light and now she has to wait for the light to change in order to turn right. Of course. *Fuck*. "Then what?"

"Then we go downtown. I know one person who may be the key to it all. One person on the inside who I think I can flip. If we're going to bring down this house of cards, we'll need this guy."

"Who?"

Mitch told her.

Kate nodded. "What's the end game, Mitch? What exactly are we trying to achieve?"

Mitch knew what she was asking.

"Your father's going to jail."

"And the Russian?"

"He's mine. I'm going to kill him."

Molly nodded through tears. "Fucken-A right."

64

The girls parked and waited. About a thousand cars in the Sun Dome parking lot so Mitch thought it was as good a place as any to blend.

Cameras were everywhere. Most were hidden. The ball cap and shades shielded him from the software that captured iris images at distances of five meters and conducted face data comparisons from as far away as half a kilometer.

He needed to turn on. Losing the ability to search the Grid as part of his memory left him feeling incomplete, unsure… *empty*. He wanted it back. For himself. *InSyte* was his and it had been taken.

Mitch remembered reading an article as a kid that described highly addictive online computer games. The article listed case after case of poor sad sacks who chose games over true life. A thirty six year old lost his job and destroyed his marriage. The man was not much of a role model to his young children, but he progressed to Level fifty-eight as Madrid, the

Great Shaman of the North Land. That's all that mattered.

A word was coined to describe such electronic addiction – heroinware. Online self-help groups sprung up to deal with the fallout. Online forums swelled with refugees from online worlds. All had harrowing stories of runaway gaming habits, lives ruined, friends lost, marriages broken. Madrid, the Great Shaman of the North Land, was so obsessed over getting to level sixty that he fatally neglected his youngest child and the game was implicated in the death of the infant.

Game manufacturers were analogized to drug dealers. The first dose was free. Download and play. If you like it then, you know, come back and register, dude. Plenty more where that came from.

Mitch smiled like a man who'd gone all in, everything he had. More than he had. All he would ever have. Then watched his four aces get beat by an improbable straight flush. Because of the wild cards. The Joker. Casinos called them bugs. He had developed a physical dependency to the Grid. His Grid. He tried to avoid the word *addiction*. He'd thought the chemical that Russian bastard used in the parking garage caused his cramping and nausea. Now he knew better.

He tried to look online for an old Steppenwolf song and felt momentary panic, like a man reaching for his pack of cigarettes who finds an empty shirt pocket. Mitch tried to remember the lyrics and couldn't. He shook his head and focused on searching his actual memories instead of the Grid. His mind resisted like it didn't want to make the effort. Or had forgotten how. He concentrated harder and the lyrics came.

The pusher is a monster, not a natural man. Goin to sell you lots of sweet dreams. The pusher will ruin your body but he'll leave your mind to scream. God Damn the pusher man.

OK, a little downside to *inSyte*. A technical hiccup, if you will, Mr. Buyer. Nothing to worry about. Sort of like biting into a juicy steak with a pink center that melts in your mouth and the only problem, minor point really, it's crawling with death because it's got this germ deep inside that will huff and puff and blow your house down.

But it'll leave your mind to scream.

Mitch circled the optics lab twice from a distance looking for anything out of the ordinary. Now the building appeared sinister, like a stingray waiting to strike. But it was just the optics lab and nothing looked out of place. No uniformed troopers, no lunatic, no suspicious lawn crews or window washers. Satisfied, Mitch approached the entrance. He pulled the bill lower to hide his face from the ever present cameras.

He opened the main door and walked to the bank of elevators. He went to the lower level and walked to the set of double doors on the left. He walked past the doors and listened carefully for any sound. Nothing. He ducked into the men's room. Painfully relieved himself. Washed his hands. Exited the men's room and walked down the hallway toward the double doors on his right. He opened the doors and entered his own world, just like he had done a thousand times before.

65

The young trooper couldn't believe the photograph of Dakota Fanning. What an absolutely prime piece of blond ass. Celebrity Sleuth was usually nothing more than a tease. The rarest and the barest, my ass. But this issue. My-oh-my. Twenty four and there's so much more, Dakota my darling.

The door to the lab opened and the Trooper glanced up from the magazine. His mistake was not recognizing Mitch immediately even though he had a picture of the suspect on his police radio. But the trooper's mind was still on the picture of Dakota.

"How's it going, guy?" Mitch said with a smile.

"Got some ID? Let me scan your micro and that'll be fine." The Trooper glanced at Mitch's hands, noticed the index finger was wrapped, dropped his magazine and reached for his taser.

Just one trooper. Mitch had gambled and won.

The lab was shared by about a dozen grad students and two professors. So a trooper wouldn't be on his toes every time the door opened. Two or more cops and he would be caught. A single trooper and he had a chance. With cracked ribs he'd only get one shot.

When he was a boy there were a lot of TV shows where one man rendered another unconscious by a karate chop to the neck or some similar manner of fuckery. His personal favorite was the Vulcan neck pinch. For some silly reason he had always been tickled by the idea, especially in SEAL combat training, of attempting to incapacitate someone using a neck pinch. He imagined pinching the base of a person's neck between four fingers and the opposing thumb. A pause, then the pincher and pinchee look into each other's eyes, throw back their heads and roar with laughter. The sheer idiocy of the situation somehow transcends for a moment all animosity.

But this was real life. The lab would be watched and he planned something other than the neck pinch.

Although it varies with how hard you land it, the uppercut is always a devastating punch. He generally avoided use of an uppercut. You could seriously damage a person. He'd seen people on the receiving end bite through tongues and swallow teeth. Nonetheless, he was unaware of any punch more effective at causing the other person to instantly stop whatever it was they were getting ready to do.

He stepped forward and put the trooper down with an uppercut to the jaw. The man was fumbling to release his taser and didn't see it coming. Eighty percent was plenty of force. He leaned down and examined the trooper's face on the floor. Nothing appeared broken. Nothing obvious, anyway.

Mitch had to move. Impossible to say how long the cop might be unconscious or how often he was checking in.

Six minutes to locate and reapply enriched e-resin to his right index finger. Another six minutes to activate Grid connectivity through a rogue IP address using a proxy server in Bolivia. Not bad for nine fingers. He allowed himself two minutes to revel in the great release of tension, the injected information flowing through his brain. He shut his eyes and flew past ones and zeroes and images, wonderful images in his mind. Sweet relief, profound satisfaction. Peace. Power. Happiness as strong as you'd get from a warm needle. Or a warm gun.

He searched under the deep sink at the far end of the lab, found his bio-box tucked behind the tall-form beakers. He moved his right index finger across the sensor and the box opened. Thank God Kate painted the green resin on his left hand. He retrieved the contents and tucked them into the waistband of his swimsuit.

He grabbed a spectrum generator, powered it on and slipped it into his pocket.

The next several hours were do or die. He'd entered the lab a victim. Hitting the cop changed everything. Now he was the criminal. The aggressor. The hunter. And he had some hunting to do. Some prime asshole hunting.

He met Kate and Molly in the parking lot and they laced through traffic on Fowler Avenue. Disabling the cameras in a rolling five hundred meter radius prevented Kate's vehicle from being identified as harboring a fugitive.

66

"I take it you disposed of all your trash?" the Mayor asked.

"All of your trash, da. Devoured."

The Mayor nodded.

"My services are complete per our agreement," Cheslov said. "I now require payment in full."

"Lordy, Lordy. I come out to your boat last night to pay you and help you send him off. And you let him get away. Then you assault me. Now you ask me for money. Unbelievable. I'm not going to pay you shit, son. You're lucky I don't have your ass locked up. That's where you belong, you goddamn animal. Your incompetence is approaching legendary proportion."

Cheslov listened to the Mayor from the comfort of his cabin on *Chorny Volk* back at the pier. Audio only. He had no desire to open a video channel and see the Mayor's piggish face. The fool would get around to asking about the boy and girl in his own good time. Cheslov sipped cold vodka and waited patiently.

"Tell you what. I'll throw you a bone, son. A bone for redemption. More than you deserve. You do one more little favor for me and I'll pay you twice your original rate. Then we're done. One hundred ten percent finito. How does that sound?"

Cheslov quietly sipped Stoli.

"I want the boy. Downing. And my daughter. I want them both. Bring them to your boat. I'll meet you there and transfer payment in full."

"Why don't you have your police pick them up?"

"Don't play games with me, son. I'm telling you how it is. If you want to get paid then you'll do this. Just that simple. And don't forget, I still have the audio file."

"I do not have the time for such nonsense. I have appointments up the coast."

"This won't take any time at all. I'm tracking my daughter's hybrid as we speak. I'll send the data to you now. Get her. Bring her to your boat. I'll meet you in an hour and pay you half. Provided you have Kate. We'll talk about how to get that other fucking son of a bitch when I see you."

The Mayor ended the call. Cheslov beamed Kate's coordinates to a wall monitor. She was driving west on Kennedy Boulevard downtown. Twenty minutes away. He decided to fetch the girl. His reasons were simple. That crazy Mayor still had the file.

And Cheslov needed the money.

67

Kate dropped Mitch downtown, two miles from the Tampa Municipal Government Building. He watched her pull away and disappear, then opened a channel to the only man who could help.

"Hello, this is Paxton."

"Hello, Paxton."

Silence.

"You're alive," Phelps said.

"That's right."

"I hope you believe me when I tell you I'm happy to hear that."

"I'll let you prove it. I need your help."

Silence.

"What can I do for you?" Phelps asked.

"You can start by meeting me."

"Where are you?"

Mitch hesitated. Here it was. Time to put it all on the line. If Phelps couldn't be trusted then Mitch would be caught and arrested. No choice. He had to trust Phelps and he knew it.

"Downtown. Two miles from your building."

"That's good. Come on over and I'll meet you out front. I guarantee your safety."

"You can't guarantee shit. You're in this as deep as the Mayor."

"Then why are you calling me?"

"I need your help."

"I thought you just said you couldn't trust me."

"I said you can't guarantee my safety. I didn't say I couldn't trust you."

Silence.

"Why do you think you can trust me?" Phelps asked.

"Because you have a conscience."

Silence.

"What do you need me to do?"

"Meet me," Mitch gave him the intersection.

"Look, I want to help you. This has gone way too far. But if the City cameras catch me talking to you then I'm just as guilty."

"That's not going to happen. I have the video oversaturated."

"If you can disable the cameras, then why don't you meet me in front of the Government Center?"

Mitch chuckled. "How long do you think it takes before the area's crawling with troopers if the cameras go white in front of the Center?"

"I see your point."

"I've lowered the transmit power on my spec-gen. Only cameras in a fifty meter radius are out. Good enough to prevent someone from seeing us together and tight enough not to arouse immediate suspicion."

"Alright, Mitch. I'll leave now and see you in ten minutes."

"Wait."

"What else?"

"I need you to bring something."

"What?"

Mitch told him.

"You have got to be kidding. I can't do that," Phelps said.

"Sure you can. You're the Chair of the City Council."

"You think that means I have access to what you need? Think again. I'm a bureaucrat. A suit. I can't get near that stuff."

"I know you can do it. Be creative. Get it done."

"If I give that to a citizen I could lose my job. At a minimum."

Mitch sighed. "Did you see what he did to my friend?"

Paxton shut his eyes. Did he see it? He couldn't get it out of his head.

68

Kate dropped Molly off at her place then kept driving, per Mitch's instruction. Besides, she didn't know what else to do. She couldn't sit still. To say her world had been turned upside down in the past twenty-four hours was an understatement. She wished she were back on top of the Ferris Wheel with Mitch. Better yet in his bed eating peach ice cream.

A horn sounded sharply and she saw the light was green. She pushed the amp pedal and suddenly realized she was famished. He last meal was the peach ice cream, come to think of it. When was that? Yesterday? Seemed like a lifetime ago. She turned into a Spanish café on the corner of Kennedy and Fremont. She pulled into the lot behind the building, drove to the back corner beneath a shady Oak. She leaned back and shut her eyes for just a moment. She needed time. Time to unplug. To think. To not think. She needed to pull it together before going inside.

She didn't see or hear the dark, electric Jag pull in quietly behind her. She was equally oblivious, of course, to the over-saturation of the parking lot cameras.

She heard a car door close. Felt a car door open.

Her car door!

She opened her eyes as Cheslov lifted her like a bag of leaves. He wrapped one arm around her chest and held her parallel to the ground with her arms trapped against her sides. She felt like a mannequin, lifeless and helpless to control her world. A large hand clamped over her mouth. Something wet and odorous filled her face and she gagged.

"Hey man!" a strange voice.

"What are you doing to the senorita?" Another voice.

"Let her go, motherfucker!" the first voice.

Kate was released and fell to the ground. Gritty asphalt stung her legs and arms. She didn't have the strength to push herself up so she just lay there. She turned her head and watched two heavyset Hispanic men striding toward the giant Russian.

Under different circumstances Cheslov would have enjoyed the encounter. He would have taunted the men and looked deep into their eyes to determine if they were born with courage or false bravado. But on this particular day at this particular moment Cheslov had neither the time nor the patience for interference. He pulled his Makarov and pointed it into the face of the first man. Pulled the trigger. Only a soft *piiiffft* and the man's head disappeared in a thick puff of red mist. The headless body fell to the ground like a puppet with strings suddenly severed.

Kate smelled an intense aroma of gun powder and copper.

She was dizzy from the chemical and she couldn't help it, she smiled at the second man's eyes large as golf balls. Another soft sound then his face with the Titleists also disappeared in a thick red blur.

She tried to rise but the wet hand covered her mouth so instead she slid into a deep hole. Even though she knew it was all a dream she decided life was a lot like death. It sort of happened to everyone. Ready or not.

69

Phelps parked two blocks from the intersection and started walking. He carried a soft-sided briefcase with a noticeable bulge. The burnt umber color of the briefcase was a nice match for his light Spring jacket. He'd purchased the jacket and shirt combo from Brooks Brothers last weekend in Hyde Park. He so admired the color and cut of the jacket. He hadn't seen this shade of cornflower blue and he simply couldn't escape the image of Cheslov killing that boy. He took him down from behind like an animal. Like a goddamn mountain lion on a sheep. But that wasn't the best part. The punch line was … wait for it … the Russian had actually *eaten* the boy's face.

Phelps was having a hard time with that part. He thought he may have actually gone a little insane by the act of merely watching the atrocity. Wrong place at the wrong time. Bad, bad luck. After Cheslov roared off in the boat, Phelps stood and watched the absurd Mayor shout and cry and shake his fists at the wake while his ass bled. Phelps sprinted across the dock to his car, removed his clothes on the drive home, scampered into his recessed marble shower and scoured head to toe with a brand new loofah. He could tell from a steamy shaving mirror he wasn't getting clean so he decided to use some bleach. Just a mild solution.

He noticed folks stared as he walked down the street. He smiled with secret pride because he knew how good he looked in his new jacket and shirt. Brooks Brothers was the best of the best and the way the Russian killed that boy was just a mind bender. Tackled him like a northbound jackal on a southbound gerbil. You had to see it to believe it.

He had a sudden hopeful thought. Maybe the images weren't actually in his mind? Maybe they were somehow imprinted on his corneal lens? If he went home after lunch to apply the bleach solution directly to his eyes, that might help.

Mitch stepped from an alley, grabbed Phelps by the shoulder, spun him round.

"What happened to your face?"

"What do you mean? Nothing." Phelps said.

Mitch wasn't surprised to see the post traumatic reaction in Phelps. He'd seen it in seasoned veterans from Iran. And what the bureaucrat witnessed was in many ways worse than anything he'd seen in Iran.

"Paxton, look at me. I need you to focus." He grabbed Phelps' jaw with his right hand and squeezed, forced him to look into his eyes. He watched the confusion drain from the man's face, replaced by a reluctant awareness that wanted nothing more than to run and hide. The chemical burns were slight. He didn't think they would hurt the man's career. Phelps probably had bigger problems going on in his head, anyway.

"I know what you saw was horrible. It was shocking. But you cannot let it beat you. You have to rise above it. I know you want to hide. Believe me, I have been there and I have done that."

Phelps struggled to look away and Mitch tightened his grip.

"Owww," Phelps cried.

"Listen to me. You have to fight. If you try to hide it will follow you everywhere you go. And it will devour you." He stared into the older man's eyes. Phelps finally focused.

"OK. OK. I get your point."

Mitch stared for a moment longer, dropped his hands. "Did you bring it?"

Phelps handed the device to Mitch. "Wasn't easy, but I got it."

"Tell me how you got it." Mitch needed to know how much time he had. He needed to know how soon they'd come looking for it.

"Don't worry. It won't be missed. I told the armory guard I needed to check inventory to validate purchasing records. Boring stuff. He couldn't care less."

"You told him looking the way you look?"

"Over an audio feed. He unlocked the door remotely."

"How'd you get it out?"

"Front of my pants. My new jacket covered the bulge. No worries."

Mitch nodded. "Tell me where they are."

Phelps hesitated. "Are you sure you want to know? That motherfucker is *crazy*."

Mitch smiled and thought about a time so long ago in Iran. "He's a wolf. That's OK. Takes one to kill one."

"I think you know where they are," Phelps said.

Mitch nodded again. He thought Phelps would be OK, he was one of those guys who looks like a dweeb and acts like an asshole but he's strong. Sneaky strong. He'd met more than a few SEALs with the same trait.

"Give me your keys," he said.

Phelps handed them over. "Space twenty-six, lot four."

He turned to leave.

"Mitch?"

He turned back.

"Kill the crazy son of a bitch."

"You can count on it."

"Oh, and Mitch?"

"Yes?"

"Thank you."

He knew what Paxton meant. "You're welcome."

70   Tuesday July 15, 2014
Bushehr, Iran

The temptation to close his eyes and accept the fall was overwhelming.

But Mitch wasn't ready. He propelled his arms and kicked his legs and swam against the stream, against wet snow. He felt rather than heard something far away and kicked toward it. Shouts and distant explosions then bright sound and intense color and he hungrily gulped a lungful of air like a man bursting through the surface from an impossible depth.

And there, waiting for him at the surface was the smiling face of a dark animal.

Mitch detected a flash of motion, watched Woody whirl and put two bullets between the eyes of a dark Mullah warrior crouched two steps from their position. Powerful waves of pain surged through Mitch's body. His lungs felt squeezed. His breath was short and painful. He climbed to his knees and willed himself back in the game.

"Surrounded by warriors. Request immediate air support and evac. Roger that. Over." Mitch crawled back into position and resumed firing.

"Did you get through?" Woody shouted.

"I think so," Mitch whispered hoarsely. "Cavalry's on its way."

"How fucked up are you?" Woody shouted.

"I'm good," Mitch whispered. Then once more, a little louder. "I'm good." He felt like he lay in a puddle of maple syrup. Somehow the bullet must have missed his vital organs which was nigh near a miracle. He was bleeding but he'd hold out as long as he needed. Passing out was not an option.

He kept firing and imagined some kid at Creech Air Force Base in Nevada sipping a cup of coffee, manning a joy stick, wreaking cubicle warfare. Probably a professional gamer, maybe won a contest or two. Flying a Reaper from twelve thousand kilometers away, watching the desert landscape unfold on a computer screen. Controlled by humans but as close as it gets to a machine that kills autonomously. Come on, baby.

Mitch heard the shot from close range and Woody's right thigh burst into a bright crimson fountain. Mitch whirled and shot three of the men from the Samshiri in rapid succession. A fourth raced around the corner and Mitch threw a grenade with all his strength toward the retreating warrior. The waffled steel clacked off the wall and past the corner, then exploded. Woody and Mitch were protected from the blast.

"I hope like hell it killed you, you little prick," Mitch growled. "And all your friends."

The dumpster exploded and Mitch was blown back into the alley. Diverting the SEALs' attention from the street for only a few seconds was all the time the fighters had needed to get an RPG into position. He tumbled head over heels and lost consciousness for a moment, came to, thought he'd lost his eyesight. What was it, third time today he thought that? Then he realized his face was covered in debris that continued to rain down. His rifle was hidden somewhere in the huge pile of trash. Bad, bad, bad. They were dead ducks without the M25's.

Incredibly, his Sig lay inches from his head and he believed with all of what was left of his heart that at that moment on that day God wanted him to have that pistol.

And the high capacity fifty round clip that lay next to it.

Back in action.

Mitch looked toward the street as the dust cleared and was horrified to see his friend's body crumpled on the sidewalk, just beyond the mouth of the alley.

Mitch flipped onto his stomach and fired into a group of fighters crossing the street. Three fighters fell and the rest dove for cover.

He crawled toward his friend and continued firing, a focused killing machine. *Red dot on a forehead, pull the trigger. Watch the head explode.* Bullets thudded into the ground and walls around him, kicking up dirt and mortar and waste from the exploded dumpster. *Red dot on a chest, squeeze twice. Watch the body pinwheel into the gutter.*

He grabbed Woody's boot and pulled with all his strength to drag his friend to the alley. Woody didn't budge. Mitch holstered his Sig, stood and yanked Woody's boot with both arms. An AK round hit him in the gut and he couldn't breathe but he kept tugging because this time the bullet didn't penetrate his vest and finally Woody's body moved. Mitch dragged him into the alley, tore off his own bloody cloak and wrapped it around Woody's wet thigh.

A black-eyed fighter lined up an RPG across the street. Mitch drew his Sig Saur, lit the man's throat and tore it out from forty meters.

He whispered into Woody's ear. "Wake up, Woodman! I need help."

Woody's eyes opened wide, his massive head shook once, twice. He held his rifle in one hand. He flipped over and blasted away up the mouth of the alleyway.

Three rounds then his rifle fell silent.

"That's it, man. I'm out."

Mitch shook his head and couldn't suppress a little grin. "If I'd known you were out of bullets I wouldn't have wasted time dragging your ass back to the alley."

"Suits the shit outta me. I was dreaming about a blonde. We're smoking a bone. Then you wake me up and here I am in this shit storm with a weapon firing fucking blanks."

"Sig?"

Woody reached for his holster, shook his head.

"Gone."

Now their backs were literally against the wall. They had maybe thirty seconds before those bastards overran their position since they couldn't enforce their perimeter with rifle fire.

Mitch glanced at Woody's face. Dirty and bruised, freckled with blood. Woody grinned, winked, pulled his bayonet. Mitch grinned and pulled a grenade. If this was it then so be it. They'd come into this outfit as brothers and that's the way they'd go out, by God.

The street swarmed with fighters. The fusillade of bullets coming into the alley intensified. Several men positioned RPG's. Mitch removed the firing pin and sailed a grenade, hook shot style, into the swarm.

The street exploded in a blinding flash. A lot more than Mitch expected and then he tried to laugh and it hurt. He laughed anyway. Wondered if these guys had ever seen a demonstration of American air power. Impressive, eh? Enjoy the fireworks, boys.

Two drones softened the target with Hellfire missiles. Multiple strafes. Important to clear the RPG's before the Apache showed. The military was reluctant to overtly bomb Iranian cities. But Bushehr was known to be heavily sympathetic to Al Qaeda. And terrorists were no longer considered criminals. Since 911 they're classified as combatants in a worldwide war. Killing them is part of warfare and the battlefield is the globe. The US made it clear they would drone Al Qaeda anywhere, anytime. So the Team commander on the carrier had made a quick decision. To hell with the collateral damage, just get my goddamn SEALs.

The gray Apache attack helicopter hovered overhead like a lumbering hippo rocking in the water. The Chain Gun beneath its great nose showered the street with five thousand thirty millimeter rounds in less than a minute.

Six SEALs fast-roped into the alleyway and moments later Mitch and Woody sailed over the clouds toward the Nimitz. Medical corpsmen cut away what was left of their clothing to cleanse and treat their wounds. Mitch's organs were shutting down due to lack of oxygen from blood loss. His cardiac system was trying to conserve precious blood by constricting vessels.

The corpsman flushed his body with fluids to increase blood pressure. They beamed video of Mitch's chest wound to the Lieutenant Commander on the Nimitz, who directed the chopper to land on the task force hospital ship, USNS Mercy. By the time Mitch touched down it was all-hands-on-deck in the infirmary OR. Two surgeons and three nurses worked seven hours to save his life.

The lead surgeon told one of the attending nurses it was a miracle. He'd never heard of a man shot through the chest from close range with a three oh eight Kalashnikov and not one major organ punctured. The bullet just went in through his chest and out through a neat little hole in his back. Didn't strike any bone. If it had it would've ricocheted around inside his chest, torn through his organs and killed him.

"Someone's watching out for this kid. No doubt about it," he said to the nurse.

"I'll say," she agreed. "God bless him."

The cracked right shoulder was a mystery until Woody leaned in, thigh wrapped following surgery to remove his souvenir AK slug, and told the Doc about the initial grenade launch on their truck.

The surgeon rubbed the back of his head and let out a low whistle. He was glad these goddamn SEALs were on his side.

71   Thursday March 12, 2020
Tampa, Florida

"How do you intend to find him?" Mayor Delaney asked.

"I do not intend to find him," Cheslov replied.

Mayor Delaney and Cheslov were in *Chorny Volk's* main cabin below deck. Kate sat at the galley table and watched the two men argue. Her hands were tied behind her back and her mouth was taped shut. On the table in front of her she saw a half empty bottle of Stoli, a large unlit cigar in an overflowing ashtray, and a dark medicinal jug. CHLOROMETHANE R-40 was laser-printed across a scarlet label bonded to the jug.

"Wrong answer. I'll say it again. How do you intend to find him?"

Cheslov said nothing. He looked at the Mayor and smiled his dark smile.

Kate realized her father did not know what he was dealing with. She was still delirious from the Chloromethane and didn't understand how implicit her father was in this sordid mess. She thought he was still her father and the Russian psychopath was to blame for everything and she needed to warn her Daddy and why couldn't she talk? She shouted at him to watch out but all she heard were strange muffled sounds.

The Mayor glanced at his daughter irritably. The way an impatient man might glance at someone else's crying infant.

"Angel, you need to keep quiet. We'll leave soon but right now I need to take care of some business." He looked back at Cheslov. "Listen you son of a bitch. I should haul your ass in on assault. I been soaking my butt in peroxide. You think that's how I wanted to spend my morning?" He leaned toward the Russian and slapped the table.

Kate moaned louder through the duct tape. Her eyes were wide with fear. *Oh Daddy, don't you see he's a python and he's about to strike don't lean toward him lean away you need to call the troopers the whole fucking department of troopers.*

"Honey, I told you to shut the fuck up. One more interruption and I'll have to do something I really don't want to do."

"The swimmer is not my concern," Cheslov said.

"I'm making him your concern. Come on, Cheslov. I need this one. Isn't that what you do? Don't tell me you're having a sudden conscience attack. After what I watched you do last night?"

A small tic darted across Cheslov's stoic face. Just for a moment then it was gone.

Kate saw it and moaned desperately in an effort to warn her father who was treading water like a man inside a fuel tank, lighting matches to find his way out.

The Mayor backhanded his daughter with his right hand. The force of the blow knocked her head sideways and strained two cervical vertebrae high in her neck. She couldn't raise her head back to center.

"Quit fucking around, Cheslov. I need you with me on this one. Think! Where did that boy run off to? I have his apartment staked. I have his whole school staked out. Goddamn, I can't believe that trooper let his guard down. Letting a kid get the drop on him like that. Goddamn pitiful. He sure as hell ain't with her," the Mayor pointed toward Kate who sat with her head hanging sideways like a broken doll.

Kate could not believe what was happening. She couldn't actually comprehend the situation. Intellectually she knew this meant her mind was checking out, her body going into shock.

"WHERE DID HE GO?" the Mayor roared.

Kate's body gagged involuntarily. She felt as though she were suffocating.

Cheslov slowly sipped Stoli. Straight from the bottle. He decided to humor the fool.

"He will undoubtedly have contacted your prima donna. You should stop hitting her. Instead you should question the girl. She will tell you where the swimmer hides."

The Mayor looked at Kate, as if only realizing she was in the room.

"Hitting her? What are you talking about? I'd never hit my little girl." He reached out and absently stroked her chin. She looked up and tears spilled down her cheeks. Her father tenderly wiped them away.

"She will tell you where your swimmer hides then you can hunt him down on your own. I am retired. As of now."

The Mayor nodded thoughtfully. He gripped the edge of the duct tape and tore it from his daughter's bloody face. She winced but didn't make a sound. Her head was clearing from the chloromethane and she stared at her father through furious eyes.

"Angel, I need you to concentrate for Daddy. Going to ask you a question. Stand up and look at me." The Mayor pulled Kate to her feet. She stood unsteadily, head hung to her side, hands tied behind her back.

"Angel, I'm only going to ask you once. OK? I want you to listen and answer Daddy. This is important." The Mayor spoke as though addressing a young child. "Where's your boyfriend hiding? Where's Mitch? It's important that Daddy find him. For his own safety. I need you to focus and tell me where he is."

Her sandals were in the floorboard of her car back at the Spanish cafe. She drove without shoes and hadn't have a chance to put them on in the parking lot before Cheslov interrupted her lunch plans. But even without her shoes she was still as tall as her father. She whispered something so soft he couldn't hear.

"What?" the Mayor moved closer and once again she said something too soft for him to hear.

He leaned close and Kate bit down on his ear hard as she could. She expected the ear to feel rubbery the way a toy might because in her mind she couldn't convince herself that she was really biting her father's ear. But it didn't feel rubbery. It felt like warm wax paper and she couldn't get a grip so she ground her teeth to get more traction.

The Mayor screamed and tried to shove his daughter then realized that pushing her away only caused more pain so he dropped his arms and shrieked louder and begged her to stop grinding her teeth and for Chrissakes to let go of his ear.

Her neck was in agony but she held on tight.

Cheslov threw back his head and laughed heartily, literally slapping both knees with his open palms. He'd initially regretted his decision to come back into port but the sight before him was indeed worth his trouble. He leaned back in his chair, tipped the bottle upright and drained the last of the vodka. He chuckled and wiped away tears of cheerful amusement then cut the top from a Cohiba Maduro. He inhaled the fine aroma. Rich, creamy and chocolaty with nuance of vanilla, cedar and caramel. He reached into a pocket for his Zippo then looked up and there, leaning against the open hatch and holding what appeared to be a flare gun, stood Mitch Double-Downing.

72

Mitch was sure he'd seen stranger sights but couldn't remember where or when.

Kate stood next to the table barefoot but wearing the same loose fitting Tee over faded jeans that she wore earlier. She looked the same except her knees were torn, her hands were tied behind her back and the lower part of her face was red with what appeared to be tape burns.

Her face was also red with bright blood that evidently came from her father's ear which she held firmly between her teeth. Most people pulled back when their ears were bitten. Mitch noticed the Mayor'd had the good sense to lean close and hold still. Quick thinking had in all likelihood saved the man from losing his ear right then and there.

Both Kate and the Mayor were motionless. Since the ear was still connected to his head it appeared that Kate held the advantage. The way a terrier held the advantage over a rat. There was a tenseness in the

Mayor's eyes born of an awareness that she might shake her head viciously at any moment.

Across the room, relaxed and calm with a cigar in his mouth and an empty bottle of vodka at his side, sat Cheslov. Mitch watched him smile his shit-eating grin as he lit the long, dark Cohiba.

"Going to the beach today, my young friend?" Cheslov asked. "Perfect weather."

Mitch pointed the gun. "Kate, let go of your Dad and come on over here."

She opened her mouth and felt the ear slip wetly past her lips. She stepped toward Mitch and was grabbed from behind by her father.

"Drop the gun, son," Mayor Delaney said. "You're a fugitive and a criminal and it's time to end this. Put your gun on the table and we'll talk. No reason we can't all get what we want here."

Mitch looked at the Mayor then looked at Cheslov then looked at Kate. He felt the beginning of a headache, tendrils slithering through his mind.

"Kate. Hit the deck."

She threw her body sideways in a quick motion like a volleyball player sliding for a sand save. The Mayor struggled to hold her with only one arm around her waist. His other hand held his bleeding ear. He let go of his ear and just managed to hold her off the ground in front of him. It was excruciatingly painful for Kate, and Mitch wasn't sure how much longer he could keep the Mayor and Cheslov covered with Katie in that compromised position.

Then he didn't have to because Cheslov surprised him.

Upon seeing the Mayor use his daughter as a human shield, Cheslov's dark face contracted upon itself in a massive muscle spasm. Once. Twice.

Cheslov stepped forward and grabbed the Mayor's throat. He lifted the Mayor off the deck and shook him like a saddle blanket. The Mayor immediately released Kate and she fell onto the hard deck.

Mitch thought about a lot of things in the next moment. He thought about his Dad and he thought about his Mom. He thought about his brother, Bobby. He thought about all the people he'd known and all the people these bastards had killed but more than any of that he thought about his best friend, Woody.

This one's for you, bro.

He pulled the trigger of the Goodbye Gun and held it. A band of white formed on his trigger finger.

He aimed head high and hoped the tight dispersal pattern of the beam prevented Kate from taking a direct hit. But she was smart and rolled forward which then allowed him to thoroughly soak the Mayor and Cheslov.

The Mayor screamed, turned, tried to scramble up the back wall which, of course, he couldn't. Mitch thought of the third rat trying in vain to scale the glass to escape from that python. The Mayor's shriek climbed several octaves as though he were being dipped in molten lava.

Cheslov dove to the side, away from the beam. Incredibly the cigar stayed in his mouth. Mitch followed him with the spray. The indifferent microwave energy formed small blisters on Cheslov's face and arms. Cheslov snarled at Mitch like a cornered wolf as he sank to his knees. His face bloated and his skin smoked then thirty seconds were up so the weapon shut down and Cheslov collapsed.

The Mayor hobbled toward Mitch and Kate.

She looked at her father and froze.

It stepped forward and its skin was mottled and brown. Hands reached toward her with black fingernails. The eyes were a vivid blue that she recognized.

"Come back here, Kate. God damn you, stay away from him."

No, no, no, no, no. This is a dream.

"Come over here, this instant!" the Mayor spat. "I am your father and you will obey me."

Wake up, wake up, WAKE UP!

"Kate, come to me or I'll split you from your---"

An effective head butt can be performed with a forward motion of one's head but is even better when the forward motion of one's opponent is leveraged. The chin is generally a bad position to attack since it can lead to mutual damage.

Unless striking from below. As it happened, Mitch timed it perfectly.

He drove upwards with all his strength into the bottom of the Mayor's chin. Similar to an uppercut with a two by four. The Mayor's teeth slammed together hard enough to break against each other after biting through his tongue.

The Mayor dropped like a butchered bull, a pool of blood spread from his open mouth.

Mitch turned toward Cheslov ready to fire the Goodbye Gun again on a partial charge if necessary.

It wasn't.

He walked over and stood above the fallen giant.

Cheslov slumped low with his back against the bulkhead. The big Russian's arms were covered in broken blisters that oozed blood. Burnt skin cracked off his face in sheets like marshmallows left too long over open flame. Mitch thought of the rat caught in the python's noose. The rat was doomed and its pink eyes knew it. Cheslov had the same look in his black eyes. One Mitch had seen many times.

Resignation.

Mitch found a chef's knife in a galley drawer and cut through Kate's bindings. He helped her to her feet, then carried her up the ladder to the top deck.

He returned to the lower compartment and knelt next to the Russian.

"Volchionok." Cheslov's voice was a reedy whisper.

Mitch found the lit cigar. He picked it up, dusted it lightly, placed it between Cheslov's burnt and bloody lips. Cheslov's eyes focused and Mitch read gratitude in their blackness.

"Rostov, eh?" Mitch asked.

Cheslov nodded. He inhaled weakly and coughed blood onto his shirt. His lungs were damaged from breathing superheated air.

"By the Black Sea?"

Once more a flicker of surprise in the dark eyes.

Mitch glanced on-Grid. Studied the satellite images for a moment. "Little village two miles from the sea."

"Impossibly muddy in Springtime. Rutted from … wheels of cart … hooves of oxen."

"They paved that road half a century ago."

Cheslov raised what was left of one eyebrow and nodded. "Sorry to … kill friend."

"Woody," Mitch said quietly through clenched teeth. "Woody Logan."

"Strong boy." Cheslov chewed his cigar. "Sorry you and I did not … meet different time."

Mitch remembered the long ago camping trip. "I think maybe we did."

"Cut from same cloth. Would have… been good together."

"Unlikely partners," Mitch said. "Like machine guns and barbed wire."

Cheslov thought of horses caught in wire and slaughtered. Machine guns and warwire. Unlikely partners indeed. A distant memory, a dream where he would be devoured by prey. That day had come. This utterly defiant little wolf. His black eyes rolled toward a puddle in a corner of the compartment.

His eyes rolled back to Mitch and he winked a partial eyelid. "*Dasvidania.*"

Cheslov tossed the cigar.

Chloromethane cut with the proper amount of sulfuric acid is a colorless liquid with a slightly sweet odor that's on par with lighter fluid. The corner of the room ignited in a soft *whhuuummmp.*

Air rushed past Mitch's head, pulled toward the sudden flame. He continued to gaze at the Russian. "What did you do with his body?"

"Burial. At sea."

Sonofabitch. Fed my brother to the sharks? Mitch reached beneath his shirt and drew the Sig Sauer P226 he'd retrieved from his lab. He tickled the blue trigger softly, the way a man might caress his lover. God had granted him this weapon. And as far as Mitch could tell, God wanted him to use it. He pulled back the slide to cock the hammer. Cheslov was very lucky to have killed Woody while Mitch was unconscious. If he'd awoke while Woody was alive, he would have ripped Cheslov's fucking head off. Then used that bayonet to cut off his fucking scalp and hang it on his fucking belt. So Cheslov got to live a little longer because of blind luck. But only just. Because killing Woody made this inevitable.

"It's time for you to die," Mitch said.

Mirth sparkled deep in Cheslov's black eyes.

"I can't."

To Mitch it sounded like a plea.

He released the slide and a nine millimeter round shoved into its chamber with a metallic pop. He pushed the barrel beneath Cheslov's jaw.

"Maybe I can help."

The force of the bullet entering Cheslov's chin slammed his head into the bulkhead. The bullet exploded out the back of his skull along with a significant portion of brain and his head rocked forward. The Sig's barrel slid into the hole in his chin while the bullet ricocheted off steel and zinged through the compartment. Mitch instinctively ducked, then slipped the wet barrel out of Cheslov's chin. His fault for using wadcutters. Frangible rounds would not have gone straight through his head like that, but they were just so damn expensive. Mitch knew that point blank shots against flesh resulted in blood and gluey fat splashing back against the weapon. So he carefully worked the slide to properly chamber the next round.

Fire climbed the bulkheads and engulfed the table. Mitch angled the Russian's head so as to avoid another ricochet. Be ironic as hell if he shot himself with his own bullet.

He pressed the barrel against Cheslov's ear. Pulled the trigger. Twice. Security rounds. Violently expanding gases from the muzzle blast were directed into Cheslov's skull while the actual bullets blew his brains out. Wet matter sprayed across the compartment, hissing in outrage as it roasted and was devoured by hungry flame.

Cheslov's noticeably lighter head hung twisted at an odd angle. His empty eyes were a stunning shade of blue. Mitch stuffed the wet pistol into his pants, threw the Mayor over his shoulder and bounded up the ladder ahead of the flames.

"Come ON," he shouted to Kate. "Let's get off this boat!" He took her arm and together they climbed down the ramp to the dock. "Let's GO, let's GO! I think he has a major weapons stash onboard!"

Mitch held her hand and they stumbled up the dock until the explosion then they flew as the enraged air lifted them off their feet and threw them toward the street. Mitch pedaled backwards while he sailed into an obsidian maw and he remembered the first rat trapped in the mouth of the python. His last thought was that the freight train finally arrived in his head and he was going to die.

73   Epilogue

One week later everything had changed. Mayor Delaney was arrested and arraigned on charges of murder and conspiracy to defraud the government. He faced serious prison time as well as oral surgery followed by months of drinking through a straw.

Paxton Phelps was acting Mayor. Cheslov's death broke the spell and Phelps was mostly back to normal. He applied make-up to cover his bleach burns and his first decision as Mayor was to fully exonerate Mitch Downing of any and all charges.

His second decision was to reverse the wireless award, which he announced to the Planetcom team in person. The firm's corporate attorney was outraged and threatened to sue. Bud Colt became so enraged he spit on the wall then kicked one of the desk's claw feet hard enough to crack his big toe. The lawyer piped down when Phelps had Bud tasered and arrested on the spot for destruction of private property and spitting in public. Phelps explained to a prostrate Mr. Colt that an old law on Tampa's books since

1925 prohibited spitting in a public office. Spitting was only allowed from trucks.

The New Light representatives were ecstatic until they realized Phelps had no intention of making an award to either vendor and Wireless World was officially dead. Phelps directed the city's bid team to refocus their efforts on creating an RFP to craft technical training programs. He challenged them to target conversion of twenty percent of the Nomad population to working members of the information society per year over the next five years. The idea was to create a perpetual motion event. Once the homeless converted to working citizens, the new tax revenues would fund education of the next group and so on and so forth.

Phelps placed an immediate order with AM General for sixty Humvees with FRAG 10 armor kits to protect against roadside bombs. He outlined a plan to ramp police trooper strength and recalculate key patrols throughout the city. He appointed the son of Jane Woodall to lead the task force.

Kate and Mitch were treated in Tampa General Hospital. Doctors were puzzled by the acute physical withdrawal symptoms observed in Mitch. His blood tested negative for opiates. Nonetheless they prescribed mild codeine for three days to calm the baffling cramping, nausea, and fever.

Molly spilled the beans that Mitch Double-Downing was an ex-Navy SEAL. She told Kate how he saved Woody in Iran. At Kate's absolute insistence, Mitch told her accounts of his time in the Navy, tales he had never shared with anyone. Mostly they were heroic stories about Woody.

Kate remained angry at Mitch for deceiving her. She tried to forgive him. She wanted to forgive him. She just couldn't find the next step in the staircase to make it happen.

The day before they were to leave the hospital, Kate lay in her bed. She wore a heavy neck brace. Mitch joked that it looked like an Elizabethan ruff. He rolled to her bed in his wheelchair. She followed him with her eyes. His color was better, but his eyes looked too dark. As always, he needed a haircut. But much, much better than when he hobbled out of McDonalds last week.

"How you feeling?" he asked.

"My throat is dry," she said.

A water pitcher rested on her side table. Mitch filled a plastic cup and stood to hand it to her. She tried to sit up and fell back on the pillow with a little sigh. He held the cup carefully to her lips. She drank half then shook her head. He placed the cup on its blue plastic saucer on the table.

"You're serious?" she asked. "They couldn't find any trace of his body?"

Mitch shook his head. "Nope."

"I don't understand. Where did it go? We stood there and watched that boat burn into the Bay."

Mitch chuckled. "Maybe you did. I was slightly unconscious."

Kate remembered climbing to her knees and watching the flames devour *Chorny Volk,* its prow slipping beneath the dark water like a corpse. She shivered.

"What do you think happened?" she asked.

"I think he got away."

"What do you mean? You shot him in the head! What, three times? How the hell could he get away?"

"I didn't say he's alive. I blew his brains all over that stateroom and in my book that means he's dead for sure. But his spirit was trapped. It had been for some time. I set it free."

"What are you talking about?"

"I'm not sure I can explain it any better than that."

"I don't want any part of him to be free. He doesn't deserve that."

Mitch thought about wolves running free in the wild. Chewing off their paw to escape from traps, their survival instinct that strong. "You can't blame an animal for its nature."

"He killed Wanda. He killed your best friend. Tried to kill me. I watched him kill two men in that parking lot. The man is … was a raving psychopath."

"In the end he saved you."

They were quiet for several minutes.

"What about your Dad?" Mitch asked.

"What about him?"

"Have you spoken with him?"

Kate managed a tight smile. "He's on major pain killers, totally unstable. Missing his tongue and a little more than pissed off about it. Oh and did I mention insane? No, I haven't spoken to my father."

"You're right, he's pretty messed up at the moment. But that's not the question. The question is, will you be able to forgive him?"

"Could you?"

"He's not my Dad."

"That's not my question."

Mitch thought about his father, who he never had the chance to know. "I think I'd try. He's a sick man but in the end he's still your Dad. I understand he was hooked on a derivative of anti-dorexal."

"Don't forget the single malt."

"If he could get better and he makes the effort and I could see he was making the effort then yes, I believe I could forgive him. In time."

"I don't know that I can. If he could take what I offer, my terms, and consider it's better than nothing, then maybe. If I could tell him---"

"Do you love him?" Mitch asked.

"---don't reach for too much because you won't get it. But that's not the kind of man he is. He likes things on his terms."

"But you love him."

"Yes, I suppose I do. Problem is, now I hate him as well. So no, I don't think I'll be able to forgive him."

"It's important to try."

"Why?" Kate asked. "Why is that so important?"

"I can't say. I just know it is."

She looked away. "Honestly, Mitch, I'm not sure what forgiveness is, anymore."

He said softly, "Forgiveness is the scent the rose leaves on the heel that crushed it."

She turned to look into his eyes. The bruising made his eyes look darker, almost black. But they were the same eyes she'd fallen in love with. "Is it you this time, or am I still talking to a computer?"

"It's me, Kate. I'm off-Grid. Now. Forever."

She nodded slowly. "Mitch, why didn't you tell me? Why didn't you tell me you were plugged in like that?"

"I should have. I'm sorry."

She thought about the photograph in the worn metal frame in his apartment. The little boy growing up to be a man without a father or a brother. Trying to take care of people, to rescue everyone else and finally her heart melted just a little.

"The Doctors said keeping it on all the time was like going without sleep. Even when you thought you were sleeping that thing in your brain processed information subconsciously. Your body was building a tolerance and the device was responding by demanding more data. They said it would have killed you." Kate shook her head slowly and tried her best not to cry. "Oh, Mitch. I do love you."

He took her hand gently in his. A small tear trickled down the end of his nose and dropped onto her sheet. "I love you, too," he said hoarsely.

She brought his hand to her soft lips.

"What about your invention, Mitch?"

"*InSyte*? I'm going to destroy it. I don't need it anymore. It's funny. My whole life I thought some level of something was unfolding just out of my reach, just around the next corner. And I was missing it somehow."

"Always looking beyond the next step in the staircase?"

"More than that, Kate. I've spent my life searching for something that doesn't matter. That's not even real."

"There's nothing wrong with looking forward."

"There's something wrong when it blinds you to what's already right in front of you," he said. He smiled and she squeezed his hand.

"So like I said, I'm going to destroy *inSyte*."

"Don't be ridiculous. You can't put the genie back in the bottle. You released it, Mitch. Like it or not you have a responsibility to tame it. You didn't invent anything you just found a way to do something before anybody else. But don't you realize it's just a matter of time before the next person figures it out? So we'd better figure out how we're going to control this."

Mitch smiled. Here was this woman who didn't care what he knew. He didn't need to protect himself from her. He just needed to share himself with her.

He softly rubbed her wet cheek. "You'd better get some rest. I'll come back later."

"Promise?"

"Promise." He kissed her forehead, lowered to the wheelchair and rolled into the hallway.

When he first awoke in the hospital, *inSyte* had been running, churning, doing its thing. But there were no visions. No burning streets, no mutilated bodies. Mitch was satisfied the future was safe so he'd unplugged.

Finally his head felt clear, free.

At least during the day.

He spun into his room and shut the door.

Nighttime was a different story. The dreams were bizarre. No doubt a symptom of withdrawal.

He was back in Iran. But he wasn't trying to escape the Mullahs.

He was *hunting* them.

Running through bright urban jungle that transformed into dark forest. Shadows grew long and night fell and he couldn't see anything but that didn't matter, he just ran fast, incredibly fast, pushing with his legs, pulling forward with hands digging into soft earth.

Mitch rose from the wheelchair and looked down at the odd contraption. Designed to put men in motion who did not have the strength to move independently. He walked to the sink and splashed water onto his face.

Who needed light when the sense of smell lit an area better than fifth gen night vision? No blooming, no bright spots. Funny how in his dreams it was easier to run in the absence of light. Peaceful, relaxing. Utter control. The way a man should run through a forest.

Mitch wondered again about Cheslov's soul. He knew he'd set it free. But where would such a soul go once liberated?

Mitch looked into the mirror and was momentarily startled by the black eyes watching him through the glass.

THE END

ABOUT THE AUTHOR

Greg has been happily married since 2001 to the beautiful and inspirational *Serena,* and has two wonderful and beautiful children – Grace and Miller.

Greg Kiser graduated from Southern Polytechnic University in Atlanta with a Bachelor of Science in Electrical Engineering. Greg also earned his MBA from the University of South Florida. He is currently a Technical Director at Cisco, a high tech firm that makes the equipment upon which the internet runs, lives, grows.

Greg has written extensively for fortune 50 high tech firms in describing next generation networks and painting pictures of the true evolution of technology for the consumer.

Greg's short story – *Did They Tell You?* – was selected for the 2010 San Francisco Writer's conference Anthology.